D0223902

UNLOADED 2

ALSO AVAILABLE

Unloaded: Crime Writers Writing Without Guns

UNLOADED 2

MORE CRIME WRITERS
WRITING WITHOUT GUNS

EDITED BY ERIC BEETNER

DOWN&OUT
BOOKS

Compilation copyright © 2018 Eric Beetner
Story copyrights © 2018 by Individual Authors

All rights reserved. No part of the book may be reproduced in any form or
by any electronic or mechanical means, including information storage and
retrieval systems, without permission in writing from the publisher, except
by a reviewer who may quote brief passages in a review.

Down & Out Books
3959 Van Dyke Rd, Ste. 265
Lutz, FL 33558
www.DownAndOutBooks.com

The characters and events in this book are fictitious. Any similarity to real
persons, living or dead, is coincidental and not intended by the author.

Edited by Chris Rhatigan
Cover design by Eric Beetner

ISBN: 1-946502-59-6
ISBN-13: 978-1-946502-59-9

For the women, children and men
who have been victims of gun violence.
And to the families left behind.

CONTENTS

INTRODUCTION
Sara Paretsky

In 1985, I was in Kate's Mystery Books in Cambridge, on tour with *Killing Orders,* when I met my first real-life private eye. *Killing Orders* was the third novel in my series. My following was small, but they were a happy bunch. I knew they were happy because they were in the store's front room, drinking and laughing. I was in the back, alone.

Kate's occupied the ground floor of an old Victorian house; Kate herself lived on the upper two floors and usually had room for visiting writers to sleep. Unless you were the writer alone in the back room, it was a wonderful place to be. The store is long gone, one of the many victims of the onslaught of the chains and e-commerce.

When Michal (1), the private eye, came into the back room at Kate's and said she wanted to talk to me about my books, I tensed: her manner was stern and I wondered what criticism was about to head my way.

Actually, she said, VI Warshawski dealt with cases similar to those she herself handled. Michal worked for defense attorneys whose clients were often poor, African-American or Portuguese, and who were facing an uphill battle in the criminal justice system.

"I like VI," Michal said, "But she shouldn't carry a gun."

In my early books, I hadn't thought through the question of guns; I had unwittingly absorbed the popular meme that detectives never leave home unarmed.

1

Michal explained that she owned a gun and that she felt confident using one. She had an up-to-date license, and she often practiced at a gun range. She said she stopped carrying her gun on the job because she found having a weapon made her unconsciously escalate encounters, as if her unconscious mind wanted an excuse to fire her weapon.

"When I started leaving my gun at home, I began thinking of smarter, less confrontational ways to handle encounters with witnesses or families of perpetrators," she explained. "Even though I go to some of Boston's most dangerous neighborhoods, I've never been in a situation where I wished I'd had my weapon."

After my conversation with Michal, I didn't get rid of VI's Smith & Wesson, but I had my detective lock it in her safe. She would only get it out if response to an investigation made her life seem actively at risk.

I thought of Michal's assessment when the United States moved 55,000 troops into Kuwait and Qatar in the winter of 2002-2003. We also shipped thousands of tanks and other armaments to the region and moved the Fifth Fleet into the Persian Gulf. Although I wrote, marched, and even prayed for peace all that winter, I knew that my government had already determined on war. The weapons were in hand, the itch to escalate confrontation too extreme. Nothing would make them put all those troops and weapons back in the DoD's holster.

We live in a society obsessed with weapons. "Make my day" was one of the first President Bush's happiest campaign slogans and the crowds, which had worried he was too much of a Yale boy, too soft on abortion providers, were delighted: at heart he was really a Dirty Harry kind of guy. Bush's largely white supporters knew the subtext: in the movie, Clint Eastwood assassinates a diner full of African-Americans.

Guns have become part of our national narrative. Although the United States is eighty-three percent urban, we like to think it's 1850, when we were eighty-three percent rural and everyone (supposedly) needed a weapon to chase off Betsy de Vos's famous grizzly bears. Or, although we don't say it out loud, European settlers needed to kill people of color, whether indigenous or enslaved.

One of the most extraordinary aspects of America's obsession with guns, assault weapons, rifles, and so on is our lack of interest both in facts and consequences.

More than thirty thousand Americans die from gun wounds every year, but we think laws controlling access to weapons are worse than AIDS or snake bites. Thirty thousand plus deaths from opioid addiction is called a national emergency in Washington, but over eleven thousand annual gun homicides and nineteen thousand annual gun suicides are apparently a testimony to America's frontier spirit.

Every year, almost thirteen hundred American women are murdered by their domestic or dating partners. Most of the murders are committed by guns. In homes where guns are present, women are five times more likely to be murdered than in homes without guns.

The USA Patriot Act allows law enforcement agencies to go into libraries to see what books Americans read, but it prohibits tracking purchases of guns, even by people who are on terrorism watch lists. Apparently books and ideas are more powerful than a Colt 45, which perhaps is reassuring to writers and philosophers, but not to the many hundreds of thousands of families who are grieving the deaths of their murdered loved ones.

The annual cost of gun violence, including medical bills, court and prison costs, disability payments, lost wages, and other indirect costs, is about $230 billion. Exact data aren't available because gun lobbyists have pressured Congress to limit the Centers for Disease Control from tracking these costs (2).

* * *

As a society our reaction to these facts is either denial or rage or some combination that leads gun enthusiasts to troll researchers, or even the families of murder victims. The families of the Sandy Hook children in particular are targeted by trolls who claim that the massacre never happened.

The authors included here, and in the first volume, have boldly decided to try to change the national narrative on guns. Like all change, it starts with slow steps, and one of these steps is a series of anthologies in which guns cannot be used, either by perpetrators or by investigators.

This is the second such volume and the stories range from horror to humor, as is always true with crime writers who give their imaginations free range. I get to write about guns in the introduction: Lugers, Walthers, Glocks, Uzis, Mannlichers, SIGs—guns! guns! guns!—but no one else can.

I actually don't own any guns, rifles, machine guns, grenades, or even nuclear weapons. They all frighten me, never more so than as I write this essay while the United States president says my country is "locked and loaded" against North Korea. He has the weapons and he is aching to escalate the confrontation so he can use them.

It's definitely time for a change to our national narrative.

---

1. Michal is a pseudonym; she doesn't want her actual name used in print.
2. http://www.motherjones.com/politics/2015/04/true-cost-of-gun-violence-in-america/

FROM THE EDITOR
Eric Beetner

I wish this book didn't exist.

But here we are. In the time between publication of the first volume of *Unloaded*, gun violence in America has continued unabated and we've witnessed yet another record setting number of dead in that ever-shifting tally of "America's deadliest shooting." No legislation on a national level has been enacted to curb the use of guns in attacks, suicides, robberies. If anything, those who see the solution to gun violence as more and wider access to guns have gained more allies in Washington and have set about dismantling what state laws restricting gun purchases that do exist. As ever, "now is not the time" to discuss gun violence in Washington, especially in the wake of a tragedy—which is nearly every day.

So we've collected another group of crime and mystery writers to raise our voices and sharpen our pencils in a call for a reasonable, calm, and fact-based discussion of guns in this country.

For those of us who often use guns in our writing, we wanted to make clear the line between our fictional worlds and the real world we all live in together. By writing crime stories with all the excitement and suspense readers love about the genre, but without guns, we want to express that guns aren't necessary to the plot, and indeed in our lives.

Instead of guns you'll get everything from apes on the loose, androids, punk rock shows, and murderous housewives.

You'll also find a story written in ever shortening sentences, a feat of authorial magic, and a true tale of a near-tragedy.

For the writers included here, and in the first volume of *Unloaded*, we aren't content to sit by and watch nightly news reports of mass shootings, home accidents, or teen suicides without taking up our pens and making our voices heard.

In many ways the most tragic thing about the time that has passed between volumes is the lack of media coverage regarding gun violence. While the number of gun deaths hasn't decreased in America, the reporting on it has. It's become so second nature, so common and expected, that it simply isn't news anymore.

That's chilling. We're normalizing the enormous scale of gun violence in our society.

So do we expect to change the hearts and minds of those far on the other side of the issue? No. But for those of us in the middle—the reasonable ones, the sensible ones with children and hope for a future, we want to start the conversation.

Both sides of the issue can be drawn into hyperbole and vitriol. We want reason and research. All the charts in the world about how outsized our level of gun ownership, gun violence, gun accidents, gun suicides are compared to the rest of the world don't mean a thing if we don't listen to each other.

No one here is trying to repeal the Second Amendment. No one here is trying to take guns away from legal, responsible owners. As with volume one, we have here a representation of both side of the political spectrum, both gun owners and non-owners, all with the common goal of a rational discussion about a clear and present danger in America.

Let's hope we don't need a volume three.

CON SEASON
Chris Holm

We pulled into the strip mall a little after four in the afternoon on Christmas Eve. The lot was empty. Dry wisps of snow swirled across the pavement in the bitter wind. The storefronts were dark and stripped of signage, but years of grime had darkened the building's façade, so the lettering was still visible in negative. Inside, I saw evidence of renovation. A stepladder. A floor polisher. Stacks of drywall, half swallowed by the gloom.

Dad scanned the parking lot—his eyes wide, his pupils pinpricks—and frowned. The nervous drumbeat he'd been tapping out on the Caddy's steering wheel ceased. The car was shit brown inside and out, and reeked of cigarettes, even though Dad didn't smoke. It was on its fifth owner and third engine, but Dad loved it just the same. He'd always said that when he made it, he'd drive a Cadillac. Then one day, three months out of prison, he came home with this late eighties monstrosity.

Mom was furious. Said, "Christ, Jason, what were you thinking? The price of gas alone'll break us." She'd been weird about money ever since Dad got out—partly because he couldn't seem to keep a job, and partly because the owner of The Music Box had bumped her from the dancing lineup not long before, when he found out she'd turned thirty. She still worked there, tending bar, but claimed the tips were shit because her customers would rather give their money to the girls on stage.

Dad wouldn't hear it, though. He was so goddamn happy, I didn't have the heart to tell him that driving a Cadillac didn't necessarily mean he'd made it.

I sighed and stopped poking at my smartphone for a moment. "You told Stick you'd meet him around back, remember?"

"Around back," he said, rubbing idly at his nose. "Right." He tapped the gas. The car lurched forward. His drumming resumed.

He always got like this before a meet. A bump for courage. Then another because the first one felt so good. Maybe a nip or two to ease his jitters. Next thing you knew, he could barely keep his shit together. No doubt in my mind he would've rabbited by now if I weren't here. I'd like to think that's why he brought me along, but I knew better. Truth was, Dad figured nobody was gonna pop him in front of his kid. I wasn't the brains of the outfit—I was his insurance policy.

Still, I'd be lying if I said I didn't like being invited along.

Behind the shuttered strip mall, the lot was narrow and unlined. No parking spaces, just loading docks and dumpster enclosures. A chain-link fence woven through with dying weeds marked the edge of the property. Dense forest encroached upon it from the other side. Steel doors with heavy locks led into the building at regular intervals, one for every storefront. Every three doors or so there was a picnic table and a pair of those silly outdoor ashtrays that look like big beige plungers. Each of the tables was chained to a metal loop anchored to the side of the building as if the people who'd put them here were worried someone would steal them. Honestly, they didn't seem worth the effort—and if they were, a cheap padlock wouldn't be much of a deterrent.

Out front, sodium vapor lights began to blink on one by one—on a timer or a sensor, I supposed. The sun had yet to fully set, but the sky was thick with clouds the color of smudged newsprint. The lights back here must be manual, I thought, because they remained off. The orange glow out front cast a halo around the building and blanketed us in shadow. My cell phone's screen bathed the interior of the Cadillac with ghostly light.

Dad hit the brakes—a little harder than intended thanks to his nerves. Cold pavement crunched beneath the Caddy's tire treads as we rocked to a halt.

"Where the fuck are you, Stick?" Dad licked his lips. Reached across me and opened the glove compartment. Removed a crumpled envelope and a pint bottle of Old Crow. He stuffed the envelope into his jacket pocket, uncapped the bottle, and took a swig. When he was done, he offered it to me. I shook my head.

"Oh, c'mon. Fourteen's plenty old for a drink."

"I don't like whiskey," I replied—which was true enough, I guess, even though I'd never tasted it before. Also, I was thirteen. I appreciated the gesture, though. He was an idiot, but he meant well.

"Suit yourself." He returned the bottle to the glove compartment. I closed it with a knee, grateful bourbon was all he'd brought to fortify himself. Open containers weren't illegal here—but, last I checked, cocaine still was. Possession with intent is why he missed my last five Christmases. I wasn't about to let it fuck up this one.

Turned out Stick's panel van was parked beside one of the dumpster enclosures. It was midnight blue and nearly invisible in the long shadows of the building. When Stick realized we couldn't see him, he flashed his lights. Dad pulled in beside him, but left the engine running. I put my phone in my pocket and pulled on my gloves. Then we both got out of the car.

The air was cold and dry and smelled of coming snow. It froze my nose hairs and burned in my lungs. My breath plumed. Dad cupped his hands and blew on them to keep them warm, his wedding ring a dull reflection of the sky. Plat-

9

inum, to hear him tell it, although it looked like sterling silver to me. Mom had kept it in her sock drawer for him while he was away. She'd kept her wedding ring there too.

Stick rolled down his window, pot smoke billowing into the night, and broke into a toothy grin. "J-Man. Doogie. Funny meeting you here."

Stick always fucking called me Doogie, even though my name was Andrew. I think it had something to do with a TV show that was on the air a million years ago. He told me once it was because I was so smart. "Only in comparison to the company I keep," I'd muttered in reply. If he'd heard me, he'd been too baked to take offense.

"You bring the stuff?" Dad asked.

"You bring the paper?" Stick countered.

Dad removed the envelope from his pocket and waved it in Stick's face.

"Well, all right, then. Let's get down to it."

Stick reached for the envelope. Dad pulled it away. "Not until I see the goods," he said.

Stick climbed out of the van, sauntered around back, and threw open the rear doors. The cargo area was piled high with all kinds of random shit: leather jackets, unboxed PlayStations, a surf-green Telecaster. Stick rooted around for a minute, found a Barbie-branded tackle box, and slid it toward Dad.

Dad opened it and whistled. Instead of fishing lures, each compartment contained a single piece of women's jewelry.

"Now," Stick said, "lemme see if this paper of yours is half as convincing as you say."

Dad handed him the envelope. Stick tore it open. Inside was a thick stack of twenty-dollar bills. He pulled one out and held it to the light. It was an older design, dog-eared and creased as if it had been circulating for years.

Now it was his turn to whistle. "Jesus, Hank. This shit's no joke. If I didn't know better, I'd think it was the real deal."

"That's kinda the idea."

"How much is this?"

"Three G's. You can count it if you'd like."

Stick liked. His lips moved as he thumbed through the bills. "Where'd you say you got these again?"

"I didn't. A buddy of mine made 'em. Guy's a goddamn artist."

I swallowed a laugh. That was a bit of an exaggeration. The guy in question was a screen printer who made his living selling novelty tees online.

"Damn, dude—even the feel is perfect."

Dad smiled. "That's because he makes 'em from bleached ones." The pride in his tone was evident. Dad was the guy who supplied his buddy with all those one-dollar bills. You wouldn't believe how many vending machines he had to knock over to gather 'em all.

"What about the security features? These things won't stand up to a black light, will they?"

"They don't have to. All those bills are based on a pre-nineties design. That means no microprint and no security strip."

"Fuckin' A. Whaddya want for 'em?"

"What're you offering?"

Stick thought about it—or did some math, more like. "Tell you what; I'm feeling generous. Pick a piece, any piece. It's yours."

Generous. Right. Whether Dad realized it or not, he was doing Stick a favor. Stolen jewelry is notoriously difficult to move.

Dad took his time looking through the items in the tackle box. Occasionally, he'd hold one to the van's rear dome light for a closer inspection, then set it down—his mouth a thin straight line. Stick, cold and anxious, shifted his weight from foot to foot, his hands thrust deep into his pockets.

Eventually, Dad held a ring up to the light and smiled. Then he extended it to me. "What do you think, kiddo—will she like it?"

I pulled off my right glove and took the ring. It was a square-cut sapphire framed in diamonds and set into an elegant white-gold band. Sapphires were Mom's favorite, which is why she'd chosen Sapphire as her stage name.

"It's perfect," I replied. "She'll love it."

"A fine choice for a fine woman," Stick said, drawing out the second *fine* until it sounded all skeevy. "Seems we got a deal."

Stick offered Dad his hand, but before they got the chance to shake, the night erupted in a riot of shouts and sirens and screeching tires, blue lights splashing all around. Next thing I knew, I was on the ground—my left arm in a hammerlock, cold asphalt like sandpaper against my cheek.

Four hours later, I was sitting on a bench along one wall of the police station, waiting for child services to show. Beside me was a guy in a filthy Santa suit, fake beard askew, blood seeping through a cotton bandage on his cheek. Nobody paid the two of us any mind. The precinct's bullpen was hopping, their phones ringing off the hook. As if I needed reminding the holidays aren't always so jolly.

Dad and Stick surrendered without a fight. The cops cuffed 'em both and loaded them into separate cruisers. After a quick pat-down, I rode upfront in a third. When we arrived here, the cops stuck them each into their own interrogation room. Nothing fancy, like on TV, just two old offices repurposed for the task.

One of the cops sat me down in a wooden chair beside his desk to take my statement. He typed slowly with two fingers as I spoke. When I finished, he asked if he could call my mom to pick me up. "Good luck finding her," I replied.

He took that to mean she was out of the picture, which was handy, because it meant I didn't have to lie to him. The fact was, I didn't want Mom to find out about tonight if I could avoid it—and I was pretty sure I could. Even if they tried to track her down, it'd take a while. Our apartment was an illegal sublet. Our cell phones were prepaid.

When I was done giving my statement, one of the cops handed me a Styrofoam cup of instant hot chocolate—clumps of undissolved powder still clinging to the sides—and pointed me toward this bench. With the exception of a bathroom break an hour or so ago, I'd been parked here ever since.

Eventually, the door to Dad's interrogation room swung open. One of the detectives he'd been talking to held it for him, although he didn't look happy about it. The other—still seated at the table—shook his head in disbelief, his thick mustache bent into a frown.

Dad headed to the front desk to sign some paperwork, after which the uniformed cop behind it handed him his car keys. Then Dad trotted over to me. His face was tight and expressionless, but his eyes glinted with barely contained delight. He looked as if he'd just been dealt a royal flush.

"Drew, get your things—we're going."

I put on my coat and hat without a word. Picked my gloves up off the bench and stuffed them into my jacket pocket. Then we walked out of the precinct together.

The temperature had dropped significantly while we were inside. The snow had come and gone. Now the sky was black and full of stars. A fine dusting atop the Caddy glimmered like diamonds beneath the streetlights. We brushed it off as best we could and climbed inside.

Dad drove carefully for a while and said nothing, his gaze darting from mirror to mirror as if he thought we might be followed. But once we were a few miles from the police station, he banged the steering wheel and whooped with joy.

"Did you see that, buddy? Your old man just put one over on the fuzz but good."

I muttered noncommittally.

"Aw, c'mon," he said, jabbing me playfully in the ribs with his elbow, "you can do better than that! You just witnessed a goddamn Christmas miracle. Holy shit, was walking outta that precinct a rush. I mean, obviously, I feel bad Stick's gonna take a fall for all that shit he stole, but that's his problem, you know? I was more worried what'd happen when they laid eyes on the fake-ass twenties in my pocket. Guess Wally's bills are even more convincing than I thought!"

"Guess so," I said, even though I knew damn well they weren't. Wally's counterfeits were shit. Every one had the same serial. The shade of green was close, but not quite. That's why I swapped 'em for real bills—taken from Mom's secret stash, which she hid inside a tampon box beneath the bathroom sink—before the meet.

Full disclosure: I'm the one who called the cops. Well, texted, actually, as we pulled into the parking lot. I wanted Stick out of the picture because he and Mom had been banging on the sly for over a year. Dad, God love him, was oblivious. He's never been the most observant guy. Anyway, I'd hoped that Mom would break it off once Dad got outta jail. When she didn't, I decided to take matters into my own hands.

Look, I'm not a fucking idiot. I knew going in my fix was tenuous at best. If Mom found out that someone had replaced her secret cash reserve with counterfeits, she'd flip her wig—and it was only a matter of time before Dad wound up back in jail for real. But I had to try. If everything went to shit the twenty-sixth, at least we spent one Christmas as a family.

Halfway home, Dad's face fell. "Son of a whore," he muttered.

"What's wrong?" I asked.

"I just realized—without that ring, I don't have nothing to give your mother tomorrow."

"About that." I took my left glove out of my jacket pocket, stuck two fingers through a narrow hole between the shell and lining, and tweezed out the sapphire ring Dad had been eyeing.

"Well, would you look at that," Dad said, a smile spreading across his face. "I do believe my boy just saved Christmas."

"Yeah," I said. "I guess I did."

ENDGAME

Laura McHugh

He'd always imagined he might die in the electric chair, arms and legs secured with thick leather straps, his skeleton rattling inside his skin as the life was fried out of him. It would be a worthy exit.

He'd come close, only once, to a death he hadn't planned for. Number Six had managed to get a pocketknife out of her little beaded purse, spilling everything else in the process—lip gloss, tampons, library card, a shiny tin of Altoids that popped open and scattered across the grass. She gouged the blade into his belly, cutting through his shirt and piercing the skin. It smarted, though he didn't realize until later how badly she had wounded him. He'd been too caught up in that extraordinary moment, when it felt like all the windows in his head had been opened and the breeze was blowing through. He kept the pocketknife in a red lacquer cigar box, along with other mementos: an incomplete set of glitter-flecked acrylic nails; an orange eraser shaped like Garfield the cat; an opal earring; a Swatch watch, the battery long dead; a frayed friendship bracelet stiff with blood.

Had the girl with the knife somehow killed him, it would have been the end of his winning streak, the conclusion to a fabulous game he had played for many years, and he would have died doing something he loved. While not ideal, he could have appreciated such a death. What he could not appreciate, nor anticipate, was melanoma.

It was merely an inconvenience at first, taking time out for the surgery, tending the large wound on his forehead. Then the lymph node biopsies and removals, and the news that the cancer had spread, that surgery had come too late, even though he still felt fine. The sun, from all those years on the midway, that's what would kill him. Ridiculous.

The doctor had proposed an aggressive treatment plan he couldn't possibly afford, including infusions of an immunotherapy drug with the dire, laughable warning: *can cause serious side effects in many parts of your body which may lead to death*. Even then, the odds weren't good, and the extra time it might buy him wouldn't be pleasant. The doctor scolded him for waiting too long to seek treatment in the first place, and he wanted to press his thumbs against her trachea and squeeze, to watch the tiny blood vessels burst beneath her skin. He could almost feel the hard knobs of her vertebrae beneath his fingertips as he imagined his hands closing around her neck, but he didn't touch her.

Instead, he went home and made arrangements. He listed the house—a modest bungalow he'd once shared with his aunt—well below market value in exchange for a cash sale, and then packed his station wagon with only the necessary supplies. He slid the red lacquer cigar box under the driver's seat to keep his treasures close by. Everything else he hauled to the curb for the garbage man or neighborhood scavengers. It didn't bother him to leave the house behind, to pile his aunt's dishes and photo albums and Beanie Babies in the damp grass by the mailbox, a bag of her scuffed-up shoes spilling over into the street. His own possessions were few and betrayed very little about him: navy blue Dickies work pants and shirts, barbells, an assortment of tools, a broken VCR.

He was going to take a final road trip, though instead of visiting national parks or kitschy roadside attractions as some might do, he was going to revisit spots that were special only to him, places where he'd felt that click of latches releasing and the windows in his head flung wide open to let in fresh air. The game wasn't over yet; he might have time to play one more round.

He retrieved his road atlas from the crack between the console and the passenger seat, where he had stowed it next to a package of licorice whips and a bottle of Nestea. He'd thought about buying a GPS, considering the scope of his trip, but he was wary of any electronic device with tracking capabilities. The right person or computer program might be able to decipher his movements, to distill a constellation of sorts, each point of light coming from a star that had gone dark years before and largely been forgotten. He kept the map in his memory and never recorded it in any permanent way, though he would sometimes sketch it out on the shower door, sliding his fingertip through the condensation and watching the trail vanish moments later.

It had been easier back when there weren't cameras trained on every street, sidewalk, and parking lot, and readily available to everyone who carried a cell phone. Things changed so rapidly that he'd had to relearn the rules after a stint in prison, to be careful not to end up in the background of some idiot's selfie as he trailed a girl past a bar. He supposed it didn't matter so much now, being careful, since the end would be coming soon. He'd die before anyone could figure out who he was, what he'd done.

His Nebraska driver's license said Thomas Dean Fenton, a borrowed name that fit him well enough. In the washed-out license photo, above his thin nose and tufted eyebrows, you could make out the splotch high on his forehead that would turn cancerous, that had since been cut out and replaced with a grinning scar. He had other licenses from other states: Jacob Crandall, Brent Merriman, Jim Welch. Without his aunt around to call him Miles, his given name could easily be forgotten.

Already his legs were a bit swollen from driving, a side effect of lymph node removal, the doctor had said. She warned him that there were no guarantees; his condition could worsen rapidly as the cancer spread, or he might linger for half a year. She felt fairly confident, though, that he had at least a couple of good months left. He didn't dwell, as he drove, on his dwindling number of days. There was another, brighter number in his head.

Fourteen. The number glowed inside him like a neon carnival light. Fourteen spots to visit on his final trip, if he had enough time. He spread open the atlas and brushed his hand over the red and blue highways, a network of arteries and veins. He'd make his way across Nebraska, heading northeast toward the upper part of the Mississippi, and then follow the river down to the southern tip of Iowa.

The wind barreled across the plains, buffeting the station wagon as he pulled out of the QuickStop parking lot with a full tank of gas and an empty bladder, on his way toward Number One. It bothered him a bit that he couldn't do them all in order—too much backtracking required—though Number One was indeed the first, the closest to home: Seventeen-year-old Cassie Montgomery from Galesburg, Nebraska, home of the Chatham County Fair. She'd been dead for forty years.

He chewed on a licorice whip as he drove through downtown Galesburg, with its tidy town square and red brick courthouse and a banner announcing the upcoming Galesburg High homecoming parade. A man driving a tractor waved at him when they met at a four-way stop, and Miles waved back. He rolled down the windows and turned onto the blacktop road that led out to the fairgrounds. Cornfields crowded the road on either side for miles, the stalks eight feet tall and beginning to wither.

The fairgrounds were deserted this time of year, a clearing

of worn dirt amid the fields. The late afternoon sun slanted weakly over the livestock barn and the grandstand, and he imagined, in the empty spaces, the Ferris wheel and the cotton candy vendor and Cassie Montgomery slipping into the corn, into the darkness away from the colored lights. Anticipation simmered in his gut.

He walked along the back edge of the barn, half expecting to feel a magnetic pull when he neared the spot where he had killed her. When he reached the far end of the building, he cut into the field, pushing through the narrow gap between the rows of corn until he was surrounded on all sides and couldn't see his way out. He stroked the opal earring in his pocket, listening to the stalks rustle in the wind, a flurry of whispers. The stalks had been whispering the night he found Cassie, who had gone into the cornfield to pee because the line for the toilets had been too long.

She was a skinny thing with bell-bottom jeans and straw-berry blonde hair that hung all the way to her belly button. She reeked of beer, and she told him she had spilled it down her shirt and that her dad would kill her if he found out she'd been drinking. Cassie wasn't scared of Miles. He was twenty-one at the time, though he looked young enough to be one of her high school friends, especially in the dark, and when he asked her if she wanted to smoke some weed, she'd followed him deeper into the corn, singing to herself, a song by the Steve Miller Band. He'd strangled her mostly to keep her from screaming, but once his hands locked around her throat, he felt the click and release, and his head, which often thrummed like a wasp's nest in a sweltering attic, cooled and cleared as if the night air had swept through his skull.

Cassie's body had been found the next day, when a farmer noticed buzzards circling the field. He was back home then, at his aunt's house one county over, one of Cassie's opal earrings hidden under a flap of loose carpet in his closet. He realized, from watching the news, that no one had any idea who had killed her.

He knelt down and breathed in the rich, damp scent of the field, trying to slip back into that moment: Cassie's body shuddering and then going limp; her silky hair matted with dirt and tangled around his hands; the muted sounds of the midway that, going forward, would always trigger a sort of arousal. He felt a slight rush, as he always did when he thought about a kill, but he'd expected it to feel different at the scene of the crime, more intense. He couldn't quite work himself up to the heightened state he wanted to achieve; it was frustrating and a bit disappointing, like trying to get an erection after snorting cocaine.

He wondered if it was partly because Cassie's body had been recovered. Later, as he became more careful, more methodical, he would make an effort to hide his victims, some of whom had never been found. Maybe the hidden graves would prove more satisfying, the remains waiting where he had left them, below ground or weighted down underwater.

He removed the opal earring from his pocket, remembering how it had looked, nested in the pale flesh of Cassie's earlobe, before he ripped it out. Ordinarily, nothing could make him part with a trophy, but since Cassie was no longer here and he would never return, he wanted to leave something behind. He dropped the earring into the dirt, where it would get swallowed up by the combine at harvest time or plowed under in the spring, a secret offering that, even if it were found, would never be traced back to him. Maybe, he thought, he would return each treasure to the spot where he had taken it, so that when he reached the end of his journey, there would be nothing left to link him to his girls.

By the time he made it back to the car, he was fatigued and short of breath. He told himself that he was simply out of shape, but he had to wonder how quickly the cancer could spread to his lungs. His current plan had saved Number Ten for last, the southernmost point of his trip. Now he decided that if his condition grew too dire, he would change course to ensure that he reached Burlington, a personal favorite, before the end.

His back ached from sleeping on flaccid motel mattresses, and he was sullen after disappointing visits to numbers Four and Seven. He'd never learned the name of Number Four, a brash, curly-haired girl, possibly a runaway, whose disappearance hadn't even made the news. When he drove to the pine forest where he'd buried her, he discovered that the trees had been replaced by a shopping center with a massive parking lot, which interfered not only with his ability to recapture the moment, but also with his desire to leave a trophy at the grave. Irritated, he'd tossed Number Four's Swatch watch out of the car near the Home Depot, then instantly regretted doing so. No one would pick it up and guess at the mystery behind it; no one would sense that the curved band held echoes of a fading pulse, that it had clasped the freckled wrist of a dead girl. The watch meant nothing to anyone but him.

Number Seven started out a bit better: Jenny Pike, snatched near the Apple Festival in Haddock, Wisconsin, and weighted down in the Chippewa River. Her skeleton had eventually been found downriver by hikers, but the wilderness where he'd dumped her remained largely unchanged, and he could stand on the riverbank and remember the weight of her slack body in his arms, the scent of her strawberry lip balm. He took her wire retainer from the red lacquer box and pitched it into the slow-moving current.

Then, on the way out of Haddock, he'd gone through the McDonald's drive-thru for a large iced tea. He'd been feeling dehydrated no matter how much he drank. The drive-thru girl gave him an insincere smile, her chapped lips refusing to part and expose her teeth.

Do you ever get scared working the late shift? he'd asked

her, their fingers touching as she handed back his change. *Do you worry someone will snatch you out of the parking lot, like what happened to Jenny Pike?*

Who? she asked.

Jenny Pike, he said. *The girl who was murdered.*

The drive-thru girl had shrugged. *That was a million years ago.*

He pushed thoughts of the drive-thru girl aside as he maneuvered his station wagon into a narrow parking spot at the Eau Claire public library. He had a fondness for libraries, and he knew he would feel at ease as soon as he entered the building. With a plain brown cap covering his scar, he didn't stand out in any way, and no one gave him a second glance as he signed in with a fake ID for an hour of internet time. He cracked his knuckles and typed in the address of a site that kept tabs on missing persons cases and unsolved murders, including, though not limited to, the ones he alone could solve.

The discussion boards were his favorite part, and he left comments using an assortment of personas. Rod Foreman wanted every predator to burn in hell, preferably after a prison rape and public hanging. Betty Hernandez prayed for everyone, her text in all-caps, each line punctuated with an exclamation mark. Doug Ferguson addressed his deadpan comments to the families of the victims. *When will you stop looking for your daughter? Don't you think she's dead by now?*

He noticed a flurry of activity on the Kenner forum, which had been quiet for a while. When he scrolled through the latest thread, he saw that Katie Kenner, dedicated victim advocate and younger sister of the missing Joy Kenner, had moved back into the childhood home from which Joy had vanished. A reporter was writing a book about the case, laying out his theory on how Burlington factory worker Mitchell Crane—long suspected but never convicted—had gotten away with murder.

Miles had always prided himself on remaining invisible, yet he felt a twinge of envy as he read through the scores of comments about Crane, who was falsely credited with one of the most well-known, unsolved child abductions in the country. Fame was not something Miles had ever wanted, and it was strange to be thinking about it now, accompanied by unwarranted bitterness at Crane's notoriety: he himself had many names, and when he died, not a single one would live on.

As he hunched in a grimy motel bathroom that night, cursing the havoc the pain pills were wreaking on his bowels, he considered how pathetic his little farewell tour had become. Wheezing when he walked too far, napping in the car every afternoon, visiting empty graves, purging his trophies so there'd be no evidence left in the end.

He wanted to leave something behind, a legacy, and he wanted it to be more than a list of things a dying man had done in his distant past, things that everyone else had forgotten. Burlington was already the end of the line, and it provided the perfect opportunity for a memorable finale: he would pay a visit to Katie Kenner, and feel the fresh air rush through his skull one last time.

Miles drove as fast as he dared along Route 26, also known as the Great River Road. His skin appeared ashen when he glanced at himself in the rearview mirror, his bones startlingly prominent beneath his dwindling flesh. His condition had declined rapidly in a matter of days, and he wondered which internal organs the cancer had infiltrated. The doctor told him there was a fifty percent chance of melanoma metastasizing to the brain. He could experience seizures, numbness, impaired motor function. His cognition would be affected, too, and toward the end he might begin to hear things, see things that weren't there, lose the ability to speak.

It would have been worse, he reminded himself, had he chosen aggressive treatment. He would have spent each of his last days lying in bed, nothing to look forward to. Instead, he had a chance to finish the game. He wouldn't linger pointlessly like Aunt Margaret.

He hadn't realized until he returned from prison just how ill his aunt had become. She had hidden it from him, writing cheery letters, telling him about the new Beanie Babies she'd acquired, asking if he was getting enough to eat. By the time he came home, she was confined to bed, slowly dying of congestive heart failure.

He'd been planning to return to the carnival circuit, but she asked him to stay with her, promising that when she was gone, everything she owned would be his. She didn't have much besides the house and the station wagon, which she likely would have left to him anyway. She seemed to realize, though, that she had to bribe him, that he wouldn't stay just because she needed him, or because she had taken him in and raised him as her own.

She called him into her room one night after the nurse had left and asked him to help her die. Her favorite Beanie, a white bear with a halo and iridescent angel wings, sat propped on her pillow. From the look in her eyes, it was obvious she'd known what he was capable of all along; she knew he would have no qualms about taking her life. Part of him was angry that she was now acknowledging it, that she had been faking her belief in his innocence all this time. For his entire life, she had vehemently defended him against every accusation: *Miles would never do that! He's a good boy!*

Will you help me? she'd pleaded, her chest gurgling. And he'd shaken his head. He who lived to kill withheld death as a petty punishment.

The sky was streaked with pink feathery clouds as he drove into Burlington, the sun on its way down. Miles found the Kenner house easily, a fading Victorian beauty on the bluff above the Mississippi River, and parked down the street to wait for nightfall. He reclined the driver's seat a bit so he could rest while he waited, the heater cranked as high as it would go. His appetite had diminished to the point that he couldn't think of food without feeling nauseated, and his hands and feet were freezing. Despite the chill in his extremities, the pain glowed like embers in his bones, and he imagined his skeleton burning through his flesh and disintegrating into a pile of ash. He knew he didn't have long, but he didn't need much more time.

When the sky was sufficiently dark, he emerged from the car with the red lacquer box under his arm. There were still a few items left inside that could help unravel the grand puzzle he would leave behind: his fake IDs, the bracelet stained with Number Twelve's blood, and a silver barrette that clasped a hank of Joy Kenner's hair, roots and all. As a bonus, his fingerprints all over the box's shiny lacquer.

It was clear and breezy, a perfect night to finish the game, if it had to be that way. There were lights on in the Kenner house, and Miles crept across the lawn to the backyard, ducking behind a shed to catch his breath and decide what to do next. He could wait until the lights went out and try the doors and windows, smash the glass if need be—or, hell, he could just ring the doorbell. Now that he was no longer concerned about getting caught, he didn't need a careful plan. As he peeked out from behind the shed, he heard someone call out to him.

"You're trespassing." He could make out the silhouette of a young woman, her long hair undulating in the wind. "I'm sick of people coming here to gawk."

"My dog got away from me," he rasped, limping toward her. "And I think I twisted my ankle chasing after him. Maybe you could help me...?"

She came closer, quickly closing the gap between them, and he felt a flicker of anticipation. She was making it easy. He could shove her into the hydrangeas alongside the shed and strangle her there, leaving his trophies to be discovered with the body.

He tossed the cigar box aside in preparation, then found himself collapsing on the lawn, unable to breathe, his gut bright with pain. In his confusion, he didn't immediately realize that Katie Kenner had kneed him in the groin.

"Stay off my property, or I'll call the police," she said. Miles lay on the grass and watched her walk back into the house, his vision blurring. It took several minutes to even attempt to get up, then he only made it to his knees. He expected to hear sirens at any moment, but they didn't come. His treasure box had landed downhill and spilled into the darkness near the old-fashioned iron fence that marked the edge of the bluff. He crawled toward it, spying and collecting his IDs as he went, searching for the most valuable of his trophies, the one that would ensure his legacy would live on long after he was gone.

He caught sight of it, the billow of Joy's hair as it was lifted by the wind. It slipped through the fence, the barrette catching briefly, and he scrambled after it, panicked, using the last of his failing strength to hoist himself onto the fence and reach out as far as he could. His balance shifted, and the fall was long enough for him to understand his fate and to rage against it. There were no witnesses save the river, which shrouded him and began, without ceremony, the indifferent work of forgetting.

PAN PANISCUS
James W. Ziskin

The adolescent bonobo named Bingo escaped from the zoo in the early hours of an October morning. His keepers described him as a sweet-natured, mischief-making scamp who'd steal your heart if you weren't careful. But his headstrong behavior, no matter how adorable, had been well documented by the primate curator, Dr. Halberstam, and earned the little fellow a red "caution" circle around his name in his file.

Prone to kleptomania, Bingo especially liked snatching children's baseball caps, their ice cream cones, as well as the termites being consumed by other apes. Usually gentle and gregarious, he nevertheless displayed some behaviors uncharacteristic of bonobos. Among his many quirks, Halberstam had observed in Bingo an irrational fear of elderly humans, a strong dislike for giraffes, and a deranged response—backflips and screeching—to flash photography. This prompted the zoo's director to post large signs prohibiting the practice around the primate village. But visitors routinely disregarded the interdiction, some through cluelessness and others through a perverse fondness of rule-breaking. An online guidebook once described the spectacle of Bingo's reaction as comical, and, as a result, tourists—particularly the Dutch for some reason—enjoyed setting off the little ape by machine-gunning flashes in his face. Bingo didn't help his cause any; he might have learned to run away from the taunting but, instead, held his ground, flipping and screaming until a zookeeper appeared to chase away the flashing Dutchmen.

* * *

On the night of Bingo's escape, security cameras captured grainy images of him squeezing through a tear in the mesh canopy above the primate enclosure. Once he'd climbed down to the ground on the other side, he quadrupedaled through the zoo park for an hour, picking snacks from the garbage and befouling one of the zoo's kiddie train cars, before finally slipping through the bars of the main gate. Like a shadow, he melted into the darkness and disappeared into the city.

Married just three years, with a one-year-old daughter and plans for a second child as soon as practicable, Mitch and Fiona Hirsch had recently moved from a one-bedroom apartment in the University District to a four-bedroom house on two acres of hilly land in the suburban Bellevue section of town. The neighborhood offered excellent schools, low crime, and unmatched vistas of the city below. The nearby zoo provided a lovely bonus for families with children.

The Hirsches bought the house with the help of Fiona's father, an obscenely wealthy hedge-fund manager. Mitch had accepted the money for the down payment reluctantly and only on the condition that he would pay it back as soon as his expected promotion and bonus came through. Fiona wasn't as confident about his future at the firm of Travers and Gregson. She knew he sometimes let his idealism interfere with his success. In fact, Mitch was forging a reputation as a bleeding heart. Committed to socially conscious and progressive causes, he believed he could make himself rich without compromising his principles. But his billing told a different tale. After some early successes, he'd become more interested in human rights and pro bono asylum cases, and those weren't impressing his boss, Fred Gregson.

"Can't you just take the gift Daddy's offering us?" Fiona

had asked Mitch on closing day. "He wants to help us get out of that awful neighborhood."

"Awful because of the dark-skinned people?"

"Awful because of the crime. We've got a child to worry about now. And this is the perfect place to raise a family."

Mitch had to agree.

"Daddy's a product of his generation," concluded Fiona. "And just because he's for strong borders doesn't make him a racist."

Since the day they'd met, Mitch and his future father-in-law, Arthur, had clashed on political issues from taxation to abortion to states' rights. But the subject that sparked the most animosity between them was immigration and, by extension, race. Fiona, daughter and wife, found herself caught in the middle of the two men she loved most in the world. After each ugly partisan brawl, father and husband ended up begging for Fiona's forgiveness. They sued for peace and promised never again to argue.

Until the next time.

By nature, Mitch was quick to anger and slow to redress offense. He hated to apologize or admit fault, and rarely did. The lone exception was with his darling Fiona. She was the one opponent he could never defeat or bear to offend, even when he felt right was on his side.

Fiona had captured his heart the first time he spotted her in the university library ten years earlier. Something in the way she curled her hair just so behind her ear as she read. He'd watched her from across the room that day and the next, before mustering the courage to approach her. Her eyes, so bright and intelligent, so clear and blue, cast a spell over him. And, somehow, against all odds, she too found him irresistible and fell in love.

Mitch indulged her spoiled-little-rich-girl affectations, accepted the coquettish airs she assumed. Her feigned pout, a mannerism designed to win some desired favor or token of devotion, rendered him powerless. He'd even come to tolerate her expensive tastes and shallow friends, with whom she spent the third Thursday afternoon of each month discussing books and drinking wine. Privately, Mitch suspected that the club was an excuse to engage in the latter more than the former.

After several hours exploring the area surrounding the zoo, Bingo spied a ginger cat named Rusty on Osage Avenue and, unable to contain his excitement, he approached his new friend at a dead run, chirping and squeaking as he went. No fool he, Rusty wanted nothing to do with the little beast and found sanctuary just beyond the ape's grasp beneath a low-slung car. Bingo flattened himself on the road, twisting and stretching in vain for several minutes to reach the cat before finally giving up. Saddened and confused by Rusty's standoff-ishness, he reluctantly moved on in search of other diversion.

He scaled a wooden fence that separated two homes. At that very moment, an octogenarian grandmother was enjoying her afternoon stroll in the yard. Bingo vaulted the fence and nearly landed in her arms. The old gal loosed a scream that sent birds to flight and Bingo rocketing off in the opposite direction. He bounded over a parked car—denting the hood and tearing off a windshield wiper in the process—before crashing through a hedge and scampering across another yard into a tree-lined alleyway. There, he cowered behind a bush, wheezing for air.

In time, Bingo concluded that the old lady must have given up the chase, and he allowed himself to relax. He spotted a short man across the alleyway trimming some trees with a pair of hedge shears and, riveted by the spectacle, Bingo wondered if he might be able to lop off the tail of a giraffe with one of those things. He pictured the one who lived in the enclosure next to the primate village. The one the keepers called Jerry. Bingo hated that fucking giraffe.

The man was dressed all in green, much like Kenny, Bingo's favorite keeper at the zoo. But Kenny, who spent many hours teaching him sign language, stood a full two heads taller than this fellow. And, since Bingo had no fear of short humans— just old ones—he emerged from behind the bush and advanced toward him. While the little bonobo was eager to make a new friend, the human—like the cat—was not. The gardener dropped his clippers and ran toward a gate, just as it swung open and an SUV emerged. The woman at the wheel stomped on the brakes.

"Evelio!" she called through the open window. "Are you all right?"

Barely taller than the hood of the car, the gardener stammered something half in Spanish half in English.

"*Cuidado, Señora!*" he managed finally. "Watch out to the monkey!"

"Oh, my," said Fiona, raising her window.

Once safe behind the glass, she smiled at Bingo, who regarded her with curious interest. How cute, she thought, and retrieved her phone to snap a photo of him. Evelio tapped on the window from the passenger side and asked what he should do about the monkey.

"It's not a monkey. It's a chimp," she said.

"Kills monkey?" he said, keeping a watchful eye on Bingo.

"No! Don't kills monkey."

Fiona could barely suppress a giggle. She often made gentle sport of Evelio's odd English. A couple of weeks before, she'd asked him to get rid of some pesky pocket gophers that were tearing up the lawn. In due course, Evelio presented a handwritten invoice that itemized "kills rack" for thirty-five dollars. Fiona was never sure if it was the service he was billing them for, or some device, such as a trap or a smoke bomb. And never mind the linguistic hoops he must have jumped through to arrive at "rack" for "pocket gopher."

Mitch, on the other hand, found nothing amusing about

Fiona's jokes, and he scolded her for her insensitivity. He'd known, of course, that Evelio was undocumented when he hired him, but he'd felt sorry for the little man who was struggling to build a better life for his wife and young son. In fact, Mitch was exploring options to legalize Evelio's status.

"Chase him away but don't hurt him," said Fiona through the car window. "I'll call the zoo."

She sent the photo of the little ape to Mitch with a caption that read, "My new boyfriend." She was so pleased with her wit that she forgot to phone the zoo. Glancing at her watch, she gasped. It was nearly two, and she was going to be late for her book club. Fiona hadn't even read the first chapter of that month's book, *Being Mortal* by Atul Gawande. At least there would be wine, she thought.

Mitch was tied up most of the afternoon in a deposition. The rural township of Bakersfield was suing Fischer Oil and Gas over the methane in its groundwater supply, contending that the company's fracking practices had turned residents' faucets into veritable flamethrowers.

While deposing Fischer's chief science officer, Mitch produced a bottle of brownish liquid he'd drawn from a Bakersfield tap and asked the man to drink it. The witness blanched and refused, blurting out to the dismay of his lawyer that he wasn't about to drink that *lighter fluid*. When the session adjourned for the day, opposing counsel pulled Mitch to one side and asked if he'd be receptive to a settlement offer. Sensing an opportunity to score a major financial judgment for the firm, Mitch turned him down, saying he liked his chances with a jury.

Happy with the positive turn of events, Mitch stepped outside and checked his phone. He saw the picture of the cute bonobo and phoned his wife to get the details.

"He just appeared in the alleyway behind the house," she

said.

"Did you call the zoo?"

"Of course," she lied, cursing herself for having forgotten.

"I've got some work to finish up in the office," said Mitch. "I'll be home by nine."

As soon as she'd hung up, Fiona dialed the zoo, but it was past closing time. She promised herself she'd try again in the morning.

"Sorry, girls. I've got to run," she announced.

"Just one more glass," said the hostess. "This New Zealand sauvignon blanc is delicious."

It was nearly six. The babysitter wasn't going to be happy; Fiona had been due back at five. Blasting the horn at dawdling motorists, she raced home, speeding and crossing double yellow lines when necessary to pass slower traffic.

After he'd chased off Bingo, Evelio resumed his gardening duties. With the leaves starting to fall, he'd stayed later than usual to finish raking them. He collected them into a great pile, which he set on fire near the toolshed.

Burns leaf, he thought, satisfied with his work.

Nearby, Rusty was patrolling the area, keeping an eye peeled for any of several neighborhood dogs whose owners flouted the leash laws and let their beasts roam the streets like a canine death squad. The coast was clear. Rusty took a seat on the curb and began to wash his face. He'd barely licked his paw when a high-pitched cry ripped the calm of the evening. Without waiting to discover the source of the noise, Rusty bolted from his standstill and, ears back, darted across the street into a tree-lined alleyway. Calling out for the cat to wait, Bingo followed close on his heels, chattering as he galloped along. Then a car, approaching at high speed, appeared ahead of them.

Fearing a collision he could not win, Rusty changed course and ducked into the bushes. When he emerged into the yard on the other side, he noticed a blazing fire near the old toolshed where he sometimes slept on hot days. He also recognized the figure tending the pyre. It was Evelio, the nice man who never failed to greet him warmly and scratch him behind the ears.

Bingo burst through the brambles, tumbling into the open yard. He quite nearly landed on top of Rusty. The cat sprung into the air like a Harrier jet before settling back to earth a few feet away and darting off toward the protection of his friend the gardener. Buoyed by a second wind, Bingo resumed the chase.

Fiona careened through the back gate and roared into the long drive, reaching forty-five miles an hour in a matter of seconds.

If Evelio enjoyed spending the occasional moment petting Rusty, he found himself reluctant to do so once he'd spied the deranged ape barreling directly toward him on the tail of the fleeing cat. The gardener uttered an oath, dropped the rake, and ran.

Distracted by the burning leaves, Fiona never even saw the gathering commotion to her right: a small ape chasing a streaking orange tabby across her lawn.

She felt a thud. A small dark form caromed off the fender, slammed into the windshield, then spiraled over the top of the car in a palsied cartwheel, leaving behind shattered glass, blood, and a tuft of matted black hair. Fiona skidded to a halt and turned to look back. All was dark.

"Oh, God," she said, breathless. "I killed the damn monkey."

Not far off, Rusty vanished into the bushes, happy to have escaped with his life.

* * *

Fiona phoned Mitch, but he didn't pick up. She left a message on his cell, then another on his work line. She even tried his secretary, Kendra, but she'd already left for the day. Desperate to reach him, she sent a text.

Something terrible, she wrote. *That chimp from the news. The one from the zoo. It was dark. He jumped in front of the car. God, I think I killed him!*

Fiona sobbed into Mitch's chest as he comforted her. He questioned her as gently as he knew how if anyone had seen or heard the accident. Fiona shook her head.

"What about the sitter?"

"No. She was parked out front. She couldn't have seen the monkey."

"Ape," muttered Mitch, staring off through the window as he took stock of the situation.

"What?"

"It was a bonobo. An ape, according to the news. Not a monkey."

"Who cares? I killed him!"

A pair of headlights lit up the window. "I called your father," he said. "Here he is now. I'm going to go cover up the body."

Mitch tramped down the long back drive, illuminating the way with a flashlight. He knew he should inform the authorities, but what about Fiona? He'd smelled the alcohol on her breath. The police would certainly do the same. Running over an erratic and unpredictable ape could be forgiven, but not if the driver had been drunk. Damn it. How many times had he warned Fiona not to drink at book club?

About halfway down the drive, Mitch stopped and squinted to see in the dark. He could just make out a mass on the ground ahead. It wasn't moving. Had he not known better, he might have mistaken it for a pile of leaves that Evelio had forgotten to burn. But the sinking feeling in his gut told him it was not *recortes de jardín*. And when he reached the still figure crumpled on the ground, Mitch realized his worst fears had not been dire enough. He gaped at the body at his feet. It wasn't an ape. It was a man. It was the gardener. It was Evelio.

"What are we going to do?" asked Fiona through her tears.

The three of them—father, husband, and she—sat in the study. Arthur and Mitch glared at each other, as if somehow the other was to blame.

"We have to call the police," said Mitch.

"No," said Arthur. "They'll arrest Fiona."

"Then what do you suggest we do? Bury the body and pretend nothing happened?"

"That's exactly what I propose."

Arthur laid out his plan. They would load the dead man into the trunk of his car and drive out to the state forest about fifty miles away. No one would ever find the body there. At least not before it had decomposed beyond all recognition. The gardener was an illegal, after all, and there would be no way to identify him. Mitch would then clean up the SUV with bleach, carefully remove every last trace of blood and tissue, and take it across the state line two hundred miles away to have it repaired quietly.

"Tell them you hit a deer," said Arthur.

"You realize that's not an animal out there," said Mitch. "It's a man."

"Yes. Very tragic," said Arthur. "But what about your wife? My daughter? Would you have her go to prison for this? Because some wetback stepped in front of her car?"

"He's a man, Arthur. He's married, and he's got a kid. What if his wife comes looking for him?"

Arthur huffed. "You'll say you don't know where he went. He just ran off somewhere. Do as I say, and we'll be all right."

The three of them stewed in silence for some time. Then Arthur, growing impatient with the long faces, told them to stop worrying. "For God's sake, you'll get another gardener."

That night, husband and father cleaned up all evidence of the accident. They packed the gardener into Arthur's car and drove to a remote spot. There, using a shovel they'd taken from Evelio's truck, they buried him in the forest. Mitch called in sick to work the next morning and took Fiona's SUV to be repaired.

"What do we do about his truck?" he asked once he'd returned hours later in a rented car.

"Too risky to move it now. We'll leave it where it is and stick to our story. He disappeared. We don't know where or why."

The woman stood like a statue, short and stout, legs bowed and face baked by the sun and the hardships she'd lived. For more than an hour, she stared at the house, as if trying to decode a cipher, before Fiona noticed her.

"Mitch, who's that woman outside?"

He drew the curtains to one side and peered out. "I have no idea."

"Can't you do something about her?"

Mitch pulled on a sweater and stepped out onto the porch where he called out to the woman. She said nothing. Her eyes gazed back at him from beneath a deep, furrowed brow. Determined to get an answer, Mitch strode across the porch, down the stairs, and approached her at the curb. It was then that he noticed the small boy hiding behind her. Tiny, dark, and thin, like a miniature adult—like a baby Jesus in a gothic painting—the toddler smiled at Mitch and extended two sticky fingers as a greeting.

"May I help you?" asked Mitch, ignoring the child.

The woman straightened and stood tall—all four feet nine inches.

"I am the wife of Evelio."

This was what Mitch had feared. Not only that the wife would turn up, but that Evelio's son would be so cute as to break his heart. He wanted to help them, but knew it was too late for that. He lied instead, swearing that he had no idea where Evelio was. But the woman either didn't understand him or refused to accept his answer. She kept repeating in Spanish something that Mitch took to mean, "Where is my husband?" Over and over in an off-key, half-strangled monotone.

That evening, the woman and her son were still holding vigil in the rain. Inside, Fiona wept, demanding that Mitch do something.

"They're giving me the creeps. Get rid of them!"

Mitch ventured out and tried again to convince the woman to leave. He even offered her money. She refused it. Pushed his hand away and repeated, "*Mi esposo. Mi esposo*" in that same eerie drone.

Afraid Fiona might be nearing a breakdown, Mitch stayed home the following day and the day after that. The woman showed up again, always at different times, with the child in tow, appearing and disappearing like a specter. Fiona's reaction grew more disturbed with each new sighting. On Tuesday morning, she screamed at Mitch that if he wasn't going in to the office, he could at least chase away the "the monster and her spawn."

On Wednesday, Mitch shooed away the widow with some Spanish he'd found on the internet. She left for a few hours, but came back when Mitch was on the phone trying to explain to an angry judge why he'd missed an important hearing the day before.

Like his wife, Mitch felt control slipping away. There were several unanswered messages from his boss, each one more urgent than the last. He put off responding, wanting to get a handle on this crazy situation first. And so on Thursday, despite a full docket of court dates and meetings, Mitch called in sick to work again. He waited at home for the monster to appear.

But she didn't show. Instead, a city police car pulled up in front of the house, and two officers climbed out.

"We're making inquiries about a missing man by the name of Evelio Barcenas," said the taller of the two cops. Mitch and Fiona stood in the doorway, side by side, hand in hand, displaying a united front to the policemen.

"Evelio?" said Mitch. "He worked here for a short time, then he just disappeared. I assumed he moved on to work somewhere else."

"We found his truck parked in the alleyway behind your place. About a hundred yards from your back gate."

"That's odd. We haven't seen him since…" Mitch turned to Fiona. "When was he here last?"

"A week ago," she said, almost whispering.

"That's right. Last Thursday, the day you texted me about the ape." He turned to the cops and explained that she'd spotted the escaped bonobo.

The officers exchanged a look. "Anyway," continued the taller one, "the wife thinks something terrible happened to him. She was reluctant to come forward since they're both undocumented aliens."

"Really?" asked Mitch, trying desperately to affect surprise. "I should have asked him for papers."

The cops nodded, though they hardly seemed convinced. "And you didn't see him that day?"

"I was working late at the office," said Mitch. "And, darling, wasn't that your book club day?"

Fiona nodded. "I saw him as I was leaving. And the bonobo, too. I told Evelio to chase him away."

Again the look between the two policemen.

Then Mitch's cell phone rang. He glanced at the screen and, seeing his boss's number, said he'd only be a minute. He excused himself and stepped back inside the house.

"Finally," said Fred Gregson. "Where the hell have you been?"

"I'm sorry, Fred. I've been dealing with a personal issue at home. I'll explain everything to you tomorrow."

"Judge Beecher's screaming at me because you missed a hearing the other day. And the Bakersfield people want you off their case. They said you turned down a generous settlement offer from Fischer Oil and Gas. What is going on with you?"

"Just give me till tomorrow. I'll explain everything, Fred."

Silence whistled down the line.

"There is no tomorrow for you, Mitch," said Fred at length. "We're letting you go."

"What?" snapped Mitch, loud enough for Fiona and the policemen to hear at the front door. "You can't be serious. You're firing me?"

Mitch stood there, holding the phone to his ear long after Fred had hung up. He felt numb. He was scared. Scared that his life was hanging by a thread. Everything he'd fought to achieve was now circling the drain. And his odious father-in-law would be there to rub his nose in his failure. All because of some insignificant, foreign gardener he hardly knew.

His fear swiftly turned to anger, then rage. He marched back to the doorway and rejoined the others. Heaving for breath, eyes blazing, Mitch fixed the two cops with his glare.

"Goddamn illegal aliens!" he yelled. "They're ruining our country!"

"Take it easy, sir," said the taller officer.

"And you come around here harassing innocent people like us instead of rounding them up!"

"No one is harassing you, sir," said the other cop. "We only asked you some questions about a missing man."

"A missing *illegal*," fired back Mitch. "We have nothing more to say to you. Get off my property, and don't come back without a warrant."

The officers exchanged one last glance, a silent acknowledgement, born of years of responding to domestic disputes and crime scenes together. They'd come to develop a shared instinct, one that exists between experienced partners: a certainty that the man they were interviewing was lying.

"Good job, Mitchell," said Arthur, raising a glass of whiskey to his son-in-law. Fiona had taken a sleeping pill and gone to bed.

"I'm afraid it's going to be a while before I can pay you back for the loan," said Mitch with a sigh.

"Forget it. You don't owe me a cent. And you'll come work for me. I could use a smart lawyer like you."

"Thanks, Arthur. That's very generous of you."

"Never mind. Just be glad this thing's all over."

Mitch wasn't so sure. "I didn't like the way that cop was staring at me. Like he knew I was lying."

"So what? There are no witnesses. We're the only ones who know, and we're not telling. There's nothing to connect you or Fiona to any of this. Not even the car. It's already been repaired."

"I just hope we haven't overlooked something."

* * *

Certain that Mitch was lying, the patrolmen reported their suspicions to the captain, who remained skeptical. They managed to convince him, however, to have a detective request the Hirschs' cell phone records from the service provider.

The actual text and voice messages were gone, but their digital footprints had remained. Having interviewed the two police officers, Detective Carla Torres was well acquainted with the details of the case. She reviewed the phone logs and zeroed in on the day Evelio Barcenas disappeared. A flurry of activity on Fiona Hirsch's phone jumped out at her immediately, and she took her findings to the captain.

"No luck on the texts," she said. "But look at this. Last Thursday evening, Fiona Hirsch made three calls in quick succession, then sent a text to her husband."

"Yeah, so?"

"The first call was to Mitchell Hirsch's cell phone at 5:57 p.m. Lasted twenty-one seconds. The second, a minute later, was to his office phone. Thirty-eight seconds. Then the third to Hirsch's secretary. A hang-up. And finally, she sent him a text at 6:00 p.m."

"And you're thinking maybe she left a voice message."

Torres nodded.

The captain pursed his lips. "I'm not convinced these people have done anything wrong. But let's say the wife did leave a message. I'm sure Hirsch has deleted it by now."

"Maybe not the second call," she said. "The one to his office phone."

"Why wouldn't he have erased it?"

Torres smiled. "Maybe because he got fired and never had the chance."

The captain leaned back in his chair, studying the detective. "I see you've thought this through. Is this because he's Hispanic?"

"I beg your pardon?"

"The gardener. He's Mexican, isn't he?"

Torres stiffened in her seat. "Salvadoran. What difference does that make?"

"Okay," said the captain with a knowing smile. "We can play it that way if you like. But I gotta say, Torres, I don't see probable cause for a warrant."

"But, Captain…"

Kendra knocked on Fred Gregson's door. It was past six, and she'd stayed late to pack up Mitchell Hirsch's personal items.

"I've finished," she said.

Gregson didn't even look up. "Thank you, Kendra. See you Monday morning."

She stood in the doorway, twisting the engagement ring on her left hand. At length, he became aware of her lingering presence.

"Was there something else?"

"Actually, yes." She swallowed hard. "There's a voice mail message on Mr. Hirsch's line. I think you should hear it."

"Thank you again for calling me," said Detective Torres.

Fred Gregson frowned at her across the conference table. He cleared his throat. "Naturally we want to cooperate with the police in a situation like this."

"Can you play it again?" she asked.

Gregson pushed a button, and Fiona Hirsch's shaky voice came through the speaker.

"Mitch, where are you? Something terrible has happened. Oh, God, I just ran over that monkey from the zoo! He's dead. I killed him. Call me right away!"

"I don't get it," said Gregson once the message ended. "I heard on the radio that there was another sighting of that chimp in Bellevue just this afternoon. This message is from last Thursday. Fiona Hirsch couldn't have killed that bonobo."

"Precisely," said Torres, thinking of the crow she was going to feed to the captain. "But if she didn't kill the ape, who *did* she kill?"

With the days growing shorter and the nights colder, Bingo missed his comfortable home in the primate village. After nine days on the lam, roaming the streets and scavenging for his meals, the little fellow was cold and hungry. He'd had his fill of adventure. It had been fun and exciting, except for the horrible night when the car ran over the man dressed in green. That was scary. And the worst part was that the kitty had run away.

The zoo was closing as Bingo tramped up to the front gate. Some departing visitors stopped to marvel at the sight, stepping aside to let him pass. Children squealed with delight, even as their parents sheltered them from the wild animal. Then, realizing the little ape posed no danger to them, they watched with glee.

"Careful. Don't scare him," said one lady.

"So cute," observed another. "I wish I could take him home with me."

Then a Dutch tourist snapped a photo of him, flash and all, and Bingo, shrieking bloody murder, backflipped his way through the gates and into the safety of Kenny's arms.

THE NEON PUNCH
An Eddie Flynn Short
Steve Cavanagh

Everyone's got a plan until they get punched in the face.

That's the first thing I learned in the ring. You spend hours working on your combinations, getting the breathing and stance just right then—*wham*. Your plans follow your ass to the canvas. Doesn't matter how much you've prepared. Maybe you've studied your opponent for weeks, figured out his weak spots. I've always found it real easy to see an opening. A guy drops his shoulder half a second before his glove moves, his eyes lock onto a target, or maybe he tucks in his chin before he throws. You do enough study, you can read people like a map.

Sometimes it doesn't make any difference: there's just no way to see that bunch of knuckles tearing over the horizon and coming straight for you.

Before I was a trial attorney, I had a different life. I'd learned to read people. It came in handy when I was reading witnesses and jurors.

But those kind of lessons come with a price. A painful one.

On this particular night, seventeen years ago, with this particular punch—well, nobody saw it coming.

Vegas.

Caesar's Palace. Poker. Texas hold 'em. Three in the morning. I'm five whiskey sours down and forty-five grand up. Only one opponent left at my table. He's two stools away, on my right. This man is a professional poker player and an amateur asshole. He's north of fifty-five, but he didn't look a day over seventy. Half a gallon of Jim Beam and four packs of Marlboro Reds a day for thirty-five years had aged him like a lemon left in the hot dessert sun. Deep, dark folds of bile-colored skin formed ruts around his mouth and brown eyes. The whites of those eyes had a yellow tinge to them, to match his pallor. The pale, button-down shirt only accentuated the sickness oozing out of his pores. When I met him for the first time that evening, I didn't know whether to shake hands or call a paramedic.

His name was Rubin Wachowski, a semi-retired second-hand car salesman from Poughkeepsie, but he never used his real name when he was playing cards. In the dessert, he called himself the Cat. Stupid, I know. Las Vegas had that effect on people. The entire town was a neon fiction. A shiny, inviting mirage of sex, gambling, drugs, and very few rules. It still had the feel of a pioneer town, even though the corporations were running it. Nothing seemed real in Vegas. Not even time. No clocks on the walls of the casinos, no reminders of the hours and the dollars slipping through your fingers.

They liked it that way.

I did too.

The Cat threw in five grand.

"Call," he said.

I turned and studied him. His lips were drawn tightly together, the edges curling upwards in a permanent feline grin. He had big eyes too. Round. Liquor yellow. Cat's eyes.

The cat-like effect would've been more pronounced if Rubin hadn't weighed over three hundred pounds. Both sides of his ass fell off the edge of the stool.

A big cat.

I checked my cards. An ace and a jack.

A strong hand if the flop fell right.

And it did.

Three cards were dealt face up. Two kings and a jack.

I had two pair. Kings over jacks. Ace high on top. Possible full house. Possible straight.

The Cat gave nothing away. Didn't check his cards again, didn't react. I watched his thick, bloated fingers. He reached for his chips and started messing with them, rearranging his stack.

It was an impressive sight. Ten rows of black and red chips made up fifty grand. And behind them, two chip bars. The chip bars were around the same size as a playing card, a third of an inch thick and colored silver. Each bar was a hundred grand.

Each hand I'd played that night was a step closer to getting my hands on those bars. Now was the time. My stack was much smaller. Sixty grand in total. There was already seventeen grand in this pot alone. I threw down ten thousand in chips.

The Cat took a pull on his cigar, let the smoke escape from his mouth like his stomach was on fire. He hesitated, didn't look my way, answered the ten grand and raised ten.

My gut told me it was a bluff. In this game, you play your opponent as much as you play the cards. It's a skill game. A confidence game. Right then, the Cat was betting like he held the other king in his hand. If he did, I was screwed. Three kings beats two pairs.

I called his ten grand, said, "You're bluffing."

He didn't react.

There was fifty-seven thousand dollars on the table when she walked into my line of vision. A blonde. Tall, slim, with Saturday-night eyes and lazy Sunday-morning lips. She wore a short, red dress tight enough to send a man to war. From the bucket of change in her hands, it looked like she'd been feeding the one-armed bandits all night.

"Sweet Jesus, would you look at *that*?" said the Cat, nodding toward the lady.

"I don't think she's a cat lover," I said.

"Why not? All the ladies love the Cat," he said.

I gave him a look. The kind that asked if he was serious.

Turns out, he was. She passed by our table.

"Hey, darlin', can I buy you a drink?" he called out.

The blonde stopped dead, fixed those eyes on him, then approached the table. She stood next to me, close enough that I could smell her perfume. Then she leaned over and stared hard at the Cat.

"You're the Cat, right?" she said.

"The one and only," he said.

"You're the son-a-bitch who cleaned my boyfriend out of our apartment deposit last week," she said.

The Cat raised his hands and said, "My bad, but you should think about ditching him anyways. Get yoursel' a real man."

The cigar bobbed up and down between his lips as he chuckled at that one. The lady didn't take it kindly.

"I wouldn't sleep with you for a million bucks," she said.

I could tell where this was going. The dealer spotted it too.

"Ma'am, please calm down," said the dealer, a dark-haired kid in a black waistcoat.

This was a distraction. There was money to be made on this table. I'd about had enough.

"Look, lady, I've got a game going here," I said.

She took a step back, smiled.

Maybe it was the perfume. Maybe it was the smile. Or the dress.

Didn't matter. Whatever the distraction was, it worked. She hit me in the chops so hard and so fast, Sugar Ray would've been proud. A straight right hand. Deep out of nowhere. Strong enough to send me flying sideways off my stool, right into the Cat. I tried to grab onto the table as I fell, and sent all the chips flying across the green baize.

The Cat stayed upright, but my head hit the carpet. For a second, all I could see were luminous streams of color—lines of glossy light whirling in front of my eyes. I shook it off.

Tried to focus on the dark, navy carpet. Something small and white lay in a pool of red on the floor. I knew what it was without even picking it up.

My tooth.

A pair of hands grabbed hold and hauled me to my feet. The man who'd picked me up wore a Hawaiian shirt, decorated in a pool ball and palm tree motif.

"You okay, buddy?" he said.

"I just need to sit," I said.

Somehow I made it back onto my stool. A security guard appeared beside me, started looking at my head. I heard him call for a medic.

I closed my eyes, tried to stop the ringing in my head.

Then I heard the blonde, "Take your hands off of me! I'm going, alright?"

She tried to shrug off two members of security.

"Let her go," I said, "no harm done."

They released her arms but walked her off the premises. Only when she'd disappeared behind a bank of machines did I hear the Cat's laughter.

"She really laid you out," he said.

"She did, too. I fold," I said.

The Cat stopped laughing. He wasn't going to ask me to reconsider, or give me time to recover. Easiest hand of poker he'd won in a decade.

Three minutes later I held an ice pack on my face, a bundle of cash sat on the passenger seat and I was steering my car, one handed, along the strip. Thankfully, even after I'd folded that hand, I still left the casino ahead. Anytime you drive out of Vegas with more money than you came with is a job well done. I even had my tooth in a napkin beside the envelope of cash.

An hour out Vegas I pulled over by the side of the road. I'd left the interstate a half hour ago and lit up the desert road with my Chevy's headlights. I kept the lights on, and for another ten minutes, I watched the bugs dancing in the beams.

Two cars pulled up behind me. I tensed up, gripping the wheel. The engine purred, ready to take off if I didn't like who got out of the cars.

A man with a patterned shirt appeared from the first car, and a woman in a red dress from the second. They stood, baking in the red glow from brake lights.

I opened the driver's door and got out.

The man in the Hawaiian shirt said, "I put half on black. We got lucky."

I'd met Roosevelt two years before. He had light fingers. A smooth palm action and balls the size of watermelons. Well, you needed them if you wore Hawaiian shirts in Detroit in December. When he'd picked me up off the casino floor, I slipped him the two one-hundred-grand chip bars that I'd swiped off the Cat's stack as I went down from the punch. Roosevelt then turned and went straight to the roulette table. He was supposed to go to the cashiers.

He opened a hessian sack with the casino's logo in the side.

Three hundred grand. Split three ways.

"I hate this hair color, and I hate this goddamn dress," said Boo. Ex-hooker, professional con artist, and owner of a mean straight right hand.

"At least you didn't get punched in the face," I said.

"Oh, honey, that's my favorite part," she said.

In the excitement, and the shock of a beautiful woman laying me out, it took a while for the Cat to notice that he was down two big chips. By that time, I'd already left.

"Next time just cash out, like we agreed," I said.

Roosevelt put his hands on his hips and said, "We got lucky."

I nodded.

Luck didn't last. Not in this game.

I put the false cap back onto my tooth, took my cash, and got behind the wheel. We went our separate ways.

Until next time.

YOU KILL ME
Terry Shames

I knew what I faced when I got home, so I couldn't force myself to hurry. For a wild moment I even considered never going home at all, but I had nowhere to go and no money. Although I'd been the only breadwinner for the last few years, Will always insisted that my paycheck be sent directly to his account. He declared that women don't know how to manage money. It was easier to agree than to fight with him.

I lingered on my way to the bus stop, pausing to peer into store windows that I usually ignored, trying to find comfort with the thought of buying myself something nice—a scarf maybe, or a pair of shoes. But instead of comfort, the idea of having something new to wear reminded me of my loss. How could life change so fast from bearable to hopeless?

As soon as I opened the front door, Will started calling me from the bathroom. "Leona, come in here!" No escaping that braying command.

Every day when I left for work and when I got home, Will was soaking in a bubble bath, listening to the radio. The second he heard me come in the door, he would start hollering for me. I once asked him if he wasn't afraid he'd be waterlogged from lying in the water so much, but he told me he only stayed in the bath a half hour at a time. "It helps me relax."

I walked into the bathroom, steeling myself to tell him my news. He was lying back in the tub as usual, surrounded by bubbles and grinning. I could hardly stand to look at him, with his big belly poking out of the water like a mound of dough. "I know something you don't know," he said in a singsong voice. Nausea seized me. Will already knew what I dreaded telling him. I tried to look expectant.

"Guess what I just heard on the radio?" He didn't wait for me to guess. "Your boyfriend is retiring. What do you think about that?"

"My boyfriend?" I struggled to keep my voice light.

He snorted. "You wish. Your big boss, Killian. The guy you dress up for every day." I was waiting for the line, and sure enough it came. "Leona, you kill me. You thought with his little wife dead he was going to take up with you and whisk you away with him. Don't deny it."

"Will, that's ridiculous."

"Now he's going to leave you high and dry." He nodded toward the radio perched on the edge of the counter. "Radio says he's retiring and the company is going to be sold. And you're going to be out of a job."

"I think the new owner will keep me on," I said, determined to hold my voice steady. "After all, I have a lot experience, and they'll need it."

"You are so naïve." His face was positively gleeful, even though it meant our income would be slashed.

"Will, do you need anything? I'm tired. I'd like to take off these shoes."

"No, hell no, why I should need anything? I'm just the husband. I'm good for nothing. Just trying to get you to see things the way they really are."

I crept out of the bathroom and closed the door behind me. I was shaking. I had to go in the kitchen and sit down at the table. I'd suspected for days that something was up with Mr. Killian. He was quieter than usual and had trouble meeting my gaze. But his announcement to me still came as a shock. He was senior vice president of one of the biggest companies in Denver, and he was barely sixty. It seemed impossible that he was walking away from the job.

Will's singsong voice echoed in my head. "Leona, you're so gullible, I don't see how Killian can trust you to do anything." The first hundred times Will said that to me, I didn't like it, but I thought it was just something he was saying to tear me down and make himself feel better. I thought once he found another job, he'd stop picking at me. I couldn't have known I was going to hear it so often that it got to be like a dentist's drill hitting a nerve every time it came out of his mouth. He told me I was a naïve fool so many times that I started to believe it.

Instead of becoming less malicious as time wore on, Will started making something nasty out of everything I said or did. "Leona," he said last week when we were getting ready to go to a neighborhood party, "who do you think you are, some fashion queen? Nobody else is going to dress up for this little afternoon party. Oooo—" his face lit up, "—I bet you're wearing that fancy dress in case Mr. Killian is there. Maybe he'll want to sneak you into the bedroom and take it off you. You know he's not getting any you-know-what since his wife died. I bet he's hot to trot. And I'll bet you think it's you he wants to do the dirty with."

"Will, stop it." I had been looking forward to the party, but he took all the pleasure out of it.

There was no possibility that Mr. Killian would be there. He doesn't live anywhere nearby. He's a wealthy man and I expect he only keeps company with other rich people. There's no way he would know anyone in our neighborhood. Not that he's stuck up. He's always been friendly and kind.

"Leona, where are you?" he called, breaking my reverie. "Can you bring me a beer?" I couldn't make myself get up. Every last ounce of my energy had been drained by Will's constant humiliation.

Last month Mr. Killian's daughter got married, and Will couldn't get enough of poking me about it. "Leona, you kill me. You actually thought your boss was going to ask you to his precious daughter's wedding?" I knew I wouldn't be invited because Mr. Killian had told me weeks earlier that the wedding was going to be small, only family. He said he didn't want me to feel hurt and that if it had been up to him, I would have been there. But I didn't bother to tell Will, because I knew he'd just say, "You actually believed him?"

How do things go wrong between two people? You get married young and you're on fire. The sex is good and everything you do together seems fun. You run on giddy dreams. Will planned to have his own printing business, and we were going to have a pack of kids and a nice house and good friends.

We even dreamed of going to Tahiti someday. When I was cleaning out a closet recently I ran across a travel brochure from ten years ago. I looked through it, then tossed it out. You'd think it would make me sad, but it just made me puzzled. Why Tahiti? Maybe because we have the mountains here in Denver and all that beautiful, blue water was such a contrast.

Dreams run into reality, everybody knows that. Saving for a business was harder than we thought it would be. The money Will expected to inherit from his folks got eaten up with his dad's months in the nursing home. After that Will and I had to help out his mother financially.

The kids came along and instead of four or five, we stopped at two because our second child, Chris, had a heart murmur that meant multiple operations and a pile of bills. That was a tense time and it gave our dreams a punch in the stomach along with the pocketbook.

Then a few years ago, Will started having trouble at work. He complained that his boss didn't appreciate him. The economy was iffy and his boss kept saying the printing business wasn't doing well. Will said he felt like he was walking on eggshells.

It turned out Will was right to be worried. Suddenly the

man he had been working for since we got married sold the business. Just like that. He sold it to a guy who owned several print shops and had his own employees and his own way of doing things. The next thing we knew, Will was out of a job. We were sure he'd find a new job because he was good at what he did and he loved it. When it took longer than we thought it would, I suggested that I look for a full-time job. I had been a part-time secretary the whole time we were married, and I knew I could find something better.

"I don't want to be embarrassed that my wife has to work to keep a roof over our heads," he said

I was surprised. He never had a problem with me working before. "I don't mind a bit," I said. "The kids are old enough so it won't be a problem."

Will sulked, especially after I pointed out that we couldn't survive on my part-time salary.

I was lucky to find my dream job. In a way, you might say it's partly Mr. Killian's fault that things started to go sour in my marriage, because he was so nice to me and treated me like a real find. He said, "Leona, I've never, ever had a secretary that I trust so much and is so competent."

I'm careful about the way I dress, even if I don't meet the public in my job. Mr. Killian never failed to compliment me on my appearance. That's why I began to realize that at some point Will had stopped noticing.

It didn't take long for Will to get a job, and it paid almost as well as the one he left, so he said I should stop working and things would go back to normal.

"But I like working," I said. "We can put away the extra money I earn toward the business you've always wanted, and for the kids to go to college."

He said, "Leona, you kill me. You talk about putting money away, but then you go out and spend all your money on clothes." I wasn't spending any more than I ever did, but I didn't argue because I knew his pride was at stake.

Then he lost that job. Something about getting into a fight with a customer.

That's when he started being hateful. A couple of weeks later he said, "Leona, you kill me. You think that guy Killian is so nice to you. He's taking advantage of you, not paying you enough, that's what."

I told him the salary I was getting was in line with other secretaries in my position.

After a while Will seemed to abandon searching for a job. I didn't know what he did all day, but when I got home from work every day, there he was in the bathtub again. And he would start in on me.

One day, for absolutely no reason, he said, "Leona, you kill me, pretending you don't know that Killian is trying to get into your pants."

I was so shocked I couldn't think of a reply. Mr. Killian had never been the least bit suggestive to me. He treated me with dignity and respect.

Will must have hinted to his best friend, Stuart, that Mr. Killian was after me. One night when the four of us were playing cards, Stuart's wife, Karen, a thin, sharp-tongued woman, kept looking at me funny. When we went in the kitchen she said, "How long do you think you'll keep on working for that boss of yours?" Real casual.

I like Karen fine, but we've never been close. The question put my back up, and the devil got in me, so I said back, calmly, "Oh, I really love my job. I can't ever imagine leaving Mr. Killian. He's so nice to me." And I gave her a little smile.

There's no question that it got back to Will because he started twisting the knife harder. "Leona," he said last week, "you really kill me. You think you look so sexy with your skirts and your makeup. But with the weight you've put on, you're wasting your time getting dolled up. You look like Petunia Pig."

He'd be surprised what I think. I know the years have piled

up. I'm all too aware of the saggy chin and the gray scattered in my hair. I'm forty-five and I look it.

But if he wants to see overweight, he should look in the mirror. I wanted to say, "Will, you kill me, the way you think you're so sharp." I knew if I did that, though, I'd never hear the end of it.

"Leona! Where's that beer?"

I sat seething, resenting his demands. And suddenly there he was, dripping water all over the floor. "Now you're hard of hearing, too? I figured I may as well get the beer myself." I watched as he got the beer, popped open the top, and wandered back to the bathroom.

This afternoon, when Mr. Killian told me he had decided to retire, I felt my world falling away from me. He said now that his daughter was married, he planned to move out to Idaho where he had a little cabin. He loved fishing and he surprised me by telling me he's an amateur artist and that he wanted to devote his time to painting. I knew that with him gone my life would be blighted. There would be no one to be nice to me, and that's all that had kept me going.

Eventually I got up and started dinner, going through the motions. All evening I tried not to show how upset I was, knowing that Will would take advantage of the opportunity to rub it in. If I thought sleep would give me a rest from my torture, I was wrong. I kept waking up, half dreaming that Mr. Killian had said, "Why don't you go with me to Idaho?" I almost convinced myself that he said that and in my dreams made my plans to pack my bags and walk out on Will, leaving him to holler after me.

This morning as I was leaving for work, Will called me into the bathroom. He was lying in the bathtub again for a morning soak, as he called it. He smirked and petted his belly like it was some little animal. Then he said, "I'll bet you're awfully disappointed. You probably figured your boss would ask you to run away with him." It was as if he had read my mind as I tossed last night, yearning for Mr. Killian to ask me to throw caution to the wind and run with him. He snickered, glee in his voice. "I got it right, didn't I? Oh, Leona, you just kill me."

So I did. When I get back from work tonight, I'll find his body in the bathtub. A shame I never could persuade him how dangerous it was to have his radio perched on the ledge next to the tub. I told him he should buy one that runs on batteries. But he said there was nothing wrong with the old one and that I was always too fast and loose with his money. His money. He never listened to a word I said. That's what I'll say, and that's what the police will believe. How could a mousy woman like me ever kill her own husband, no matter how many times he said I did?

WE HAVE TO TALK
Dave White

Anna's phone rang. It was a number out of Oyster Bay, Long Island, one she didn't recognize. She let it go to voice mail as she put her bag down and went over to the coffee pot. Teaching was hard work. She didn't realize that when she got out of the business world.

She hadn't thought of the business world in so long. Nothing felt right at the moment.

She filled the cup with leftover coffee from the morning and popped it in the microwave. Summers off and leave at three o'clock? That seemed like a godsend. Instead it was nights of grading and planning. Calling parents and making decisions about which lesson fit which kid. How many more wake-ups until summer break? Twenty?

The phone rang again. Her fingers trembled as they always did when she got scared.

Why was she scared? Just a phone call.

She walked away from the whining microwave and picked up her cell phone. The same Oyster Bay number. Anna blinked and the world went static for a minute.

This wasn't right.

Anna didn't know anyone in Long Island, nor did she want to. But she answered it anyway.

"Ms. Ackerman?"

"Yes," she said, and thought about the alliteration her parents loved—just like she did when the kids said her name.

"This is Leo Burger from Autosafe Shields, the security company. Are you related to William and Marianetta Ackerman?"

"My parents, yes. Is everything all right?"

"We are calling to let you know an alarm has gone off in your parents' home. We have not been able to contact your parents, so we have sent the police to your home."

Anna looked at the clock, only twenty after three. Both her parents—retired—should be home.

"What should I do?" she asked.

There was a short pause, then, "Nothing. But if you get in contact with your parents, please let them know the police are on their way."

"Thank you," she said and hung up the phone.

She immediately dialed her father's cell phone. It rang eight times, then went to voice mail. Anna tried her mother instead. The same thing.

After disconnecting the call, she stared at the phone. Usually her mother picked right up. The microwave beeped signaling the coffee was ready. She ignored it, and scrolled through her contacts, finding the number to her parents' home line.

The phone rang twice, then it sounded like someone picked up.

She could hear the screaming alarm in the background. Beathing on the other end.

"Hello?"

Still breathing.

"Mom? Dad?"

More breathing.

"Hello!" Her voice raised as air caught in the back of her throat.

The line disconnected. The microwave beeped again. Anna grabbed her jacket and ran for the car.

* * *

Part of her wanted to slam her foot to the floor and get her car to shoot through the red light. Her chest was tight, but she kept telling herself that was irrational. Her father probably left the door open a crack after setting the alarm. They were out for a late lunch or some afternoon shopping. Whatever it was retired couples do. Then the wind blew the door open.

She'd get over there, meet the cops, and reset the alarm. Her parents rarely answered their cell phones. This wasn't a big deal.

But the breathing on the other end of the line and the sudden disconnection rattled around in her brain. It didn't feel right.

The light turned green and she accelerated out of the light. Less than ten minutes later, she pulled into her parents' driveway. Nothing seemed askew, but her stomach went cold when she saw both of their cars parked in the driveway. The police weren't there yet.

Anna turned off the engine and got out of the car. The house alarm wailed as she walked down the driveway toward the back door they always used when they were kids. She turned right and saw the door, wide open as she expected.

"Mom?" she called out. "Dad?"

No answer. She walked up to the door and looked inside. Nothing. The kitchen was empty, and much like her mother had always wanted, spotless. Anna stepped inside and punched in the alarm code—0865—her birthdate, backwards. The wailing went silent.

"Hoped you'd get here first."

Anna turned toward the kitchen door.

Her brother Mark stood there—covered in blood.

The CEO sat behind his desk, elbows resting on it. He leaned his chin on his folded hands and stared across the table. A maze of buildings rose into the sky behind him, out the window. New York City looming as it always did when I talked with Chris DeCicco, my boss.

"We want you to leave on your own accord."

I sat back, the wind rushing from my lungs.

When I caught my breath, I said, 'What do you mean?'

Chris didn't flinch. "We want you to resign."

For an instant, the years of reports, late nights, and pitch meetings flashed across my mind. The ascent up the company ladder the only thing I wanted. How many nights, weekends, and summers in the Hamptons had I squandered? And now this—out of the blue.

"That doesn't make any sense," I said.

Chris took a long breath. The silence in the room made the seconds turn into hours.

"Yes, it does," he said. "You know it does."

I opened my mouth to respond, but Chris held up a hand. Fire burned in my stomach. No one treated me that way.

"Your brother," Chris said before I could respond.

I leaned forward. "What about him?"

"You know he's been a problem."

"Fire him then."

"After all he's done, and how you've protected him? It's the both of you."

I slapped the arm rests. "I didn't protect him. Your security camera didn't work. I pointed that out."

"He pushed Janice down the stairs!" Chris leaned forward. "Meanwhile, you're running around like a lawyer telling me about the video and that I have no proof. I hired the both of you as a favor to your father, and you've been great, Anna. But your brother..."

"He's been stressed out."

Chris shook his head and looked at me like I was speaking a dead language.

"Security will escort you out," he said.

* * *

"Where are Mom and Dad?" Anna asked. It felt like someone

had wrapped a fist around her throat. She choked out the words. "What's that on your hands?"

Mark looked at his hands as if they just appeared in front of him.

"Mom and Dad are fine." He lifted his hands up in front of his eyes. The blood glistened in the sunlight that streamed through the blinds. "And this? This is blood."

Anna put a hand on the kitchen chair to steady herself. "Where are Mom and Dad, Mark?"

Mark shrugged. "I don't know. Out? They were here when I got here."

"Then why is there blood on your hands?"

Mark took a breath. "I made a huge mistake."

Anna pushed scenarios through her head, trying to figure out what was going on here. The last she heard, Mark was hanging out on a New England beach. After Chris canned them, Mark decided to take a road trip and become a lobster fisherman. He wanted off the map. While Anna jumped right back into the game, taking alternate route classes to be a teacher, Mark wanted to find himself.

He should have been arrested. If the video wasn't fuzzy, and if it didn't become their word against Janice's, he would be behind bars.

But she saved him. And she told him to go away for a long time. He listened. Even if Mom and Dad weren't happy about it.

"What did you do?"

Mark opened his mouth and something in Anna's brain short circuited. It sounded like the words were a dubbed sound-track, his lips were moving, but the words didn't line up.

"I came home to see Mom and Dad and he was here. Chris was here. He was here, and..."

Anna shook her head. This was not happening. This was not happening.

"Tell me," Anna said. Her own voice felt disembodied.

"He's gone." Mark's hands shook as he tried to steady himself. "He's gone and it's not my fault, Anna."

When we were kids, real young, like eight or nine years old, Mark used to love playing manhunt in the summer. It was essentially hide and seek, but he waited until the last few streams of sunlight to start sinking in the west before we began to play. The last minutes of twilight would give way to evening and Mark would be hidden somewhere in the mass of trees behind their house. I would count to one hundred, then I'd begin the search.

Our parents would be inside washing dishes or putting on the Yankees game while I'd call out Mark's name at the top of my lungs. With all our friends away at camp or on vacation, this was the only game we had. On a good night, I'd find him within five minutes. On a bad night, it would take fifteen, maybe even twenty.

But one night, it took a lot longer. And it took the police to find him. His hiding spot was that good.

I remember the rock that formed in my gut as my parents screamed out his name. Dad running through the trees, his voice echoing off the branches. Mom fought back tears, the cordless phone she used to call nine-one-one barely balanced in her hand.

I remember thinking I shouldn't have gotten my parents; I should have found Mark myself.

Finally, when the cops came with their Maglites and a dog or two, they caught Matt. Three trees deep, one to the left, on the eighth branch, sprawled out like he was on a hammock. The cops made him climb down while they illuminated him. Mom wrapped him up in her arms. Dad stood off to the back, fists clenched and breathing like he'd just run a marathon.

Mark looked over at me and his mouth curled in a wide toothy grin.

"Gotcha," he said.

66

The same rock formed in Anna's stomach as she followed Mark through the house to the basement stairs. He skipped down them two at a time, like he did when they were kids. She grabbed the banister and took each step as slowly as she could.

"When I got here," Mark said, "he was on the front steps banging on the door. Mom and Dad weren't home. I never expected to see Chris. It was just time for me to come home and make sure Mom and Dad were okay. I was going to see if you wanted to get dinner after that."

Anna wanted to ask why he didn't call first, why he set off the alarm, why this was happening. Somewhere in the back of her mind was the stack of papers she had to grade that night.

She never believed Janice's accident was Mark's fault. But she also didn't believe in coincidences. When she got to the bottom of the stairs, all she could do was try to convince herself it was a coincidence.

Chris was contorted in to a pretzel and it was clear his neck was broken. A pool of blood had formed around his head. Mark stood over him, his face pale.

Anna choked back a scream.

"I swear, he tripped. Just like Janice. I swear it. But no one will believe me. You have to help me get rid of the body," Mark said. And the next time he opened his mouth, his voice trembled. "Oh God."

Anna said, "No way. I can't be a part of this."

"The cops are coming, we have to move him," Mark said. "I set off the alarm by mistake. I don't know the code."

"That's why I'm here," she said. "The alarm company called me."

"We have to get rid of Chris before the cops get here."

Too late. A red swirling light reflected off the walls and down the staircase corridor. Their sirens weren't going, so they weren't worried.

Mark said, "Get rid of them."

Anna turned and hesitated. It had been so long since she'd seen him.

"Please."

She took a deep breath and headed back up the stairs.

Early September and the air was hot and humid like a steam bath. No one told me schools didn't have air conditioning. My blouse stuck to the sweat on my skin, just at the edge of my collar bone. I tugged at it and looked down at my plan book.

Today's lesson went well. The students seemed engaged, but the other teachers on my team warned me this was early in the year. Kids bought in early; it was when the holidays started to roll around that things became challenging. Plans needed to be tighter otherwise students became distracted and misbehaved.

I wanted to worry about that in November, but their words stuck out to me. I couldn't stop thinking about them. After closing the book, I looked out the window of my first-floor room and watched the last of the school busses pull away. That was a good sign it was time to leave and I wouldn't have to sit in traffic. The first few days had flown by and getting home for the weekend would be good. At the same time, I'd miss the new routine—it kept my mind off…

Glancing out the window again, toward my car, I saw him. Mark. He was leaning against my trunk. My esophagus turned to ice. I threw my plan book and the stack of papers I needed to grade into my bag and headed to the door.

Mark saw me the moment I pushed the metal door open and let the breeze hit my face. The beads of sweat on my skin cooled and I almost felt cold, even in the eighty-degree weather.

"Why are you here?" I asked.

"I'm worried about you," he said.

He looked over his shoulder, searching the grounds. I caught a slight tremor in his fingers.

"I'm fine," she said. "I've started over."

Mark shook his head.

"You're not right," he said. "It doesn't work that way."

I dropped my bag. It hit the asphalt with a thud.

"You shouldn't be here."

"I'm here to check on you. Mom and Dad..."

"You have to leave," I said. The sweat started to pour off me. "Get out of here. Go back to Maine. Go wherever you're supposed to be. Anywhere but here."

Mark shook his head. "You've made a huge mistake. You're trying to fix it this year, but you know it's not right. You know you're not right." He pointed to my head. Like an asshole.

I felt my equilibrium shake and my knees buckle. Mark grabbed my forearms and steadied me.

"It's alright," he said. "I gotcha."

I regained my balance and put my hand on the car. Closing my eyes, I caught my breath and waited for the blood rushing in my ears to settle.

"You're going to get me in trouble," I said. "Go back to where you were hiding."

I opened my eyes and saw he was gone. I looked away from campus toward the trees in the distance.

Anna stepped out on to the front porch. Two police cars with their lights flashing were pulled to the curb. Four cops approached her, their hands on their belts. Anna put her hands up out of instinct.

"I'm the Ackermans' daughter," she said. "I got a call that the alarm went off."

The sun was in her eyes and it made her squint.

"Is everyone okay in there?" one of the cops asked.

The word caught in the back of her throat, but she forced it out. "Yes. We're all fine. I'm sure the alarm going off was just a mistake."

"No. It wasn't."

Anna turned a quarter turn left toward the sound. A man's voice, but not one of the cops. It was her dad.

The sun was like a pin in the corner of her eye. She looked at her dad, standing locked arm in arm with her mother. They were old now, gray on top, with arched backs and tired wrinkles in their eyes.

"You're in trouble, Anna," her dad said.

She couldn't tell, but it seemed like there were tears in her mother's eyes.

"Come down here," her mom said. She took a breath.

"It's not right what he did, Mom."

Her mother nodded. "Come down here," she said again. "You need help."

Janice saw me in the hallway. We were waiting for the elevator.

"Hey," she said. "You okay?"

I nodded, thinking instead about the ad I just presented for the second time in two days. The feedback was good, but revisions were needed.

"I don't really have time to talk to HR now," I said.

Janice shrugged. "I think we have to."

"I'm a little stressed out right now. I have a lot of work to do."

Where the hell was the elevator?

I shifted my weight. Just get back to my office and breathe.

"I could tell. Do you know what you said in that meeting yesterday?"

I walked toward the stairwell door. I took the stairs once a day to get some exercise. Now was as good a time as any.

Janice followed me.

"You said Mark." Janice held the door to the stairs open. "You kept referring to someone named Mark. We all noticed

it. Chris tried to get your attention. It wasn't a character in the ad or anything. You said he helped."

I closed my eyes. My fingers trembled. These days, I could still hear his voice. When things looked their worse, I could still hear him.

"I looked Mark up," Janice said. "And at your background check again. Your dad got you this job. He's friends with Chris. They thought you were okay. So they buried this. They kept it quiet. We should have known, Anna."

I whirled toward Janice. "How could you?"

"I'm worried about you. I want to help. I know someone you can talk to."

I didn't think, I stuck my hand out to grab Janice. But my hand didn't catch clothing, it just caught skin—the tips of her fingers. Janice stepped back to avoid my grasp and lost her balance.

"Gotcha," I said. The words came from nowhere. Mark stood next to me and laughed as I said it. I asked him why he was here. How that happened.

"Janice fell."

"Mark's inside. He's with Chris," Anna said. Her hands were still over her head.

"Mark is not inside, Anna. You know where he is." Her mother was using the kind of voice she'd use to ground her back in middle school.

"No."

"Yes. He's gone. He's been gone a long time. In the forest. The dogs found him. Remember? He fell out of the tree."

"Please don't say that."

"It wasn't your fault, Anna. We told you that. You were just kids. You were playing."

Her eyes burned. "He's here. He's helping me."

"No, he isn't."

Anna closed her eyes and tried to force her mother's words out of her head. She could feel Mark standing next to her. She took a step forward, down the steps.

"I gotcha," he said.

The cops rushed past her.

Anna collapsed into her father's arms. "I pushed Chris."

Her dad held her tight.

"I'm going to jail," Anna said. "What have I done?"

They broke down in tears.

"You know, now, those stories you've been telling me for months—they're just half-truths?"

"I understand."

"We had a breakthrough last week. I want to make sure you understand that."

"I pushed Janice. Not Mark."

"And the rest of those stories?"

"They weren't true. They never happened. Mark died when we were kids."

"How does that make you feel?"

"I..."

"Our time is almost up, Anna. I want to know how you feel. It's a sign we're moving in the right direction."

"I have to go back to my cell?"

"Soon. But answer the question."

"It makes me sad. I knew Mark was dead. I understood it for the longest time. But I chose wrong after college. I went into business. My dad got me the job and I took it. In advertising. It wasn't for me. I wanted to teach. The business world was too high stakes for me. And Mark started to come and talk to me. At night. He started to tell me everything was going to be okay. Whenever I got nervous, he'd calm me down."

"And what happened?"

"I don't want to tell you."

"*This is important, Anna. We're so close. We want to get you back to a normal life.*"

"*I don't deserve a normal life.*"

"*We all do. We just have to work to get there.*"

"*Janice called me on it and I pushed her. She got hurt. I got fired. But Chris was tight with my dad, so they covered it up. Paid Janice a lot of money.*"

"*And who did you blame it on?*"

"*Mark.*"

"*Why?*"

"*He was there to help me. That's what he did. Got me out of tight situations. And I tried to do the same for him. Found him before it got too dark.*"

"*Tell me about the day the police came.*"

"*I was teaching and the phone rang.*"

"*Were you?*"

"*No. I don't teach. I wanted to teach. I imagined myself teaching. After the Janice stuff, I couldn't understand reality. Living with my parents again. So I pretended to teach. It was calming. But the bell rang.*"

"*The class bell?*"

"*No. The doorbell. It was Chris. My parents were out, but he didn't know that. He wanted to talk to my dad about me. See how I was. So I invited him in, told him to wait. But he was scary. He was so serious. What if Janice was going to sue? What if I was going to get in more trouble?*"

"*How do you feel right now?*"

"*Scared. Nervous.*"

"*Is he here right now?*"

"*No.*"

"*What happened to Chris?*"

"*I pushed him down the stairs. Not Mark. Me. Chris hit his head. There was blood. I ran. I ran to the woods where we lost him.*"

"*And then?*"

"*The world went haywire. I was at my apartment. I was*"

mircrowaving coffee. The phone was ringing. But I knew it was wrong."

"Our time is up."

"I have to go back?"

"Yes."

"I don't see Mark anymore."

"That's good."

"No. It isn't."

POO-POO
Bill Crider

It was two days after Christmas, and someone had stolen Miss Ellie Huggins's cat. Or so she said. I thought it had probably just run away. In either case, I didn't want to try to find it.

"It's like we have an obligation, Tru," Dino said. "She was our fifth grade teacher, after all."

Dino has a strange sense of obligation to the past. His uncles practically ran Galveston when it was a wide-open town, but when the Texas Rangers closed down the gambling, Dino didn't feel obliged to go into some other branch of the family business. Instead he sits in his house and watches infomercials. But when an old friend, or even an old teacher, calls about some kind of problem, he feels as if it's his job to set things right.

The trouble with that is, he often feels it's a lot more my job than it is his.

"I don't want to get involved," I told him.

I was sitting in my living room talking to him on the telephone. I didn't want to go outside. It was cold and raining. I could hear the water running off the house and sluicing through the oleander bushes that surrounded it. I was drinking Big Red from a twenty-ounce bottle, reading *The Beautiful and Damned*, and staying dry and comfortable.

"Remember the last thing you asked me to look into?" I said.

"Hey, it wasn't my fault that that turned out the way it did."

Dino had asked me to look into several things, and none of them had turned out very well. He continued to maintain that it was never his fault.

"Besides," he said, "it's only a cat. What could go wrong?"

Now I was *really* worried.

"I'll help you out with it," he said. "Partners, right?"

I'd recently made the foolish statement that maybe Dino should work for me. What I did involved gathering information on people, the kind of information that I now have access to right in my living room, thanks to the wonderful world of computers. Since Dino hates to leave his house, the job seemed like a natural fit for him.

"We'd have to go outside," I said. "You can't look for a cat indoors. And have you looked outside today by any chance?"

"I know it's raining, if that's what you mean. But this is Miss Ellie we're talking about."

He had a point. Miss Ellie had been one of our favorite teachers a long time ago. Every day after lunch, she'd read to us: *The Adventures of Tom Sawyer*, *Heidi*, *The King of the Golden River*. I suppose I owed her something for that.

"And it's her *cat* we'll be looking for," Dino said. "You have a cat, too, remember?"

That wasn't exactly true. I lived with a cat, but that was as far as it went. Nameless was a big orange tabby who came and went as he pleased. He let me feed him regularly, and on days like this one, he spent a lot of time curled up on one of my chairs or the bed, which was where he happened to be at the moment. But he wasn't my cat. He pretty much belonged to himself.

"She really likes that cat," Dino said. "He's the only company she has."

I sighed, put a playing card in my book to mark my place, and laid the book on the floor by my chair.

"I'll pick you up in half an hour," I said.

* * *

We drove over to Miss Ellie's in my old Chevy S-10 pickup. The rain drummed so hard on the roof that we couldn't hear the radio, and the truck wasn't as waterproof as Dino would have liked. Rain was coming in through the passenger side door and getting his shirt wet.

"You ought to have a new seal put around this door," he said, moving over a little closer to me.

"I didn't know it leaked," I told him. "Besides, I don't think a seal would help. There's something wrong with the door."

"We could've gone in my car."

"I didn't want you to have to drive all the way out to get me."

"I think you're just mad because I talked you into looking for the cat."

"Animals seem to bring me bad luck. Remember the alligator? Not to mention the prairie chicken."

"Hey," Dino said. "That alligator wasn't my fault. You got into that one all by yourself."

I noticed that he didn't bother denying the prairie chicken, however. But it was Christmas, or only a couple of days after it, so I decided to let bygones be bygones.

By the time we got to Miss Ellie's house, the windows in the cab of the truck were misted over. That was because the heater didn't work.

"You're really driving a piece of junk, you know that?" Dino said.

"I'm sure the huge fee I'll get for finding Miss Ellie's cat will take care of that. I'll probably be able to buy me a new Ford F-150 or something."

"You wouldn't charge an old lady for finding her cat, would you? It would be more like doing a favor."

"I knew you were going to say that."

* * *

Miss Ellie lived on Church Street down toward the medical school in an old Victorian house that looked as if it hadn't been inhabited since the hurricane of 1900. Either Miss Ellie hadn't decorated for Christmas, or she'd taken the decorations down already. Seen under the dark clouds and through the rain, her home could have passed for the House on Haunted Hill. All we needed was some thunder and a lightning flash or two. And, of course, a hill. No chance of that. Galveston doesn't have any hills.

"Maybe if we sit here for a while, the rain will let up," Dino said.

I smiled. "The eternal optimist. You can stay if you want to. I'm going to get this over with."

I opened the door and made a dash for the porch. I was wearing a jacket that was supposed to repel rain, but it didn't work very well. Wet weeds leaned over the sidewalk and slapped around my ankles.

Dino followed me. He was wearing an Astros cap to keep his hair dry. I don't think it worked any better than my jacket did.

There was an old swing on the porch, but most of the boards were rotten. I wouldn't have chanced sitting in it. The screen on the door was rusty and pulled away from the bottom at one of the corners. There were three or four holes in it, and someone had stuffed cotton in them as if that would keep the mosquitos out.

I knocked on the door facing and waited, with Dino standing beside me, dripping onto the porch. After a while the inner door opened a bit and someone peered out from the darkness inside.

"Is that you, Dino?" a quavery voice said.

"Yes, ma'am. And Truman's with me."

"Well, you two may come in, then."

The inner door swung wide. I pulled open the screen and stepped through. The house smelled musty and damp. There were no lights on anywhere inside as far as I could tell.

Someone I assumed was Miss Ellie stood a couple of feet away. I couldn't see her face. She was short enough to be Miss Ellie, however. She came up to about my waist.

"Follow me, boys," she said. "We'll go into the parlor."

We followed her down a short, dark hall and turned left into a large room. Miss Ellie turned on a light, and I blinked.

There was no sign of a Christmas tree. The room was furnished with very old stuffed furniture with antimacassars on the backs of the chairs and the couch. Nothing in the room looked as if it had been sat on since Miss Ellie was a girl.

Miss Ellie still wore her hair pulled tight at the back of her head and coiled into a bun, but now the bun was entirely white, as was the rest of her hair. Her face was lined, but it had been lined long ago. The truth was that she hadn't changed much since she'd been my teacher, thirty years or so earlier. I'd thought she was ancient then, though she probably hadn't been so very much older than I was now. It was a scary thought.

I shivered slightly, maybe because the room was cold and I was wet.

"My, my, Truman," Miss Ellie said. "You've become very handsome. And you too, of course, Dino. It's so nice to see the two of you. I've talked to Dino on the phone recently, but I haven't spoken to Truman in years."

I felt vaguely guilty, as if I'd been caught rolling spitballs in the back of the classroom. I cut my eyes at Dino, who was looking virtuous, the good little boy who put in calls to his old teachers in their dotage. If only Miss Ellie knew.

"You boys have a seat," Miss Ellie said. "Would you like some lemonade?"

Lemonade? Two days after Christmas? What I wanted was to get out of there. I said, "No, thank you, Miss Ellie."

"Very well, then. But do sit down. I want to tell you all about Poo-Poo."

"Poo-Poo?" I said.

Dino sat in one of the chairs. "Her cat. Somebody stole her, remember? We're going to find her."

"Oh, I do hope so," Miss Ellie said. She sat on the couch and looked at me, her blue eyes as piercing as they'd been when I was in the fifth grade. "It's so lonely without Poo-Poo in the house."

Poo-Poo, I thought. I'm going to spend the afternoon wandering around in the cold rain and looking for a cat named Poo-Poo. Dino would owe me big time for this one. I sat down and waited for Miss Ellie's story.

It seemed that Poo-Poo, a lovely calico, had a cat door and could go and come as she pleased. On cold, wet days, she was generally pleased to stay inside, but she'd gone out some time during the night and never come back.

"Poo-Poo always comes back in the morning," Miss Ellie said. "I can't remember a single time when she hasn't come in and had breakfast with me."

I wondered if Poo-Poo had a place set for her at the table, but I was afraid to ask.

"And you think someone took her?" I asked.

"That's right, Truman. Why else would she have missed breakfast?"

She could have been run over, died of natural causes, or run away from home. I looked at Dino, and I could tell he wouldn't like it if I said any of those things, so I didn't.

"When I talked to Dino," Miss Ellie said, "he told me that he'd be glad to look for Poo-Poo and that you'd be happy to help out. I hope it's not an imposition."

I looked her right in the eye and said, "Of course not, Miss Ellie."

* * *

Water began seeping through my waterproof jacket after about ten minutes of searching. My running shoes had been soaked by the time I'd taken ten steps outside Miss Ellie's house, and my jeans were clinging to my legs.

Christmas lights that hadn't yet been taken down were red and green blurs in the rain. Santa and his reindeer sat on one lawn, looking as if they wondered what had happened to the snow. I brushed wet hair off my forehead and started up the walk.

Dino was smart. He'd gone down the opposite side of the street, so there was no way I could get my hands on him.

I knocked at the door, as I'd done at a couple of other houses, and asked the man who answered if he'd seen a stray calico cat. He was wearing a pair of old khakis and a white undershirt, and he had a can of beer in his hand.

"You kiddin' me?" he asked. "I'm watchin' a ball game."

He shut the door in my face before I had time to ask anything else.

It was pretty much the same on the rest of the block. No one wanted to talk to me about a cat or anything else. There had been a number of burglaries in the area recently, I recalled, and I didn't blame people for being a little touchy about talking to some stranger with water-soaked clothes and rain dripping down his face. Nothing spoiled the holidays quite like having your presents or money stolen.

Dino had finished his side of the street with the same kind of luck I'd had. He came across and met me on the corner.

"See any little calico carcasses in the road?" I asked.

"Don't say stuff like that," Dino said. "You wouldn't want to be the one to have to tell Miss Ellie that Poo-Poo was dead, would you?"

"No," I said. "And I wouldn't have to be the one. You would."

Dino took off his baseball cap and wrung water from it, then settled it back on his head.

"I'm not going to tell her, no way. We've got to find that cat."

"Where?"

"There's the alley, and the next block over."

"You take the alley," I said.

The house in the middle of the block was dark and the yard was choked with weeds. Not far off the sidewalk there was a Realtor's sign leaning at a slight angle.

I don't pretend to understand cats, but I thought that a deserted house might have a certain appeal for a cat if she could get inside. There was a high board fence in the back, but fences like that don't matter to cats. However, I didn't see any broken windows or open doors that might have given Poo-Poo an entrance.

Still, I thought it was worth a look. I walked into the yard and all around the house, my shoes squishing on the rain-soaked ground. Not only were the windows unbroken, they all had screens. There was clearly no way inside the house, not even for a really sneaky cat.

I was about to go back around front when I heard something. I stopped to listen and I heard it again. It wasn't loud, but it was very clear. It was a cat's meow.

Most of the old Victorian houses in Galveston are built high off the ground, as was this one, and I couldn't see in the windows. So I went up onto the small back porch and called out at the closed door. I felt like an idiot, but I said "Poo-Poo? Is that you?"

There was another meow, very close to the door, which was solidly shut. You'd think that a house for sale would be locked up, especially one that had very few prospective buyers dropping by and had been on the market for quite a while.

But I opened the screen and tried the door anyway. It swung open easily, and a cat streaked out between my legs, crossed the backyard like a bullet, and disappeared over the fence.

"Hey, Tru!" Dino yelled from the alley. "I found her!"

I decided that I'd torture him before I killed him.

Miss Ellie was so happy to have her little Poo-Poo back that I relented and let Dino live. I even let him take credit for finding the cat. Why spoil the day for him?

This time Miss Ellie offered us hot chocolate and clean towels. I took the towel and turned down the hot chocolate. After we'd dried off as best we could and listened to Miss Ellie tell us how wonderful we were and how grateful she was that Dino had found Poo-Poo, we left.

"Didn't that make you feel good?" Dino said before I dropped him off. "I mean, you were a big part of it, Tru, even if I was the one who found the cat. And you saw how happy Miss Ellie was. Something like that can really get you in the holiday spirit."

"Absolutely," I said. "It was better than watching *It's a Wonderful Life*. We should do it every year."

"You don't have to be sore just because you didn't find the cat. I gave you some of the credit."

"And I appreciate it. But what I need now is a long hot shower."

"Me too. See you later, Tru."

He got out of the truck and ran to his door through the rain.

I had the hot shower and ate a big bowl of Wolf Brand Chili for supper. I fed Nameless, read some more in my book, went to bed, and slept the sleep of the just.

Until around two o'clock, when I woke up and couldn't go

back to sleep. I couldn't figure out what was bothering me for several minutes, and then I knew what it was.

I told myself that I should have thought of it earlier, but I'd been angry with Dino, and I'd wanted to get out of the rain. The analytical part of my brain had been turned off. It was just too bad that it had to turn itself back on in the middle of the night.

The question was this: if there were no broken windows in that deserted house, no open doors, no holes in the walls, how had Poo-Poo gotten inside?

I told myself that there were plenty of ways. She could have gone down the chimney, for one thing. After all, it was the season for things like that.

Or some interested buyer could have looked at the house, with Poo-Poo sneaking inside while the door was ajar.

Or maybe there were holes in the floor, and Poo-Poo had entered the house from underneath.

I didn't really believe it was any of those things, however, so I got out of bed and found a dry pair of jeans. I thought about calling Dino but decided against it. He usually slept pretty late in the mornings, and he'd probably be groggy for hours if I could even rouse him at all.

It was much colder when I went outside, but the rain had stopped and the clouds were gone. Bright stars glittered in the black sky. I could hear the waves washing up on the beach and smell the salty Gulf. I got in the S-10 and headed for town.

At one time, many years ago, Galveston had been one of those towns that never slept, but the gambling had come to an end, as had a lot of other things. Now at two-thirty in the morning, the streets were nearly deserted. There were no cars in Miss Ellie's neighborhood except the ones parked by the curb.

I stopped the pickup and got out. The night was quiet, except for the faint sounds of the surf from beyond the seawall.

There were no lights in any of the houses around Miss

Ellie's, but Christmas lights still flickered outside in the yards of a couple of places where the homeowners had forgotten to turn them off or had decided to leave them on all night and to heck with the electric bill. I didn't see a sign of Poo-Poo or any other cat. Probably I should have gotten back in the truck and gone on home.

But of course I didn't do that. I went to the back door of the house where I'd found Poo-Poo earlier, trying to be even quieter than a cat. I tried the door again. The knob turned under my hand, and I pushed against the door.

It opened slowly at first, then very quickly, so quickly that before I could even let go of the knob I was jerked inside the house.

I managed to drop to the floor and do a forward somersault, so the baseball bat that was supposed to hit me in the head swished over me and knocked the breath out of whoever had yanked the door open. It may have cracked a couple ribs, too, if the yell the guy let out was any indication.

I came up on my feet, my bad knee almost giving way beneath me, and turned around just in time to get my hands up before the bat hit me in the face.

I would have been better off if I'd been wearing a fielder's glove, one of the bushel-basket-sized ones favored by the current crop of big-league outfielders, but as it was, I managed to stop the bat a couple of inches from my nose and get a grip on it without too much damage to my hands.

I couldn't see very well in the dark room, but I figured that whoever was trying to bash my head in couldn't see much better than I could. I tried to wrench the bat out of his hands, but he was stronger and probably much younger than I was. I didn't stand a chance.

So I shoved backward and let the bat go. The guy swinging it stumbled awkwardly and tripped over his friend, who was still lying on the floor and gasping for breath.

I heard the bat clatter across the floor and bang up against the wall, so I made a dive for it. I got to it about a tenth of a second before someone else, but that was enough time to give me a little leverage. I snatched up the fat end of the bat and jammed it backward.

The butt smacked into something hard, maybe someone's forehead or cheekbone. There was a loud groan and the thump of a head hitting the floor. Now there were two people lying there, three if you counted me, except that I was sitting.

I stood up, keeping the bat in one hand, and felt along the wall for a light switch. When I found it, I flipped it up. The light wasn't bright, but there was enough of it to make me blink as I looked down at the two young men lying at my feet. They couldn't have been much more than sixteen, if that, and I didn't feel especially proud of having put them where they were or of most likely having solved the burglaries that had been happening in the neighborhood.

One of the boys, for that's what they really were, was beginning to come around. He was holding his side and trying to sit up. Judging by the way he was looking at me, I was lucky that the two of them hadn't had anything more lethal than a baseball bat.

"Let us go, old man," he said. "Let us go, and we won't hurt you."

I wish he hadn't said "old man." I'm not that old, in spite of the way I sometimes feel. I don't even have gray hair. Well, not much.

I looked at his friend, who wasn't moving but who appeared to be developing a nice-sized knot in the middle of his forehead. He was lucky I hadn't hit him in the nose.

"I don't think you're going to hurt me," I said. "You're not going to hurt anyone for a while."

He gave me a practiced smirk. He'd probably get even better at it as he got older. He was one of the predators, one of the unhappy ones who couldn't really see anything wrong with taking whatever it was that he wanted from whoever happened to have it. Sooner or later, he would have tried taking it from Miss Ellie, or someone equally helpless, who resisted just a little too much, and the baseball bat would have become lethal indeed.

I knew that I probably hadn't changed his destiny, but at least I'd postponed it.

"How'd you find us, old man?" he asked.

"You shouldn't have let the cat in," I said.

He looked at me as if he thought I might be crazy. He said, "What're you talking about?"

I didn't bother to tell him.

"You just couldn't stand it, could you," Dino said to me the next day. "Just because I found the cat, you had to go out and be some kind of a hero so Miss Ellie would like you as much as she likes me."

We were sitting in Dino's living room, where his TV set was tuned in to an infomercial in which a man who didn't look much older than the two I'd turned in to the cops the night before was talking about how to become rich by placing small classified advertisements.

"I didn't do anything to be a hero to Miss Ellie," I said. "I like to think I'm a little beyond trying to impress my fifth grade teacher."

"So you're saying I'm not?"

"Me? I'd never say a thing like that."

Dino watched the infomercial for a minute. I wondered what kind of small classified ads you'd have to place to become an instant millionaire.

"So how'd you know they were there?" Dino asked after a minute or so.

"I didn't. But I thought they might be. Someone was going in and out of that house often enough to let Poo-Poo slip inside, and the burglaries had all been right around that area. It was a good place to hide out and wait until everyone was asleep, then break into a house. They could even watch to see whether any of the neighbors left their houses for a visit or to go to the grocery store or to a movie."

"You think they might have tried Miss Ellie's place?"

"Maybe. She was alone and she would have been pretty helpless against the two of them. She would have made a good target."

"I'm glad you stopped them, then. And I guess I deserve a little of the credit, too, come to think of it."

"Sure you do. If it hadn't been for you, I wouldn't have gone looking for Poo-Poo."

"And if you hadn't gone looking for Poo-Poo, you wouldn't have found those two punks."

"Right. So you might want to drop by Miss Ellie's one of these days and tell her how you saved her."

"I don't think so," Dino said.

"Why not?"

He looked over at the TV set. "I'd have to go outside. I think I'll just give her a call instead."

"You be sure to do that," I said.

I'LL MISS YOU, BABY
Alex Segura

Vic Souto wiped Espinosa's blood from his face and onto his shirtsleeve. He took a short, halting breath and looked around the tiny efficiency apartment. Espinosa was lying face down on the sofa-bed that took up most of the small home. Vic's elbow—which slammed into Espinosa's face, making a wet cracking sound—had sent him flailing onto the bed, splitting the mattress and shattering its flimsy frame. There'd been more after that—a few punches to the face, more blood, a mess. Then it got real quiet.

The place was destroyed. Takeout containers, porn mags, ashtrays, and dirty clothes everywhere. And that's the shit that was there before Vic showed up. Before they got to talking. Way before they got to punching.

Vic cursed under his breath. He grabbed a paper towel and started wiping surfaces—doorknobs, walls, shit he'd knocked over. He stopped. He was still breathing heavy and his white shirt was pink and red with blood. Espinosa wasn't moving. Vic turned toward the sink and washed his hands. The water pressure was low. He needed to think.

The gurgling sound, like someone coughing underwater, startled him and he turned around. Espinosa's mouth was moving like an overdubbed movie where the lips didn't match the words. He couldn't make out what he was trying to say.

He kneeled down next to Espinosa's head.

"Motherfucker…" Espinosa said. Getting a single word

out was causing him pain. Vic wasn't going to call an ambulance.

"You're dying," Vic said. "Don't waste time. Where's the money?"

"Gladys...." Espinosa said, his voice low and mangled. "Talk to Gladys."

Gladys was his boss. Or, better said, she was married to *the* boss—Tone Miranda, who owned the construction company where Vic worked. Espinosa was part of Miranda's crew. Gladys was Miranda's wife. Vic's life was getting complicated. His brain buzzed.

Espinosa's head bobbed a few times. Vic felt Espinosa's hand on the back of his neck, pulling him closer. Espinosa's fading breath on his ear. He whispered something. Vic pulled away and watched the man close his eyes and stop moving, as if suddenly pulled into a deep, warm sleep.

Vic parked his copper Toyota Tercel in the LoneStar lot. The engine clack-clacked a few more times after Vic turned it off. It was still dark outside. Pre-noon cool. The Miami sun had hit the snooze. His wife, Lisette, had been asleep when he left, their baby curled up next to her. Another Saturday.

Vic worked hard. He was a dropout. But he was strong and he was smart. His cousin Jesus had hooked him up with the job at LoneStar six years ago. First as a grunt, lifting stuff, running errands, basics. Now he was a manager. The pay was a bit better, the hours still sucked hard. Vic went through most of his day focused on whatever was in front of him. He didn't think of the big picture much because the big picture was a piece of shit.

He left his car unlocked and walked into the tiny, portable office set up near their downtown construction site. They were working on more high-rise condos near Wynwood, the artsy-fartsy strip of Miami. Vic wasn't sure why they were building more condos. People hadn't bought the ones already clogging the Miami skyline. But it was work, and Vic liked having money in his pocket.

"Miranda wants to see you."

Vic tried to not show any surprise as he nodded in the direction of Miranda's secretary, Jasmani. She was young, barely out of high school. She wore a tight shirt and short-shorts to go with her big hoop earrings and full-spectrum makeup. She looked like a skinny, wet clown. Miranda's niece or something. Vic walked past her desk in the tiny trailer-office and knocked on the flimsy door that would lead him to Miranda.

"Come in."

The voice wasn't Miranda's. At least not Mr. Miranda's.

Vic opened the door and found Gladys sitting behind her husband's desk. She was wearing a sharp gray business suit. She was smiling. The office smelled of flowers and fruit. Her skin seemed to shine, even in the dim light of early morning.

Gladys looked good. She was well put together. She gave off a vibe that screamed, "I know you're scanning me." Sharp features—dark eyes, full mouth, and a toned body. Vic wondered what a weasel, wannabe gangster fuck like Tone Miranda did to find a girl like Gladys. Then he remembered Miranda was a druglord and loanshark masquerading as a legit businessman. Lucky prick.

Vic didn't let his eyes linger over Gladys for too long. He got to thinking about Espinosa. His last words and what happened before then. The offer of a nightcap. Some coke. Then an argument. Punching, kicking, blood, and quiet. Now Espinosa was dead and Vic was trying to act cool, calm, and not-a-worry. Let's see how long that'd ride.

"Mrs. Miranda, good morning," Vic said, looking at his feet, the desk, the certificates framed on the wall behind her. He tried not to look at her. His eyes would want to stay for a while, soak her in, spend some time on every inch of her. Dangerous.

Gladys stood up and motioned for Vic to sit in one of the chairs. She walked around and sat on the front edge of the flimsy-looking desk. Vic didn't look at her legs, but he knew they were there. He felt sweat forming on his brow. He wiped at it as he sat. He smiled, his eyes on the window behind Gladys, letting her remain blurry and in the periphery.

"Vic, I need a favor," she said. Her voice was a whisper, her eyes at half-mast. She'd crossed her long legs and folded her hands over her right knee. Vic nodded.

"Have you heard from Andres?" she said. "He hasn't clocked in—he was supposed to be here hours ago."

Andres Espinosa. Vic didn't panic. If this was about Espinosa being dead, it'd be a fat fuck cop talking to him, not his boss's hot wife. He let his eyebrows pop up.

"Espinosa?" Vic said. His response rang true to him. Vic knew how to lie. He'd perfected it with his mom, his wife, his friends. Lying was easy. This was a layup.

"Yes," Gladys said. "Jasmani, our niece, said you went out with him after your shift yesterday."

That little nosy bitch, Vic thought. Still, he didn't let it show on his face. Gladys was smart, but she was playing a game—she knew something and was hoping Vic would end up there, too.

"We grabbed a beer, but that was it—at Kleinman's, down by the Performing Arts Center," Vic said. "I had to get home, though, so I left after a round."

Gladys nodded. Not what she wanted to hear.

"You want me to check on him?" Vic said.

"Could you? We can cover for you here," she said, recrossing her legs, her sleepy eyes on his. "Just hurry back and let me know what's going on."

He was gone.

Vic closed his eyes and opened them again, but nothing had

changed. Espinosa's body was gone. No longer splayed on the tiny sofa-bed. His place was immaculate—someone had come in and cleaned up the blood and Espinosa's own disgusting mess. For a second, Vic thought he'd walked into the wrong apartment. He'd been riding a nice buzz last night. But he double-checked. This was the spot.

Vic paced around. He wasn't sure what it all meant, but it wasn't good. Someone had come in and seen Espinosa dead and decided to spic and span the whole job. This was, on paper, good for Vic. But it meant that whoever cleaned up Vic's mess also knew it was Vic's mess. He pulled out his flip phone and dialed.

"He's not here," he said, his voice flat.

"That's strange," Gladys said. She didn't seem surprised, and her words rolled out slow and steady. "Not sure where else he could be."

"No clue," Vic said. "Could still be out getting high, for all we know."

He heard a click and the call was over.

He waved the spoonful of baby food in front of Ivonne's face and waited. Her eyes widened a bit, followed by an open mouth saying *okay feed me, please.* She snapped up the fruity slop and nodded for more.

Vic, sitting at the small dining table just off the main living room in their tiny South Miami studio, spooned up another dose of food for his eight-month-old daughter. Lisette was asleep on the couch, her arm dangling off the edge. He was reminded of Espinosa's body in a similar position less than twenty-four hours before. He felt a chill. It was pushing ninety outside and their AC had sputter-stopped two nights ago. He fed Ivonne a few more spoonfuls and put her down in her crib a few feet from the table. After a little fussing, she focused her attention on the plastic ring and ball she shared a cell with.

Vic couldn't sleep. This time—the late afternoon—was when he needed to rest in order to be up at dawn for the next day's work. But his head was like a chainsaw—too much noise and spinning. Someone had seen him go into Espinosa's apartment. Someone knew that Vic killed him. Maybe that person even knew what Espinosa had told him.

He laid on the floor and did a flurry of sit-ups, then transitioned to weights—checking his progress with a mirror he'd set up on the wall opposite the couch. They didn't have a TV in the apartment. Vic liked it that way. He cherished quiet. Moments like these with his wife asleep and child distracted were rare. But he couldn't fully enjoy it.

He built up a good sweat and felt himself calming down. His nerves dulling. The static in his head turned down to one. He couldn't control what anyone had seen. If anything, whoever cleaned up his mess had done him a solid.

He went into the bathroom and closed the door. He took off his clothes and hopped in the shower. It was chilly-cold to combat the heat wave outside. He heard his phone ring as he finished and toweled off. Probably Lisette's mom, checking in on the baby. Lady called three times a day. Called Vic when Lisette wasn't picking up. God forbid she use the bathroom. Vic walked into the main room, towel wrapped around his waist.

The slap was more surprising than painful. Lisette hadn't put all of her strength into it. Vic wheeled away, rubbing his cheek and looking at his wife in surprise. She was pulling back to hit him again. He lunged forward and grabbed both her arms, holding them up over her head.

"The fuck are you doing?" Vic said, his voice loud and stern.

"You son of a bitch, Victor, you fucking son of a bitch," she screamed, spittle hitting Vic's face as she pushed forward, trying to loosen his grip. "You are just a piece of shit, you know that? I can't believe you're doing this again. Get the fuck—"

"What the hell are you talking about?" Vic said, he was yelling now. He tightened his grip on her. His face stung from her first strike. The baby was crying. The neighbors would be knocking on their door again soon.

Lisette yanked her arms free and stepped back. She grabbed Vic's cell phone from the couch and waved it in his face.

"That was your girlfriend, *maldito*," she said. "Your *puta* Gladys. She wanted to see where you were. I asked 'Who the fuck is this?' and she tells me you had plans to see her tonight. And she didn't mean work plans, okay? So don't fucking try that."

"Lisette," Vic said, trying to calm her, his palms up. "That lady is lying to you."

"You're lying to me!" Lisette said, throwing the phone at Vic, which bounced off his forehead with a thunk and rattled on the floor.

Lisette moved toward the baby's crib and scooped up their daughter. A few seconds later, she was out the door. Vic fell to his knees. He heard a photo frame crash into the floor, followed by the glass.

The cheap door slammed open, shaking on its hinges as Vic sped in. She wasn't there. Fuck. The office was in shambles— papers strewn about, drawers left open. Someone had left in a hurry.

"Looking for me?"

Vic turned around. Gladys was standing in the doorway. The cheap office door was at a weird angle. She didn't seem to notice. She seemed completely relaxed.

"We need to talk."

Gladys stepped in, her heels clacking on the cheap, plastic floor—tick, tap, tick. She closed the door behind her and sat down in one of the chairs in front of her husband's desk, facing Vic. She licked her lips and looked up at him.

"Are you upset?" she said. "Because I'm glad you're here. I've been thinking about you."

"Are you insane?" Vic said. The words he'd hoped would escape his mouth as a yell came out more like a desperate whisper. "Why would you do that? She left. Lisette is gone."

"I'm sorry to hear that," Gladys said. "But I think you have something for me, and I'd be very happy to take it off your hands."

"What the fuck are you talking about?"

Gladys stood up. She was close to Vic. He could smell her perfume. It wasn't cheap. It was the nice kind, from places that Vic couldn't afford. Not pharmacy brand. She smelled like candy.

"We would be good together," she said. "We could help each other. You give me something I want, and I…"

She leaned in to kiss him and Vic felt himself start to respond, his mouth moving toward hers. He pulled back at the last possible moment, fighting the urge to step back.

Her expression changed from lustful to confused to angry. Full emotional twirl. She shoved him.

"You're seriously turning me down?" she said. Her eyes were on fire now. Vic saw her hand reaching toward the desk, as if trying to grip something. Something that wasn't there anymore.

Then it clicked in his brain. The alarm bells started to go off, loud, boom-boom-boom. Vic backed out of the office, his eyes on her as she realized he knew. Her bared teeth retreated and, for once, she looked scared.

They'd had too much to drink. Finger wagging the bartender for refills like nothing. Espinosa with J&B on the rocks, Vic slurping rum and cokes—the label got cheaper as the rounds hit double digits.

Espinosa was a paint-by-numbers thug and an idiot, Vic thought, as he pressed his foot down on the car's accelerator— weaving from lane to lane on the 836, the afternoon sun burning through his windshield. Sweat soaking his shirt, not just from the heat but from the fear. He had one play. He was taking it now. Vic knew Espinosa from work, but he wasn't a laborer—manager or not—like Vic. No. He worked for Miranda but he didn't *work* work. He did other work. Shady work. He showed up at the office or different sites without a spot of dirt on his white shirt, or a drop of perspiration on his forehead. He worked, alright. But not at anything clean.

Espinosa had asked to see him—asked Vic to hang out. Grab a round. He wanted to talk. They'd gotten along fine. Vic figured one round, quick exit, no worries. But the conversation flowed with the drinks and soon Vic and Espinosa were old pals, comparing notes on girls they knew in high school and how bad the Dolphins were. It was too easy.

Vic let out a long breath as he took the 87th Avenue exit south. He slowed the car down to match the local traffic—the last thing he needed was to get pulled over. He kept both hands on the wheel. He realized he didn't have his cell phone. That's fine. He wouldn't need it anymore, one way or the other.

The conversation got to Tone Miranda. The boss. He liked Vic. Liked his work. Thought he was a stand-up guy. Miranda needed some help. Wanted some new blood. Vic had the blood he wanted. The offer was quick: do a few jobs, Espinosa said. It's just security work, Espinosa said. No weapons needed, Espinosa said. Vic nodded, nodded and sipped, nodded again. Yeah, yeah, tell me more, Vic said.

Vic pulled a sloppy left onto SW 30th Street. The elementary school was on his right. It was midday. Kids were running laps in the field. Vic could see the fat gym coach yelling them on. They were specks in the distance but Vic still had to play it right. He parked a block down, in front of what looked like an empty house. He got out and walked, casual-like, down the street toward the school parking lot.

Espinosa dragged. His pitch sagged and swayed as he drank more. Miranda went from cool boss to kind of a jerk.

Espinosa vented. He ribbed. By last call, Espinosa was full-on raging. Miranda was the worst. He had stuff on him. His wife was a demon bitch with no soul but man was she beautiful. They hot-stepped out of Kleinman's bar and found themselves driving to Espinosa's tiny sinkhole of a residence. It made a cardboard box look swank.

"A deal went bad," Espinosa said. "I know where the money is. We can split it. We can start our own outfit here."

Nod, nod. Yeah, money. Sure, man.

Espinosa with the Cliff's notes: Miranda suspected but lacked the facts. Espinosa was skimming and had taken the whole pie on a deal he was supposed to cut with the Colombians. Big shipment of drugs came in, money went out but didn't arrive. Espinosa played dumb. Colombians were mucho pissed. Miranda was on the clock to repay. Espinosa was freaky scared—drinking himself silly. Trying to act normal.

Vic walked toward the main office. He got a few stares—teachers and staff wondering what this dude was doing. The bathroom was where Espinosa said it'd be—near the back of the cafeteria across from the big field. The hallway was empty. Vic hoped there wasn't anyone in the stall.

It all went south when Espinosa said it. Vic was drunk but not shitfaced—he could talk and drive and move and think. They'd walked into Espinosa's dumpster apartment. Espinosa was riffing on Gladys again. The things he'd do to her. The luck of that fuck Miranda—how'd he score that, man? That was all fine. Vic could appreciate a little lustful chatter between newfound bros. But then he said it, and Vic didn't remember breaking his nose, but he did.

"Your wife, man, you are one lucky sonofabitch, too," Espinosa said. *Vic's blood was revving up—going from rum-soaked to bubble-boil.* "Shit, she'd be moaning in a second. She'd forget your—"

Punch to the nose. Elbow to the face. Shove. Scream.

Vic is on top of Espinosa, pounding him—uppercut, uppercut, body blow, body blow. Halfway through, Vic hears the

screams and realizes it's not Espinosa, but him. He's crazy mad.
He jumps back and wipes his face and wide-scans the damage.

The stall was empty. The whole bathroom was clear. Vic took a second to scope the tiny toilets and urinals. No kids. He had to be quick. He found the cabinet under the main sink. The lock was easy—one hard pull and it opened. It was there— something heavy surrounded by Publix plastic, double bagged. Vic snatched it and pivoted, ready to bolt out. That's when he saw him.

"What are you doing?"

The dude was skinny—middle-aged sitcom dad style. Teacher, probably. Vic stood up and stepped closer.

"I'm going to call the police," the man said, holding up his phone, his hand shaking. "You should not be in here."

Vic plowed into him, head down. Fourth down and one, trying to break through the line. The guy crumbled, and Vic heard him fall onto the tile and let out an unpleasant moan. Vic didn't look back. He ran.

He got to his car. He was panting. He let himself look back and didn't see anything—teacher man was probably too ashamed to give much chase, but he could expect the cops soon. He moved around to the driver's side and saw that his tire was flat. Make that tires. Slashed. The wheels almost touching the street. This was a quiet part of town—residential, subur- ban. Vic took a step away from the car—time to run for a bit longer. The man standing in his path said otherwise.

"Espinosa tried to fuck me," Tone Miranda said. He was tall. Thin but strong. His features clean and clear. Buggy eyes stabbed at Vic. His hands flapped toward Vic. They said *gimme that.*

Miranda yanked the bag from Vic's hands and looked in.

He nodded.

"You tried to fuck me, too," Miranda said. Vic prayed for sirens.

"Mr. Miranda," Vic started. He was trying to get his brain started. Yanking on the string to get the motor going. Sputter, sputter. He wanted to rewind to a few days back. He wanted those problems. Annoying wife. Crying baby. Shitty job. Not this. "I didn't know this was yours…Espinosa lied to me…"

"Shut. The. Fuck. Up," Miranda said. Veins popped out of his forehead and Vic fought the urge to take a step back—to move at all. "You think I just figured this out, Vic? You think I just realized Espinosa fucked me over?"

They heard the sound of a door opening and both turned to the tiny house that Vic had parked in front of. The tiny house Vic thought was empty. They turned to find an older man stepping outside, bending over to pick up his newspaper and looking at Vic and Miranda—trying to figure out what was wrong with the picture.

Miranda shook his head. It was a brief, subtle motion. But the man seemed to get it. Despite his legit business fronts, Tone Miranda was no stranger to the headlines, and those stories reached even the quietest corners of Miami suburbia. The man stepped back into his house and slammed the door. Vic thought he heard the locks clicking after him.

"It's over, Vic," Miranda said. His voice was calm now. Relaxed. No jitters.

"Whatever she told you, is a lie," Vic said. Last ditch. Hail Mary. Ten seconds left in overtime.

Miranda raised an eyebrow. Intrigued.

"I didn't do anything with Gladys, man," Vic said. His voice was trembling. He didn't want to die. Not like this. "She lied to you. Espinosa just told me where to get the money, I was going to bring it to you. He told me he fucked you over—"

"Gladys?" Miranda said, an inside joke chuckle leaving his

mouth. "Gladys is dead. She tried to cross me, too. You really think she'd be dumb enough to call you like that?"

Vic couldn't think of anything else to say. He wasn't surprised when he felt the sharp tip of a long knife on his back. The warm breath on his neck. Lisette's cheap perfume lingered, even if it was covered by something fancier, newer.

He felt her mouth close to his ear. He didn't look back. He saw Miranda smile.

"I'll miss you, baby," she said.

She kissed his neck a second before he felt the blade slide into his side, smooth and fast.

DO WHAT HE SAYS

Dana King

Sonny Ng didn't talk much. Two weeks riding with him as my field training officer and his only words not directly related to police work were—

When he met me: "You Forte?"

When it was time for lunch: "You hungry?"

When it was time to pay for lunch: "I got this."

I figured he liked me because he paid for lunch more often than not.

Five-foot-five, maybe a buck sixty. Stocky without an ounce of fat on him. Alleged to know more martial arts than Chuck Norris had heard of. More than one cop smiled at me when they heard who my FTO was and said something along the lines of, "Do whatever he tells you. Not what he does, just what he tells you."

Friday afternoon, second shift. Sonny drove us to the late, lamented Robert Taylor projects, at the time regarded as Bad Motherfucker Capital of the World. Cabrini Green was rough, too, and New Yorkers still talked up Bed-Stuy. My money was on the Taylor. Answered a call there once and people were throwing broken toasters and stereo speakers out the windows at us. Even an old cathode ray television. Didn't care if you saw them do it. Leaned out the windows to taunt you while someone else brought the next appliance. Broad daylight. There weren't a lot of fucks to give in the Taylor project.

Sonny pulled the squad to the curb on South Federal Street. Pointed to a building across the way. "There."

Looked like any other building in the Taylor. Tall, ugly warehouse for poor black people and criminals not yet locked up. "What about it?" I said.

"Three years ago." Still pointing at the spot. "Marcus Taverner was supposed to have raped Tyrell Johnson's sister. Tyrell went to Elmo's Tombstones While You Wait, over there on State. Had one made with Marcus's name. Dated it day after tomorrow. Left it in front of Marcus's building."

Sonny put the car in Drive and pulled away. "Whoa," I said. "That's badass and all, but I know that's not the end of the story."

His Easter Island expression never changed. "Found Marcus there myself. Right on time. Laid out flat, head at the base of the stone."

"You get Tyrell for it?"

"No witnesses. No physical evidence. Wasn't like we could prove anything." Waved a kid on a bicycle through the intersection. "Remember the guy held the door for you the other day getting lunch?"

"Yeah?"

"That was Tyrell." Pointed to a building. "Lives right there. Head of the tenants' association."

There had to be more to that story and I would've asked what if a terrified young woman hadn't run out from between two buildings. She hesitated at the sidewalk. Turned the other way, then ours. Saw us and waved her arms across her body as if signaling for a plane to rescue her from a shipwreck.

Sonny pulled to the curb. I rolled down my window. She ran up like she might crawl inside with us. "Thank God you're here. You got to come quick. Luther got behind some payments and now Deion say his boy Lyndell gonna cut Luther's sister Taisha up Luther don't pay him right the fuck now but he don't say how the fuck Luther supposed to come up with the money while everyone standing there and Lyndell holding a knife and shit and please come in here before he hurt that girl. She ain't but fourteen."

That was more than I could absorb, two weeks on the job. Sonny already out of the car. "Call it in."

"Should we wait for backup?"

Sonny cocked his head toward the girl's screams. "They'll find us."

I gave our location and as much of the situation as I could while scrambling out of the car, no personal radios attached to the uniform in those days. Caught up to Sonny at the corner of the building closest to the street. It was dusk and the shadows of the apartment towers cut through the courtyard. The excitement was at the edge of a circle of light from one of the few operating street lamps. Sonny surveyed the situation with as much emotion as a man reading an out-of-town weather report.

"ETA on backup is three minutes," I said. "What do you think?"

Just then the guy I took to be Deion said something I couldn't make out. Lyndell jerked and the girl screamed at a whole different level from anything we'd heard yet.

"Watch the crowd." Sonny flicked on his flashlight and stepped off. Turned the corner of the building, identified himself, and strongly recommended everyone cease and desist.

Sonny must have appeared to be alone from Deion's perspective. With an audience already assembled, he decided to make a reputation for himself. Did an exaggerated double take and addressed the crowd. "Where the real cop? This mini motherfucker an insult to me."

Sonny gave away seven inches and fifty pounds. Didn't change his speed in any way. Walked right up and popped Deion on the middle of his forehead with the butt of that big policeman's flashlight. Hit him so hard the batteries and the bulb flew out through the shield. Deion went down with one foot still planted on the ground.

This made an impression on Lyndell. Unfortunately for him, he couldn't afford to lose face and was no smarter than his boss. Exercised the decision-making skills that probably kept him from a more responsible position, like asking if you wanted fries with that. "Back off, you pipsqueak motherfucker, or I'll cut this bitch right here. Watch me." Moved the knife toward Taisha's face.

Sonny left Deion where he fell. Turned to Lyndell. Spoke in the same tone as if asking for the sports page. "Drop the knife before I stick it up your ass."

Lyndell must have figured Sonny wouldn't try anything too radical in front of witnesses. "Listen to me, you slope-eyed motherfucker. I ain't playing here. I'll cut this bitch then I'll do you, just for fun."

As if he wasn't in enough trouble already, Lyndell had let Sonny close enough to use whichever form of kung kwan do fu best suited the situation. Separated Lyndell from the knife by breaking his arm above the wrist. Got behind him and twisted the good arm around his back. "Apologize."

Took a few seconds for Lyndell's head to clear. "What?"

"Apologize. To the girl."

Some people respond well to stress. Lyndell wasn't one of them. Instead of focusing his mind, he started making mistakes faster. Hollered about police brutality and how he wasn't apologizing for shit. Sonny used his free hand to pick up the knife. Leaned over and put his lips next to Lyndell's ear. "Do you remember what I said I'd do? Now apologize."

"Go fuck yourself, pig."

It was a good knife. Cut through Lyndell's belt with a single stroke. Sonny stepped on some loose material of the jeans Lyndell already wore half off his ass and slid back a foot, taking the jeans with him.

That brought Lyndell to the seemingly depthless limits of his stupidity. He started apologizing to people he'd never heard of for things he didn't know had happened. Sonny slid the pants back up and cuffed him. Steering him to our squad car with the hand holding up the jeans when the second unit appeared. Jerked his head toward Deion, who hadn't moved since their introduction. "That one needs an ambulance."

"What about this one?"

"We'll take him."

We were lucky that time. Deion and Lyndell were pieces of shit even by the Taylor's standards. The locals were so glad to see them get theirs no one admitted to noticing anything out of the ordinary. The few who ran with Deion and Lyndell and might have pitched a bitch bowed to peer pressure without the big dogs to protect them. The department gave us both commendations when we could have lost our jobs.

Walking away from the ceremony I asked Sonny what I'd done to deserve a citation. "We're partners," he said. "Never leave a partner behind." Still gathering myself for something adequate to say when he finished the conversation with, "It was the least I could do. They would've canned you if I fucked it up."

JULIE HEART NUMBER THREE
James R. Tuck

People already act weird in a tattoo shop.

They get intimidated by the art on the walls, prepared tattoo designs called flash from the carnival roots of tattooing where you'd paint lurid, brightly colored "flashy" designs to lure in the hicks and rubes to your show. The art in a shop screams at you. The skulls grinning at the topless ladies, the dragons and panthers and snakes and eagles all battling, angels and devils on the same sheet leering at you like the cartoon sides of your conscience. It's all id, no superego, and fuck your ego in the ass running. This shit was born in hucksterism and baptized by gypsy thieves in the carny moonlight.

A tattoo shop is alien, foreign, a subculture you come into that you aren't quite prepared for the first time no matter how many fucking shows you watch.

Hell, a tattoo shop has its own smell. All green soap and alcohol undercut with a hint of blood and ink and punk rock ways.

Like a hospital crossed with a mosh pit.

So people get weird in tattoo shops.

Here we always get the super weirdos.

It's because we're two tenths a mile from the county jail, right between the BONDS R US and the QUICK E'S 24 HOUR TITLE PAWN. There's only so many parts of town you can open a tattoo shop due to the zoning laws here. They list us as "adult entertainment" making it where we can't be anywhere near "family friendly" businesses. Most other shops cluster up on the Strip, called that because it's one long road with all the strip clubs on it.

The boss went another way, opening up here and explaining why by saying: "People will always spend money on pussy over tattoos."

He doesn't give a shit 'cause he hardly ever works. He was a BFD in the nineties, got in the magazines, worked the conventions, tattooed some celebrities (mostly porn stars and wrestlers), and even went on tour with Motley slinging ink in the back of their tour bus.

But the nineties are long gone and now he just swings by every morning, picks up the money we've made, and goes fishing to get away from his wife Esmeralda and her bitching.

Our customers tend to be people coming or going from the jail. They are cash-in-hand and celebrating their freedom, no matter how temporary it is, or getting one last "fuck you" in before they're locked down. The designs we do tend to be a mix of hard luck and outlaw anger and more than a smattering of love come, gone, and desperate. The majority of our clients are fucked up, either from the last blowout before reporting to a court ordered appearance or jacked from the concrete baseline of a stay at the Graybar Hotel.

So, when the older guy in overalls walks in at thirty minutes to close, vibrating like a live wire, I didn't think a thing about it.

I greeted him with a, "Help you?"

He moves across the lobby warily, like something will leap out at him, eyes jumping around, head on a swivel. He doesn't answer, finally getting to the front counter I'm standing behind. He stays half turned away from me, body toward the counter but his face sweeping the lobby.

"Hey," I say, "you looking to get tattooed?"

He jerks around and his eyes look lit from behind, like

they're covered in wet glass, and brighter because of the near-black circles around them. A flutter, like a tiny hummingbird trapped under his skin, has set up in the bottom corner of his left one.

He looks like he lost a fight.

And his bitter breath says he might be drunk.

"How many people work here?" His voice is a little hoarse but his words are clipped and free of slur.

"It's me and another artist, but he's got two clients so he's done for the night."

He nods and turns again. "He in that closed room?" He's pointing at Tom's station across from where we are.

I rap the counter between us with my knuckles, making him turn back to me. "You want a tattoo I'll be the one to do it. You don't want a tattoo then piss off."

"Not much for customer service are you?"

"Customers spend money."

"How much is a tattoo?"

"Depends on what you want."

He nods and looks to be thinking. I don't see any ink on him. He could have something under his clothes but usually the redneck construction guys go for their arms. His are tanned dark until they hit the edge of his shirt sleeves where a band of white skin gleams. They're stringy with muscle from some kind of repetitive motion and I take him for a hammer swinger, possibly a ditch digger, but his shoulders aren't quite developed enough for that. He lifts thick-knuckled hands and lays them on the counter. The nails are too short, blunted edges of the tips rolling up over them, and I see he does something with metal construction because the backs of his hands are covered in brick-red iron oxide dust.

"How much for that?"

He points at the design Tom left on the counter, a simple heart with the name Julie in it. Tom's a slob, leaving a trail of paper all over the counter area. I'm always cleaning up after his ass.

"You want a name in it or just the heart?"

"Just like that."

"With Julie?"

"My daughter's name is Julie."

"Where's it going?"

His eyebrows fold in and down, making a shadow over his eyes as he thinks. He reaches over, touches his forearm. "Here."

"Just like this?"

"With red."

It's just a flash heart and Coneria cursive. Tom didn't draw this, he pulled it from the wall of flash and printed the name off the computer. I have no problem doing this exact design, even though Tom's doing two of them right now. I won't copy someone else's custom tattoo but if it's flash anyone can have it. Bonus, now I don't have to draw anything.

Winner winner, chicken dinner for Julie heart number three.

I almost say eighty bucks but guys who work construction make good money. Plus, it's late and he's been weird.

"One fifty."

He doesn't blink at the price. "Okay."

He turns away as I make my stencil. He's staring at Tom's closed door.

I move around him. "Come on."

"I'll wait here."

I shake my head. I'm not leaving this joker in the lobby alone. "State regs. Customer has to watch me open all new stuff."

"There's an inspector here?"

"Could come by anytime."

"After midnight?"

This guy is pissing me off. If he hadn't gone for the up-charge I'd boot him out. "Just come in here while I set up."

My station is next to Tom's. I can hear his machine humming through the wall between our stations and someone, probably his customer, laughing. My customer drags ass inside after me and I start getting ready. This won't take long. Two machine setup, two colors, basic bullshit tattoo. I mean, I'm sure Julie means the world to him, but I don't know her from Adam's house cat. All she is to me is a payday.

I talk to him over my shoulder. "Look at anything you want, just don't touch anything."

My station is full of art and shit I've collected over the years. There's a lot to look at and it keeps the clients distracted from their tattoo.

I've just got the liner put together when he asks: "Why do you have a ball-peen hammer hung on the wall?"

I wave him over, take his arm, and begin shaving it where the tattoo will go.

"I read a book about old time New York tattoo artists telling their stories of tattooing in World War Two. It was wide open, boatloads of sailors and soldiers would come into town and fill the streets looking to get drunk, get laid, and get tattooed."

"Stewed, screwed, and tattooed?" he asks.

I lay the stencil on the freshly shaved patch of his arm, letting the carbon transfer from the paper to his skin. "Exactly."

"My PawPaw used to say that, when he'd tell his old war stories."

"Cool." I peel away the stencil paper, leaving behind a slightly fuzzy outline of the Julie heart on his arm. It's clean enough I can follow it so I motion for him to sit in the chair and pull his arm onto the armrest between us. "Yeah, things got hairy real quick back then, according to this book. All those soldiers all gassed up and off leash in a town full of sin." I pick up the machine, step on the pedal to make the connection and it buzzes to life. I keep talking. "The Moskowitz brothers, Stanley and Walter, told a story about keeping a ball-peen hammer in their tool kits. Whenever a fight would break out they would grab their hammers and wade in there. They said they kept the walls painted red so the blood wouldn't show and swept up the teeth at the end of the night."

I drop the needle, feeling it snag just right as my hand pulls the first line of the tattoo. His eyes narrow at the sensation of it but he doesn't move so I go to work. I've got the power supply up to fifteen volts and I begin light-sabering the lines into his sun-hardened skin. I pull one half of the heart in a long continuous sweep. The ink and blood trail that wells up is thin and runny as I blot it with a paper towel. He's definitely been drinking tonight but fuck it, I'm already committed to making the seventy-five bucks that's my cut of the tattoo.

"You ever have to use that thing?" He asks as I dip into the cap of black on my station for the next line.

"Not yet." The needle drops again, working the "e" in Julie first. I'm right-handed so I pull from the right. If I started with the "J" I would wipe off the rest of my stencil.

"You have to run into some bad guys this close to the jail."

I'm pulling the J, turning my hand in the cursive swoops that make the letter. "Yeah, but most keep it together since we're so close to a building full of law enforcement."

He grunts.

"Hurt?" I ask, dipping again.

"That wasn't for the tattoo."

"You don't like cops?"

"Fucking worthless." He shifts in the chair and the bottom of the heart gets a wobble in it.

Fuck.

I run the needle up and down over the wobble, thickening the line to hide it. Now I have to shade the bottom of this damn thing instead of only doing red. I almost say something and then I remember how much I'm getting paid for what will be about ten minutes of work.

"You ever read about some of the shit people get away

with?" he asks.

"I don't watch the news."

"Good for you. It's terrible shit."

I switch to my shader. It runs slower than the liner, but I turn it up so I can blast through this tattoo. I want to keep him talking so I can just work. "What's the worst thing you know about lately?"

It takes him a minute to answer. I use the time to begin working the black shading over the bottom of the heart, hiding the wobble and giving the heart some depth. Fuck it, might as well make it nice.

"Three weeks ago two brothers, fucking animals, snatched a girl off the street, a fourteen-year-old on her way home from choir practice." His voice sounds strange, almost metallic, like the computerized voices that call and tell you: Stay on the line for a very important phone call.

"They killed her?"

"They drove her to the quarry and tortured her. They were in a truck owned by their father, a work truck, and when they were done themselves they began using the tools in the back on her." He shifts again but this time I'm ready for it and get the needle out of the skin before he makes it move. "They left her in the water, tied to a cinderblock. She's still in a coma."

"That's fucking terrible." I stop tattooing and look up at him. "Did they catch them?"

"Yeah." Something in his voice.

"Surely they convicted the bastards."

"The judge knocked it all down to aggravated assault, time served and probation."

"The fuck?" I dip into the red and begin filling in the heart. When I wipe it looks like a smear of fresh blood.

"Their father is rich."

"And the girl's father isn't?"

He doesn't answer.

I keep making small circles with the needle, coloring his

skin ripe-tomato red.

It doesn't take much longer and I'm done. I wipe the fresh tattoo free of excess ink and smear a little petroleum jelly over it. "Alright, man, stand up and take a look, see what you think."

He looks down at the new tattoo, turning it in the light. "I thought that would take longer."

"I'm like lightning, man."

"Do you have to do anything else to it?" His eyebrows are folded in again and he's flushed across his forehead.

"Bandage it up, take your money, and send you out the door."

He stands in front of the mirror, still turning his arm, but looking out the door of my station into the lobby.

"You okay?" I ask.

Before he can answer, Tom's door opens and he walks out, followed by his customers. Through my open door I watch them go to the counter. Tom moves behind it as the two guys lightly roughhouse with each other. Their mouths are cracked open into wide smiles, whitened teeth shining as they laugh and joke. They're not clones of each other but they aren't far off it, both of them stocky with the same shock of light brown hair over the same frat boy features.

My customer moving catches my eye.

He has my hammer in his hands.

Oh fuck.

He's through the door before I can say the words I just thought. Tom yells something as my customer raises the hammer. The boys turn and he swings, catching the younger one in the jaw. The iron head of the hammer doesn't slow down, crumpling the bone it hits, hinging it and making the boy's chin slew sideways while the rest of his mouth stays under his nose.

Tom is pelted in the face by blood and white, white teeth.

The boy hits the counter like he's been thrown into it by a

cannon, immediately bouncing off and slamming into the floor on his crushed face.

My customer turns to the other boy and I see his face. It's gone thin and feral, all animal madness in the eyes, jaw clenched so hard I can see the outline of his molars through his cheeks. The boy screams and spins to run but he slips on his brother's blood and goes down to one knee.

My customer swings the hammer up, then drives it down.

It sinks into the boy's skull like it's made of paper mâché.

The boy's eyes roll white and his body shivers so violently that I think my customer is using the handle of the hammer imbedded in his head to shake him. The brained boy goes slack, weight pulling him down until he slips off the hammer my customer still holds and falls to the floor next to his brother.

My customer isn't even breathing hard.

He walks into my station and hangs the gore-covered hammer back in its place on my wall. "Sorry about that."

I hear Tom throwing up behind the counter. My ears are ringing and my neck is hot. The whole shop smells like iron, a micro spray of blood still hanging in the air. I swallow my gorge and manage to ask, "Why?"

My customer looks at me like an idiot. "You know why."

He reaches out to me and I flinch.

"Take it." he says.

I realize he's holding money toward me.

My fingers come away wet as I take it and hold it, not knowing what to do with it.

He looks down at his Julie heart, the third one. A streak of something dark covers the bottom of it—blood, brain, something.

"So, what do I need to know to take care of this thing?"

FLIGHT
Kris Calvin

Traffic slowed as the Uber driver maneuvered his Civic into the lane marked DEPARTURES at San Francisco International Airport. Hannah and Sam were in the back Sam was swathed in a lilac knit blanket in his car seat, his tiny face turned away from Hannah. Today marked six weeks since his birth. Hannah laid her palm flat on his chest, nearly covering it, and felt his shallow breathing as she thought back to that morning, when for the first time Sam had returned her smile with one of his own.

Despite near-constant exhaustion and the steep learning curve of parenting, Hannah felt more comfortable in the role of young mother than she had at any other time in her life. She regretted none of the decisions that had brought her here, although she tried not to think ahead to the possible consequences.

When she looked up, Hannah caught the driver watching her in the rearview mirror. He was old, at least fifty, but Hannah registered in his gaze the same thing she experienced when most people saw her for the first time, whether male or female, young or old. Hannah's pale, nearly translucent skin and dark, glossy hair served as the frame for her extraordinary eyes, a light blue ringed in a deeper turquoise. She'd been told she resembled a raven-haired Grace Kelly or Catherine Deneuve in their youth—she'd had to Google who they were.

Hannah viewed her beauty as an unwanted accident of

birth. Unlike her friends at school, she wore no makeup and dressed simply, wanting nothing more than to blend in, to be the last, not the first, to be noticed.

The drop-off area at the curb for Cathay Pacific Airlines was crowded, as others arrived for overnight flights burdened with large rolling bags, multiple suitcases, and even trunks. Hannah had only a combination stroller car seat and a large diaper bag containing everything Sam needed for the trip, along with jeans, shorts, and a couple of T-shirts for her.

Plus, the money.

Seven thousand dollars was the limit for a passenger to bring in cash from the U.S. to Indonesia. It had been easy for Hannah to find that out online. Given the low cost of living in Surabaya, it would cover a year's expenses for Sam and her, if she kept things simple. Most importantly, withdrawing the funds from her college savings, a little at a time, had failed to raise any alarms at home.

As Hannah shouldered the diaper bag and pushed the stroller through the automatic doors into the terminal, she marveled at how Sam could slumber on despite the harsh lights inside and the frequent booming announcements of flights delayed and passengers exhorted to proceed to their gates for immediate boarding.

She located the line for security. It wound beyond the cordoned-off area for at least another thirty feet. Some travelers appeared resigned to the wait, others craned their necks to look to the front, as though seeing the end might get them there faster. Hannah had paid for a modest upgrade to "economy plus" so that she would have more space to manage Sam on the long flight; it came with priority access through the line. As she wheeled Sam's stroller into the considerably shorter queue, she felt as though all eyes were on her. She noticed one couple whispering to one another as she passed.

She glanced down at her outfit, purchased for tonight, a plain black skirt that fell below her knees, comfortable black flats, a blazer-type jacket, something she thought a professional woman might wear to work. Her only jewelry was a simple, bold-faced watch with a black strap, also new.

It all seemed right to her. She took a deep breath and tried to ignore the growing nausea she felt, the light headedness. After all, it wasn't more than the attention she usually received, "Is she that actress, what's-her-name, or maybe a model?" Still, when Hannah reached the front of the line, she stiffened, and she could feel her hands sweating as she pulled her passport and boarding pass from her bag. But she straightened her shoulders and told herself there was no reason for anyone to try to stop her.

At least, no reason they could possibly know of.

"Evening, miss," the TSA agent said. He was short and solid, young and clean shaven. His eyes lingered on Hannah's for a moment. Then he studied her passport and frowned.

Hannah froze.

She'd hoped she might pass for twenty in the clothing she'd chosen, at least nineteen, but she knew with her documents in hand he could see she'd just turned sixteen. Her breath came quickly. She bent to adjust Sam's blanket. As she did so, she inhaled deeply, and reminded herself that with her recent birthday, she'd reached the airline's threshold for travel without a parent's consent. And there was no law against being a mother at her age, although she was pretty sure she couldn't marry yet.

But a wedding had never been part of the plan.

All she needed was for no one to take Sam away.

She was one long plane ride from that being a certainty, so long as she could keep the ghosts and her demons at bay.

When she looked up, the agent's frown was gone. He was smiling shyly, almost apologetically, in a way that men in their twenties sometimes did when they discovered she was underage, a small offer of contrition for the thoughts, forbidden, that had passed through their minds a moment before.

He waved her through.

Hannah was stopped again when another agent checked Sam's bottles, stowed in the diaper bag. But she'd read up on airport rules for flying with a newborn, so she was prepared for that. And the cash, split between a flat handbag and a rolled-up backpack, went unquestioned. She'd been right about restricting the amount.

Cleared to go, Hannah gripped the stroller handle and began to count backwards slowly from fifty in her head. It was a trick she'd learned to block thoughts that might otherwise lead her to panic.

She couldn't afford an episode, not here, not now; she needed to stay calm and in control.

Sam started to make small fussing sounds, ones that Hannah recognized would escalate into a cry if she didn't feed him soon. It was a welcome distraction. She located the gate and found an open seat in the waiting area where she unpacked the one bottle that was at room temperature, not in the cold pack. She hoped he wouldn't balk at it not being warmed.

Sam's tiny arms were flailing, his hands in tight fists as his face reddened and he began to cry in earnest. Hannah unbuckled the straps and lifted him gently from the stroller, seated herself, and cradled him against her chest. She touched the bottle to his lips, letting him root for it and take it in his mouth on his own. She'd read it was the best way to mimic the act of nursing. Hannah knew the advantages of breast milk over formula, and wished she could have offered him that. But she'd also read that the warmth and attention she could give him during feeding, if she took her time and held him close, was important.

As she used her free hand to smooth Sam's fine, dark hair where static from his blanket had caused it to stand on end, she noticed the time on her watch. It was a little after ten. Her stomach dropped. She wondered if the drugs she'd put in Ruth and Michael's nightly after-dinner scotch had done their work by now.

She wished she and Sam were in the air.

"What a beautiful baby. How old is he?" An elderly woman had taken the seat next to Hannah. She was ebony-skinned, small and round, her gray hair in a long braid that swept over one shoulder. She wore an elegant green sari with silver trim. When she smiled, the well-worn lines on her face deepened.

"Six weeks," Hannah said.

Sam relaxed his jaw, letting the nipple fall from his mouth. He turned his head toward the sound of the woman's voice. Hannah knew his vision wasn't yet developed to where he could fully focus, but that he could see her.

The woman's smile grew broader. She looked from Hannah to Sam, and back again.

"He's got your eyes," the woman said. "Unusual. That light blue with dark blue around it. Might mean something special, eyes like that. I bet they're lucky."

Hannah smiled at the woman. She told herself to remember those words; she was always reminding herself to remember the good things.

Sam nodded off to sleep again. While it was hard for Hannah to get used to how quickly he could go from waking to sleeping, she knew it was normal for a newborn. From the day she'd learned the results of the pregnancy test, she'd been reading books and blogs, absorbing everything she thought she might need to care for him, as though preparing for one of her finals in high school. It wasn't hard for Hannah, she was a star student, all A's, always on the gifted track. It had made her feel safe at school to know no one could question her effort or her value, that she could win each teacher's approval simply by not missing a single question on a test.

If only it had been like that at home. Hannah rocked Sam gently as she fed him, trying to block out the images pushing their way through.

Pain and fear had been constant in Hannah's early years;

"abuse" seemed an inadequate term for what went on in her bedroom, in the bath. So while Ruth and Michael Roberts may have completed the biological acts necessary to be her "mom" and "dad," Hannah had decided long ago that some roles in life had to be earned, and she never used those names for them.

The unspeakable sexual assaults stopped when Hannah was six or so, replaced by Ruth's neglect and Michael's disinterest. A nanny was hired to meet her basic needs. Still, in middle school, plagued by terrifying memories, Hannah sought out psychology books at the public library and discovered what pedophilia was. She came to understand there was no rhyme or reason to the form the pathology might take. Perpetrators weren't always drawn to one gender over another in selecting their victims; age and development of the child could be the sole determinant.

Hannah saw herself in stories of children so young that they were in diapers when first violated, and in case studies where abusers sought like-minded spouses, homes where neither parent was sane, and a sense of safety and love was unheard of.

"Are you on holiday? Do you have family in Indonesia?" the woman in the sari asked.

Hannah didn't answer. She had glimpsed, twenty feet away, the face of the young TSA agent hurrying past the shops and other gates along the concourse. He was almost at a jog as he cut through groups of passengers. He was headed her way. Hannah stifled a gasp. Had she left tracks for the police to follow, had they put out a breaking alert to stop her from boarding?

She stood abruptly, shifting Sam to one arm, dropping his bottle on the seat as she hoisted her bag over her shoulder. But it was too late. The agent had clearly seen her, his expression appeared grim.

"Ms. Roberts? You dropped your passport near security. Someone turned it in. You're going to need this."

Hannah understood now that he looked serious because

she'd left without the identification she would need to complete her trip.

A potentially important, but entirely innocent, error.

Still, her heart beat wildly, and as he extended the passport to her, she didn't trust herself to take it. Her shaking hands would give her away.

The older woman in the sari stepped forward.

"Her arms are full," she said smiling. "I'll tuck it in her bag."

When the agent left, Hannah breathed deeply. She counted backwards. "Fifty, forty-nine, forty-eight..." She prayed. But it wasn't enough. The walls had come down. Hannah walked away from the gate, Sam in her arms, no destination in mind. She was trapped in a memory, an image from when she was no more than four years old, backed against the headboard of her bed, trying to make herself small, invisible. Ruth holding the strange plastic object, Michael, a sick glint in his eyes, unzipping his pants, watching as Ruth thrust it into Hannah, the feeling that she was floating above her body as they took their turns with her, as they emptied her out and finally left her alone, often bloodied, sometimes bruised.

The memory faded, Hannah was back in the present, but the terminal was a blur and she realized she wasn't sure exactly where she was. She felt cold all over. She pulled Sam's blanket up around him, as though he, too, were chilled. When she saw a woman's restroom she ducked inside and made her way to an open stall. She locked the door and leaned against it.

Safe.

She sobbed uncontrollably, her ears ringing, Sam's cries mingling with her own. Hannah wasn't sure how much time had passed when she heard someone knocking loudly on the stall, asking if she was okay.

She had to get back to her gate. She couldn't miss her flight.

The elderly woman was standing where Hannah had left

her, one hand on the stroller. Her lips were tight, her smile gone. She was taking in Hannah's puffy face, her reddened eyes.

"It's all right," Hannah said, breathing hard, holding Sam pressed against her shoulder, patting him on the back. "I'm... I'm just afraid of flying."

"Ah, I see." The woman said, appearing relieved that it was only that. "But I think you've frightened your baby."

Sam was still crying, although more quietly now. Hannah shifted from one foot to the other, side to side, still patting his back.

"They are starting to board," the woman said. She laid her hand gently on Hannah's arm. "They will let me go first, I am slow. You can board now, too, with the baby?"

Hannah nodded. She was grateful to walk with the woman. She felt shielded, not so easily seen. The agent who checked their tickets waved them through.

When they crossed the threshold of the aircraft, a pilot in uniform, an older man, emerged from the cockpit to say something to a flight attendant.

He paused, his attention captured by Hannah and the sleepy, dark-haired Sam in her arms.

"Beautiful baby," he said, adding with a broad smile, "Beautiful mother."

Hannah started to shake her head. She almost corrected him, then realized there was no longer any need.

The woman in the sari gave Hannah her seat number, and told her to find her if she wanted a break, if she needed her to hold Sam for a bit during the long flight.

When Hannah reached her own row, an attendant helped her to stow the body of the stroller overhead while Hannah settled Sam in his car seat in the seat next to her. She entertained him with a brightly colored rattle during the safety announcements. Soon, the lights dimmed and the huge jet engine hummed, then roared, as they taxied down the runway and lifted into the air.

Hannah reflected that in less than one day she and Sam would land in a country ten thousand miles away, where they would start a new life.

Ruth, the woman who had carried in her womb first Hannah, and then Sam, her "change-of-life baby," would not rape her second child as she had her first. Michael, who had fathered the two siblings, would not fulfill his sexual needs through atrocities performed on his son, as he had on his daughter.

Hannah had made sure of that.

The dose of ketamine in their scotch that Hannah had scored from the dealer at school would have put down a horse, let alone her parents.

Ruth and Michael Roberts would never wake again.

The plane reached altitude and leveled out, the engine softened to a purr. Sam contentedly waved his arms and kicked at his blanket. Baby exercise, Hannah thought. She leaned over and kissed him on the forehead, then smiled at him and he smiled back, a precious, toothless grin.

"Coffee, tea, or soda? " an attendant asked. She noticed the bottle Hannah had tucked in the side pocket of Sam's seat. "Let me know if you need me to warm that for your baby."

"I will, " Hannah said.

No longer his sister, Hannah had shed that skin. She was Sam's mother now. It was a role she knew she would earn.

HABEAS CORPUS
Andrew Case

It was the nicest prison cell I had ever been in, and I had been in plenty. In the basement of the Sandra Day O'Connor Federal Courthouse on West Washington Street, the cell glowed museum-white and the corner toilet's chrome sparkled. And why wouldn't it? No one ever spent a night here, and no one ever shared a cell. When I had first been arrested and stayed in Phoenix's outdoor jail with six hundred others in the searing heat, guys had nearly strangled each other over half a bologna sandwich. After the trial I had housed outside Douglas, flush up against the Sonoran border. You escape from that place the wrong way and you come out in Mexico. Some guys down there would think of that as worse than being locked up. Instead of rats they had scorpions. My bunkmate found a rattlesnake in the yard once and took it back to the room. That can keep you up at night.

Compared to Tent City and Douglas, the holding cell in SDO, as they called it, was something close to heavenly. The floor was so clean you could have eaten off it. The guards were polite. Hell, the food was even pretty good, though the other times I'd been there I hadn't stayed long enough to get served any. Whatever cop had once said that jail isn't supposed to be the Ritz hadn't spent a morning in SDO.

I had now been there four times. The only reason there's a jail in the federal courthouse is so you can wait for your hearing without a bailiff or a marshal wasting overtime minding you. They rouse you at 4:00 a.m. at your regional prison hundreds of miles from nowhere, put you on a bus for three hours to Phoenix, and stick you in the holding cell for a few more hours until your hearing. Plain white, empty, and silent, just bare enough to make you go stir crazy. There were rumors of a guy in federal lockup in Florence who based his whole appeal on the fact that he acted as his own lawyer and couldn't focus because he was so sleep deprived by getting bused in to SDO every day for the trial. Last I heard that was still going on. Hey, I said it was nice for a prison. I didn't say it wasn't boring as hell.

Maybe the reason SDO looked so nice that fourth time was the good news I had just been given. It had been a long haul after the arrest, the trial, and the time in Douglas. First an appeal. Then post-conviction review. Then appeal of the denial of leave, and that went up to the Arizona State Supreme Court, and only after they told me I could rot in hell for all they cared did I even get a whiff of federal court. The lawyer said it would go slow. Habeas corpus. Bring in the body. The prisoner gets to be brought into court in person, you can't just do it on the papers.

Four visits to SDO—one so the lawyer could prove I even had the right to make the challenge, one for the first habeas hearing, once again for the appeal, then back down today for the hearing the appeals court demanded we do over—and if I heard the judge correctly, we were back at the very beginning. A whole new trial. My luck they would just find me guilty again and I would start the whole damned thing over.

I sat on the plain white bench and stared at the plain white wall. That night on East Catalina had been fifteen years ago, almost to the day. Velia had been worked up. Her son had run off again. Timmy. He was only twelve years old, already he and his mom fought almost every night. I had known the dad, lucky enough to catch the wrong end of a steak knife while awaiting trial on trafficking a half a million worth of heroin. And felony murder for the woman who OD'd when the balloon she'd swallowed burst while she was waiting to see a judge at the immigration detention center. Timmy's dad was either going to go away for the rest of his life or turn into the kind of person who never forgets. They spared him the trouble of deciding.

But that had left Timmy without a dad, such as the guy was, and Velia without a source of income, dirty as it may have been. And so every night on East Catalina the kid would threaten to leave, and Velia would dare him to do just that, and he'd storm out. And most nights he'd walk down to Long Wong's and eat a plate of hot wings and come home and that would be the end of that. I had been around for it plenty of times. I had taken to Velia, after her husband died. I'd had my share of troubles but was making my way back, cutting hair in a barbershop near the new stadium district. You work for tips mainly, but you hear some interesting stories. And it was a lot better than the kind of stuff I had been into before.

But one night on East Catalina, Timmy didn't come back after one of their fights. And he didn't come back the night after that either. And by the third night, as much as I was trying to help Velia keep it together, she was unraveling. She'd finished a bottle of wine each night, and followed that up with Jim Beam on the rocks. So long as the ice lasted. After that it was every man for himself. I stayed with her each night. And sure I'd been drinking with her too. I had given that up after a particularly nasty night in Nogales a few years back, but if I'd stayed sober around Velia as she screamed and pounded the walls, I might have lost it along with her.

Of course, drinking can also make you do things you regret. At least that was the operating theory of the Maricopa County District Attorney. I never changed my story. I tried all three nights to calm Velia down. I had left after she'd thrown the empty Jim Beam bottle at me. I didn't go to the hospital for the ding from the bottle because I wasn't in the habit of getting treatment for an inch-long cut that wasn't all that deep, no matter how much it bled. The scalp can bleed like crazy even when you're barely scratched, anyone can tell you that.

But that was my blood in the apartment on East Catalina, and those were my fingerprints on the glasses, and there weren't any other fingerprints they wouldn't expect to be there. And my hands were pretty much the same size as whoever's hands had strangled her, to the extent they can ever figure these things out. And you couldn't get a good DNA sample from the bits of skin under her fingernails, so even though that didn't point to me, I couldn't say it pointed to anyone else. And when the drunk ex-wife of a drug dealer gets strangled one night in Phoenix, and the boyfriend was there and was bleeding and is a good enough match, you don't exactly get Johnnie Cochran and a team of Harvard law students flying in to try to prove the guy didn't do it. The best you can do is a steady stream of papers over fifteen years from a local law school clinic. Just something to keep the post-conviction process open while someone tries to think of something.

Or until someone in a lab in Kharagpur discovers a way to sequence DNA off a smaller sample. And somehow those bits of skin have been kept in a freezer in Tucson for fifteen years, and now they aren't too small to sequence after all. And while that sequence doesn't point to anyone else in particular, it rules out the boyfriend. So much so that this afternoon a soft white judge in a prim courtroom in Phoenix told me and my lawyer that we deserved a new trial. The evidence didn't exonerate me exactly, he said. I was still there. There was still blood. But I should have had the chance to tell the jury that the DNA under her nails wasn't mine. Make the prosecution say that she had been scratching some stranger who didn't kill her. My lawyer said it was the best possible outcome. Odds were they wouldn't try me at all. They would run the DNA through a few more databases, call up a few possible suspects for a cheek swab, and drop the case against me entirely when they had a new one to bring.

But in the meanwhile, I would wait in Douglas. They don't give you immediate bail while you're waiting for a new trial in your federal habeas action. Someone who has been unjustly imprisoned for fifteen years can't expect to have a lot of faith in the system. Even if he is innocent. Especially if he is innocent. If they're just going to throw you prison for something you didn't do, why not make a run for it?

I didn't mind so much. I had gotten a good deal in Douglas. I had joined the Wildland Fire Crew. You get four weeks of training on containing wildfires and they send you out into the field. We would cut control lines, burn out fuel running up to them, and only call in the forest service if a fire started to burn faster or stronger than we could handle. In return, we got a dollar an hour to spend in the prison commissary. You could spend up to two weeks in the field working on a site. It wasn't like you could break out, since you were hundreds of miles away from the nearest town and would die of thirst if you tried walking anywhere. But it was the closest you could feel to being free. I remember one shift where I served as the designated lookout: climb up to the nearest ridge and watch the main blaze. Notify the team if it grows close. It was an easy job. You stand up and watch the world, and you can't believe you're actually a prisoner. Serious consequences, though.

Five years ago, the lookout for the Granite Mountain Hotshots missed a creeping fire and had to evacuate himself. As he did, the blaze swept over the firefighters' position and killed nineteen men. And those were the professional guys. Still, wildfire duty was better than anything else you could do in the Douglas Arizona state prison. Plus, if you ever get out, you have a level two license and a real shot of getting hired by the forest service itself.

The marshal was at the door to the cell.

"You have a visitor."

Maybe it would be the lawyer again. Always chipper that guy. Always had a reason that things were going to turn around. He hadn't been right in over a decade. Now I guess he wanted a second sitting to tell me how happy we should both be.

I looked up. It wasn't the lawyer. Instead it was a guy in his mid-twenties who looked a good ten years older than that. Dressed in a suit. But not dressed in a suit like a lawyer. More like a guy who never wears a suit who's wearing a suit just this one time because he's trying to impress someone—a judge or a guard or a date. He was wearing a suit the way that a convict wears a suit to his bail hearing. Hollowed out eyes. Thin hair. The nick of ink above the collar suggesting a tattoo down his neck. I didn't recognize him at first. Then he smiled a little and I saw it in his eyes.

"Timmy?"

"It's Timothy now."

"Timothy."

He'd lost his dad when he was ten and his mom two years after that. I had never spoken to him or heard from him in all the time I'd been locked up. I didn't know if he thought I killed his mom. I didn't know if he cared one way or the other. I hadn't heard who raised him, what he ended up doing with the horrible deck he'd been dealt. Kid had been through more hurt before he was legitimately a teenager than some people get in their whole lives.

"It's good to see you Timothy."

He nodded. "It's good to see you too."

The guard pulled back the grate and let Timothy in. I didn't know what the protocol was here. Some part of me felt I had to tell him that I hadn't killed his mom. But another told me that he already believed I hadn't. That he wouldn't have come here if he thought I had. So I just offered my hand and he took it.

"They tell me you're going to get a new trial."

"Yeah. That's what the judge said. Unless the prosecution appeals that and we go back to the circuit court, and maybe past that to the Supreme Court, and we get to run through this whole circus again."

"Naaah. They're saying it's legit. They're saying on the radio they got the DNA tested. They think you're going to walk out any day now. Sounds like they're just working on the paperwork."

"That's news to me."

He leaned up against the wall. He had grown up well. Looked like his dad. He had a lean face and broad shoulders and could have modeled suits that were much more expensive than the one he was wearing. He looked straight at me. He had the hard look his dad once had too.

"I guess I gotta say I'm sorry. I never came by. I never visited. I know you kept saying you didn't do it. It's not that I didn't believe you. I didn't think about it one way or the other. Because she was just as dead, you know? If you didn't kill her, then maybe one of those other guys did, and what's really the difference, you know?"

"You don't have anything to apologize for, Timothy."

"Okay. Only now, you thought about what's going to happen?"

"I got a firefighter certification. I'm still young enough. I could get a job with the forest service."

"That's nice. I mean what happens with your trial."

"I thought you said there won't be one."

"Well, whenever they match that DNA to someone, then they'll want to try that person. And once they find that person. Well, he's going to want to point the finger back at you anyway, right? DNA or no, you fought with her, you were there, your prints were on the glass. No one else's prints were in the house."

No other prints you wouldn't expect to see there. "Yeah, I suppose someone would point at me." Timmy had been away three nights when his mom was killed. They hadn't had an ordinary spat. And why wouldn't his fingerprints have been all over the apartment. And if they came back and found out that it was his DNA under his mom's fingernails, that would be the end of it. Whatever little life he had managed to put up after crawling out of the hell of his childhood would be gone. Maybe he was here to make sure that wasn't going to happen.

I looked out the cell toward the hallway. The guard had already left. He was back at his desk. It was a nice prison. The inmates didn't need babysitting. Timothy would be able to say I came at him. Or I confessed that I really had killed her and he couldn't help himself. Either way, if I were out of the way before the conviction was fully overturned, there wouldn't be any reason to open up the investigation again and hunt down new leads. Timothy looked as though he'd grown into the kind of man who didn't consider a manslaughter sentence to be hard time.

I backed away toward the door. I craned my neck; the guard was out of sight. I looked back to Timothy. Of course, he had never called. And he never doubted my innocence. How could he when he killed Velia himself?

And as he lunged toward me, those hands almost the same size as mine, I thought about how different it all could have been. As his hands locked on me and my ears started to ring and my eyes started to bulge, I thought about that moment on the ridge, looking out over the Arizona wildfire, burning against the desert sunset.

I thought about being free.

And then it all went black.

LOSING KIND
An Eoin Miller Mystery
Jay Stringer

ONE
NOW

I was used to the smell of a burned-out building. I'd grown up with it. Caravans, houses, pubs. There was a time when my family wouldn't have been allowed to settle anywhere for long.

The halal butcher on Union Street was a blackened shell. Scorch marks reached outwards around the broken windows. Water pooled on the tiled floor. The canvas awning across the front was blackened with soot. A hole had burned through the middle.

Quasim Khan had opened the shop as an immigrant back in the seventies, before I was born. He'd sold halal produce from a stand in the corner, but stocked standard meat at the main counter. When his son, Saj, took over the business, he'd focused on only stocking halal, and put the name in the sign above the door.

The attack had been on the news the night before, but I'd needed to see it for myself. Britain in 2017.

English votes for English laws.

Politics for the people.

Firebombs for the darkies.

Saj was stood near the shop. On the other side of a police cordon. He was talking to a TV reporter. Saj looked rattled.

Edgy. There was no trust in his eyes as he looked toward me, then turned away.

I didn't have any help to offer. Truth was, the town *did* feel different.

I'd only been away for two years, but everything had changed. I walked up through Union Street, to the town center. Bookies and pubs. Places I used to call home. I crossed High Bullen. A congested procession of traffic leading down to the motorway. Everyone passing through, from somewhere else, *to* somewhere else. I thought every driver probably had the fear. Maybe if the lights went red, they'd have to stay in town forever.

Heading up the hill, I found the house I was looking for. A semi-detached bungalow in the shadow of the old windmill. The front walls were painted white, and the tiled roof was dirty. The small garden was well kept. It looked like the lawn of a retired teacher. I rang the doorbell and saw movement through the frosted glass. The door opened on a thin old man. Thomas Mitchell. His hair gone gray, and his skin had faded to match. He wore a brown cardigan and slacks. I knew Mitchell was only in his fifties, but he looked twenty years older. He'd taken early retirement for health reasons, which I knew now to be only half of the story.

He smiled at me. "I always thought it might be you."

He offered his hand for a shake, and I looked into the eyes of a killer.

TWO
THEN

Suicide funerals are always difficult. It's the mix of emotions in the room. A cocktail of anger, frustration, and guilt. A few might even be relieved. Pleased that the person in the coffin is no longer suffering.

The service was for Robert Malpass. He'd left behind his

wife, Amy, and two children. We sat through a low-key sermon, with a few words from a family member. We sang "Abide With Me" and "The Lord Is My Shepherd."

When it was done, we all filed out and waited in a line to pay respects to the family. That part made me nervous. I'd been to school with Robert and Amy, but I'd said maybe three words to them in the twenty years since.

Technically, I'd been on a date with Amy. We were both fifteen, and she agreed to watch a movie with me. Genius that I was, I chose an action movie based on a computer game. Amy bought a friend along. To this day, I'd never worked out whether it counted as a first date. There hadn't been a second.

A world has passed by since then. I've been famous, and infamous. I was a crime boss for fifteen minutes, and I'd fancied myself as a private detective for a little less than that. Since then, I'd been moving around the country. Never settling for long, but steering clear of my hometown. Too many bad memories. Too many bad connections. My mother called to tell me Robert had passed away, and when I Googled the details, I saw it was suicide.

He parked up in his garage, fed a hose from the exhaust to the passenger window, and closed his eyes listening to an Oasis album.

I couldn't think of a worse way to go.

I slipped in to the back row of the service and kept my head down. There were a few faces I recognized. Each one older and rounder. There was a lot less hair on show and much more scalp. I avoided their gazes as we shuffled through to meet the family. Amy recognized me straight away. Her eyes widened, and, for just a second, a smile broke through the sadness.

"I didn't know you were here," she said, pulling me into an embrace.

For a second, it felt intimate. Two near strangers sharing a moment. Then reality set back in, and I mumbled something trite about being sorry for her loss. Outside the church, I felt the desperate need to light up a cigarette. The odd thing was, I don't smoke. I just needed a distraction. I stood away from the crowd, watching as they broke off into familiar groups. They all talked about going on to Amy's house for the wake.

Someone walked toward me, but stopped when I turned in his direction. He paused, made eye contact with me, and nodded toward the trees.

Matty Spooner. He'd been on the football team. He was small and fast, and had been a natural winger until his developing taste for weed started to slow him down. If this had been twenty years earlier, he would have been calling me to the trees to offer a toke. As I met him beneath the large oak, I found out that's exactly what he was doing.

He held out his joint. I paused before taking it. I have a bad history with painkillers and amphetamines, so I usually avoid all drugs. But I'd been looking for something to do, and he was offering. I held the smoke down, letting it find my lungs, before blowing out a cloud.

"Been a while," he said.

"Twenty years."

"Everyone's here," he spoke with a nervous edge, about to break into a pot laugh at any minute. "Social event of the season."

The line sparked a memory. He was quoting something, but I couldn't remember what.

"You back in town?"

I shook my head. "Passing through."

"I need your help," Matty said. He hesitated. "I—I don't think Robert killed himself."

That would have hit me a lot harder if the drugs weren't floating around my head. Instead I laughed, and said, "What?"

Matty reached into his jacket and pulled out a crumpled photograph. It was our football team. Fifteen young boys. The usual starting eleven, plus the four who were never quite good enough. Stood on either side of us were the two teachers who coached us. Colin Etheridge and Thomas Mitchell.

Everyone looked so young.

"Four of these people are dead now," Matty said. "Robert is the third suicide."

THREE
NOW

"What did you mean, you thought it would be me?"

The conversation had taken an awkward pause while Mitchell showed me into his living room and offered me a seat on his plush sofa. He left to fix us both a coffee, and I sat waiting, listening to the sounds of the kettle, before I could talk to him about killing.

Sometimes, there's just no escaping being British.

He handed me a cup of black instant coffee, and I blew on the dark surface to give him time to sit down before asking my question.

"I kept up on you. The whole time. Read your name in the papers. You know, I used to love that, before going to work. Sit and read the paper. See what had happened in the world the day before, then fold it up, throw it away, and get on with the new one."

"Most of what they said about me is a lie."

"Thought as much. But I know you pulled those people out of that fire."

"I pulled myself out of a fire. Other people followed."

Mitchell smiled. "You never could take a compliment."

He paused to sip from the drink. It came with a loud slurp, which went right through me. If every sip was going to be accompanied by that sound, I'd soon be wanted for murder myself.

"Didn't see you at Robert's funeral."

"No." He paused to rub his nose. "No. Didn't feel right."

"Why not?"

Mitchell stared past me, out through the front window. He seemed to be a million miles away. "Such a shame," he said, drifting back. "He's got boys?"

"Two girls."

"Such a shame," he said again. "It just keeps going round, doesn't it? A cycle. Someone gets hurt, then they pass it on, hurt others. Just carrying something for a while, until we give it to someone else."

I saw a different way in. "What were you carrying?"

FOUR
THEN

We were known as a doomed team. In our first two seasons together, from ages thirteen to fourteen, we reached the finals of four tournaments. We lost them all. In the third year, we won two cups. Everything started to improve. And then a suicide ended the whole thing.

There had been two changes at the start of that season.

First, Thomas Mitchell was added to the coaching staff. Colin Etheridge had been doing the job on his own, but he was an old-school P.E. teacher in his fifties. Most of his ideas revolved around making us run a lot, and shouting when we made mistakes. Mitchell was younger. He'd done sports science at university and was a big fan of psychology. He worked on our self-belief and would sometimes pull members of the team off the school mini-bus for a ride in his Saab. We started to enjoy our football. The results picked up straight away.

The second change was Danny Pratt.

Danny moved to us from the Catholic school across the road. He'd been a troublemaker and a bully, expelled for one too many fights. It had been a difficult transition. The message to the rest of us had been clear: *he's not good enough for the Catholic school, so he'll settle for you.*

Danny carried on with the same attitude. He would push girls around, and start fights with boys who didn't stand a chance against him. After a couple of months of this, he was drafted into the football team. The teachers figured it would give him an outlet for his aggression, and maybe bonding with the rest of us would calm him down.

It worked.

Danny was a natural in front of goal. His strength let him bully defenders, while I ran around between him and the midfield, linking up the play. He started to score, and we couldn't stop winning. From December through to March, we went through every decent team in the region. We won two tournaments and booked a place in a national competition.

And his success in the team had a calming influence on him. He started to settle into school life. He'd stay behind after training to work on aspects of his game. He was still a dick, but less so. All signs seemed to be that he was figuring himself out.

That's when Danny took his own life.

He was found by his stepfather swinging from the garage roof by his school tie.

None of us understood. Not then, and not now. Twenty years later, the shock still hit me whenever I thought about it. We didn't grieve for him, exactly. None of us had liked him. But we still had to feel *something*, and it came in anger and fights. The remainder of the team's fixtures were cancelled for the season. The school didn't enter any competitions in the following year.

Danny's sister, Jenny, was at Robert's funeral. I recognized her from a distance. Jenny had been a looker at school, and we'd messed round a couple of times in the last few months of term. She was carrying a few extra pounds, but so were all of us. Seeing her there made me decide to go on to the house for the wake. I wanted to ask about her brother. After a couple of hours of awkward conversations with people I didn't like, I found Jenny in the garden, smoking a cheap-smelling cig.

"Bring back bad memories?"

It had sounded nicer in my head.

Jenny turned to me. "You weren't *that* bad." She held the straight face for a few seconds before cracking into a smile. "How you doing?"

"Good," I said. Not really wanting *another* vapid conversation about how we were both fine and, yes, it's been a long time. You?"

Jenny smiled again. "Yeah." She went back to her smoke, but watched me out of the corner of her eye. Blowing out a long cloud, she said, "You haven't changed."

That wasn't true, but I didn't take it as an opportunity to list all the ways I'd changed in the last twenty years. Marriage. Divorce. Drugs. Riots. Murders. Gang war. None of them felt like the topic for polite conversation.

"You want to get out of here," she said, "and see what we remember?"

Yes. I decided that I did.

An hour later, as we both got dressed in the kitchen of her small flat on Park Lane, she apologized. "I get nervous at funerals, ever since. I just needed to feel something else, and I didn't have any Ben & Jerry's in the freezer, so…"

"Any time," I said. Meaning *never again*.

It had been fun but felt like I was fucking my own past out of some twisted sense of nostalgia. I sensed Jenny felt the same way.

"Did you still see him much? Robert, I mean?"

She nodded. "We'd see each other in the Myvod sometimes. They have a quiz night? We'd never be on the same team, but we'd talk a bit."

"How did he seem? I mean, was there any—"

"Sign? That he was going top himself? I'm your expert now?"

"I didn't mean it like that," I said, despite having meant it exactly like that.

Jenny hesitated. Her face was flushed with either anger or embarrassment. When she spoke, I guessed from her shaky voice it was both. "Sorry. I think, just, like I said, funerals. They put me on edge." She sat on the kitchen chair and lit a cig. After a long pull, she said, "He was always sad. Robert. He did remind me of my brother, I suppose. But, like, Danny was always angry, always. Until one day he was sad. Robert was always sad. He hid it, smiled a lot in the pub, but his eyes never smiled."

"You said Danny just got sad one day?"

"Well, it was more than that. But he changed, yeah. When he was in that team with you, he seemed happy. It was the only time I saw him relax, not trying to fight anyone. Then he was brought home by one of the teachers one day, and he was pale, sad. Mom and Steve weren't in, so it was me who saw him. He was never the same after that. Then..."

There was no sign of her finishing the thought. She sat and smoked in silence, staring at the washing machine.

"You remember which teacher it was?"

"Yeah, the one with the nice car. Mitchell?"

FIVE
NOW

"I was getting the train home." Mitchell's voice took on a distant quality. He was sat in front of me, but talking from a long time ago. "This was when I was at uni. I lived with my girlfriend at the time. I'd stayed out drinking for a couple of hours after, with some friends, then got the train. At the station, I could see a group of drunk older guys. In their forties, maybe fifties. Couldn't tell back then. I'd be an expert now."

He paused to smile at his own joke. I waited him out.

"There was a woman on her own. Not much older than me. We all got on the same train, and I saw the guys started to bother her. Not physically. They did that thing, you know, they stood around her, kept asking questions, wouldn't let the conversation drop. There were other people on the train, and the conductor was there, but nobody said anything. So, I stepped over and just said, 'come on guys, leave her alone.' Not aggressive. Because look at me. I've never been able to pull off aggressive. And they did leave her alone. Because they started on me."

Mitchell paused to take a sip from the coffee. He held the mug in both hands, shaking.

He set the drink on the floor beside his chair and stood up. He mumbled something about being right back, and returned with a bottle of Bells and two glasses. I waved the offer away. I hadn't had alcohol in over a year. Mitchell made up for it with a large measure for himself and knocked half of it back before picking up the story.

"I can still smell their breath. Feel the heat of it on my face. They stepped in close, all around me. They'd been drinking. Started telling me all the things they would do to me when we got off the train. They touched me. Groped. In front and behind. I looked at the other people in the carriage, but nobody would meet my eyes. The conductor stood there. He did make eye contact, but it was with this look on his face, like he was saying, *please don't involve me.* Nobody wanted to help. I remember thinking, I'm the odd one out, here. I'm the weirdo for wanting to help. And I remember, at the worst of it, I really wanted them to go back to harassing the woman. Anything, anyone other than me."

He swallowed.

Just when I was thinking the story might be over, he started again.

"It went on all the way to the next town. It was my stop. I was supposed to get off. But the men all got off there, and I chickened out. I stayed on to the next station. As I stepped down off the train there, this old woman turned to me, she said it was my fault. Said they would've left me alone if I hadn't pissed them off. I sat on the platform, on this bench at the end, and I cried. I sat there for an hour. I didn't want to go home. I don't know. It was like I thought my girlfriend would see me as less than a man, like she would just know."

"Must have been hard. Carrying that around."

"For years, I would volunteer as a counselor after school. At colleges and community centers. There were these seventeen, eighteen-year-old girls, and they would come to me sometimes to tell stories about what happened to them. And, you know, I saw they go through this stuff all the time. Every day. On buses, on the tram. And I'd be telling them, it's good to talk. Thanks for sharing. All of that. But I couldn't do it myself. Just, couldn't say, *help*."

"I'm sorry," I said.

"I still think about it every day. How many other people did they do that to? Did someone get hurt? If I'd just been man enough to call the police, or talk to someone, is there someone out there who wouldn't have been attacked?"

SIX
THEN

Ash Gamble had been a small kid. Sensitive and fragile, with a sheepish smile. At five-eight, he was too slight for the type of physical teams we came up against, but he was good on the ball.

He made time for everybody's problems and liked to read in his spare time. The ball was the only thing he had in common with the rest of the team. He reacted badly to Danny's death, and within a year, he was shooting up. Looking back, I know I didn't do anything to help. Like many confused kids at that age, I had more capacity to hurt than heal. I taunted him, turned my back on his problems. Ash became a joke to most of his old friends, and his new ones couldn't be trusted to steer him in the right direction. Despite what the movies tell us, most drug users live normal lives and stay in control of the habit. Office workers. Teachers. Cops. It's only a minority of people who develop enough of a taste to destroy their lives.

Unfortunately for Ash, he was one of those people.

His implosion was fast and messy.

It was no surprise when he died. He had the fatal cocktail of drugs and alcohol in his system. Rumors went around town that it was a suicide, and Matty Spooner clearly still believed that. I've seen enough drug deaths since to know it was probably an accident. I don't think Ash deliberately checked out; he was just too far gone to have any notion of looking after himself.

Even though I didn't believe Matty was right about the suicide, it didn't mean he was wrong about the cause. My thoughts kept pulling back to that final season, when everyone's lives changed.

I walked back to the graveyard to visit Ash. The plot was near the oak tree where I'd smoked with Matty a few hours before. It was a simple stone, carrying Ash's name, the dates, and *beloved*. He hadn't had much in the way of family, from what I remember. His dad had skipped out at an early age, leaving him to be raised by his mother. There were no brothers or sisters, and I don't recall him ever mentioning grandparents. There was a fresh bouquet of flowers on his grave. Either his mom had been by earlier that day, or someone from the funeral service had left them. It could have been Matty, I suppose, but he didn't strike me as the flowers type.

I bent down and whispered an apology to Ash. For looking the other way when he needed me, and for taking so long to come back. I climbed to my feet and hesitated before stepping away. There was another grave I needed to visit, but I was still putting it off.

Colin Etheridge was the fourth dead person in Matty's photograph. He'd been the second to go.

Etheridge had died in a car accident during the summer break, a few months after Danny's suicide. It was Danny's passing that had brought the football season to an early end, but it was Etheridge's violent death that had canceled the following year. *The doomed team.* It felt for a time as if everyone involved with that squad was cursed.

In many ways, Etheridge's fate was as self-inflicted as the other three. He got behind the wheel of his car with a bottle of whisky in his system. He was found in the wreckage the next day, with his skull smashed into a new shape.

I found the grave marker in the far corner. There were no flowers, and nobody had gone to much care to keep it tidy. Moss and weeds covered the ground. Crisp packets lay in small pieces, tangled in the grass.

Etheridge had never liked me. He'd called me names. *Pikey. Gyppo.* Even without the bigotry, I'd given plenty of reasons for the teachers at school to hate me. I was rebellious and cocky. I refused to listen to advice, skipped detention, and coasted through classes. Etheridge told me I'd never amount to anything and that I was lazy. But he'd needed me in the team, and football was the only thing I enjoyed, so we tolerated each other.

It had been Mitchell who'd put his arm around me. He took me to one side during training to boost my morale, and sometimes he drove me home from a match in his Saab, talking through what I'd done well and what I could do better.

Etheridge had different favourites.

He liked the boys he considered to be more dependable. The ones who would listen to him and stay after training for extra practice.

He liked Danny Pratt.

Robert Malpass.

Ash Gamble.

There was a dark stain on Etheridge's gravestone. A streak of water starting around his name and running down into the grass. I leaned in close, and could smell the ammonia-tinged scent of fresh piss.

Etheridge had another favourite.

And I knew what Matty Spooner had really been telling me.

SEVEN
NOW

"I should have known something was off when I joined the school," Mitchell said. "They already had a full staff of P.E. teachers, and a head of department. There wasn't a space for me, at first, but they hired me anyway."

"Did they say why?"

His head moved to the side, half a shake. "Not directly. The head, Mr. Prince, he said the school wanted to modernize and specialize in sport. He kept saying that Etheridge was *stuck in his ways*. Then I was asked to coach the football teams, but again, Etheridge did that, and he wasn't being sacked. It was a strange situation, the two of us working together on a job that only needed one of us."

"I remember it felt weird when we were told you were joining."

"Yeah. And there was this thing. Every time people talked about Etheridge, there was always something else there. Some subtext. I saw the way he talked to you. I'm sorry about that, by the way."

"Don't worry."

"I saw that, and I thought maybe it was because he was a racist. Maybe that's what they meant. You know, *boys will be boys*, it's kind of how it was back then. Everyone knew that racism was wrong, but the older teachers were still from another age. Nobody wanted to be the one to sack a friend for doing it, so people would be moved around, managed."

"Yeah."

"And I was doing it too. I went along with it, I mean. It

seemed natural to me, like I was thinking, well, if the only problem is that he's a bit racist...it made sense to me that they'd ask me to help out."

"But it wasn't the racism."

Mitchell paused to pour another whisky. "No." His hands shook again. "No. But nobody would talk about it. Everything was euphemism. He was just 'weird old Colin,' with his 'particular ways.' It's like, a little bit of everyone knew what was going on, but nobody let themselves dwell on it enough to fully figure it out."

"When did you know?"

Mitchell stared at the back of his hand for a moment, scratching at the skin. When he looked up at me, his expression had shifted. He wasn't quite ready to give me the rest.

"I'm not sure," he said. "When did *you* know?"

My throat tightened. The words came out hoarse. "I think I always did."

EIGHT
THEN

I was spared a trip back to the Malpass house. The seasoned drinkers had moved to the Myvod. The pub that formed the center of the social life for this part of town. I passed it on the way back to the house, and changed course when I saw Matty Spooner sat on his own at one of the tables outside.

He was quietly puffing away on another spliff, and everyone was looking the other way. I saw his pint was almost finished. I headed inside first to buy him a new one. The Myvod had been a standard old men's pub when I was at school. Full of brown wood paneling with two separate bars. The modern version was bigger and brighter. The walls had been knocked through so that it was an open plan with the bar in the middle, and the remaining walls were painted in a neutral light beige. It was my idea of hell.

Back outside, I set the new drink down in front of Matty. He looked up at me with half-baked eyes.

I took a seat next to him and watched while he finished the first pint and started on the second, raising it in a toast to thank me.

I leaned in close. "Do you need help?"

He started to cry.

NINE
NOW

I had always known. I think we all had. Some part of us. Deep down.

It was a thought that sat at the back of our minds, never wanting to fight its way to the surface. As long as it wasn't happening to us, we didn't need to face it. And to acknowledge it, to talk to the boys who were suffering....

I felt myself slump into the chair.

"It's not your fault," Mitchell said. "You were boys. You shouldn't have needed to ask for help. That's all wrong. The way we talk about victims. We always say, *don't be afraid to ask for help*. We never talk about how we should ask them if they're okay."

I swallowed and tried for a nod.

He continued, letting me sit with my silence. "It was us. The adults. We were the ones. And I went along with it, you know? Just like the racism. When I first started to pick up on the weird vibes, when I first knew, I didn't want to know. I started trying to work round it. I'd give some of you separate rides home, take you to the sides, encourage you to listen to me, not to go with him. And the whole time, I *had* to know why I was doing it. Then I found Danny crying in the showers."

His words dried up. He lifted the glass to his mouth, but held it there, not drinking. He lowered it again without taking a sip.

"I went to the head. To Prince. And he wanted it kept quiet. That's when I knew that everyone at the school had to be in on it, on some level. Etheridge coached football there for twenty years. Think how many boys passed through. After Danny..." His words sounded damp, coated in pain. "After Danny died, I just couldn't...Etheridge came to me one night, drunk. He'd downed most of a bottle of something. Stank of booze. He sounded remorseful, I thought, maybe now, maybe I can get him to quit, or turn himself in, something. But you know what he was sad about? He was upset because the season had been canceled. Because his *boys* didn't get to play in the nationals."

"What did you do?"

Mitchell's face was pale. The adrenaline rush was coming with his memories, taking him back to the feeling he'd had back then. "It was a small hit at first. Just one. I'd taken the bottle from him, but I lost my temper and swung it at his head, hit the back because he'd turned away to wipe his eyes. But that was it, like a dam burst. I kept hitting him. Harder. Harder." He almost smiled. "Never thought I was violent, but..."

"And you faked the crash."

"Wouldn't get away with it these days, I suppose. Cameras everywhere."

We sat in silence.

Mitchell worked his way through the amber liquid and poured another. For the first time since quitting, I felt the pull to join in. Other demons whispered to me. They told me I could make all the pain go away if I took a few pills. Maybe just one. Enough to take the edge off...

"What happens next?" Mitchell said. "You should turn me in, I suppose."

I breathed in deep. Held it for several seconds, feeling my heart pounding away.

"I think, to prove anything, they would need to exhume

the body," I said.

"I guess so."

"And the bottle, the weapon, I don't suppose you've been daft enough to hold onto it?"

"No."

"And even if there's still anyone working at the school from back then, they're not going to get involved. Really, your confession would be the only proof, unless they wanted to put in the time and money to get DNA off the body. It would really come down to how much effort the cops would want to put into the case. Finding justice for *that* guy."

He nodded slowly. "I guess it would be difficult to prove, if I didn't want to admit to it."

"It would."

"My word against yours."

I paused. "Only yours." I passed him a crumpled piece of paper with a phone number written on it. "But Matty Spooner could do with a friend."

I left him sat there. He was crying when I shut the front door behind me on the way out.

On the walk back down through town, I came to the halal butcher.

The tape was still in place, blowing loosely in the wind, but the cops and reporters had gone. Saj was stood out front, sweeping the water and damp soot out of the way with a stiff broom. He stopped when he saw me and leaned on the handle.

"Thought I saw you earlier," he said. "You back?"

"I don't know," I said. "Maybe." I nodded at the shop front. "What're you going to do?"

Saj shrugged. Matter-of-fact. "Fix it up, reopen."

"I'm sorry for the way things have gone around here. Wish there was something I could do to help."

He handed me the broom.

CHARACTER
IS EVERYTHING
Jon McGoran

Sitting in his cubicle in the far corner of the cavernous manufacturing floor, Roscoe Boyer kept his eyes on his screen, finishing the last profile for the spring line and ignoring the echoing clack of Doug Carter's approaching heels. It was rare for management types to venture down there. But today was special.

Carter looked straight ahead as well, as if he was determined not to look at the five hundred naked robots standing to his left. Roscoe almost sympathized. It used to bother him, too.

When Carter finally arrived, he didn't say a word. Instead, he folded his hands over the partition that separated the writers' cubicles from the rest of the floor and started tapping it with that ridiculous smart ring of his. As if his heels hadn't been annoying enough.

Roscoe tried not to look up, but as always, Carter outwaited him. A thousand robot eyes pinned on him hadn't bothered Roscoe in years. But somehow the stare of a real human—even Carter—he couldn't tolerate for more than a few seconds.

"What is it, Doug?" Roscoe asked.

"Need you to finish the character profiles on these units," Carter said, hooking a thumb at the phalanx of bots. "Then come on up to the break room. The girls in sales got you a cake."

They were closing down the character department, getting rid of the writers and handing it all over to the same god-damned bots that were marching off the line. But at least there was cake.

Roscoe laughed and shook his head.

Carter looked as ridiculous as always, with his neon green eyes and sparkly star-shaped face tattoo. Roscoe couldn't believe the guy was his boss. Well, not for long.

"I'll be done in a minute," Roscoe said as he hit the keys on his computer to take a photo with the built-in camera.

Carter stiffened at the fake shutter sound. "Did you just take my picture?"

Roscoe smiled. "Something to remember you by."

Carter squirmed but didn't protest. Roscoe liked to do odd things in front of him, watch him trying to figure out if it was legitimately weird or just something people did in the olden days.

"Just...hurry up. Okay, Roscoe?"

As Carter clacked his way back across the warehouse floor, Roscoe double-checked that he'd answered all the standard questions on the official PeopleBot character profile checklist. It was generally his last step before sending a product line to shipping. This time there was an extra step. Since it was his last one.

He told himself he was lucky to have been able to work as a writer as long as he had. His contemporaries had given up years ago. Roscoe had started out writing honest-to-God books, but he'd changed with the times—video games, social media micro shorts, story interactives. Finally this.

CharacterBots started out as playthings for the super-rich or rentals for BotSex companies. But as the price dropped, they became more common and took on different roles—replacements for absent fathers or dead grandparents or non-existent life companions. Having taken over all the manufacturing and service jobs nobody wanted to do, they took over the unwanted personal tasks as well. But looking real wasn't enough. They had to act real, too.

Roscoe thought the whole thing incredibly sad, but at least he'd been getting paid to write.

There were those who thought what he was writing was crap. "Everything you write has been written a thousand times before," Carter had said when he told them PeopleBot was automating the character department. "Ninety-five percent of it is just copied from last year's code scripts. You don't even look at it."

Carter had a point, sort of. They did start each year copying the archetypes from the previous season. And maybe the coding was ninety-five percent the same. But so what? Chimp DNA is ninety-five percent identical to human. It's what you do with the other five percent that matters.

"The bots will add onto this year's scripts, just like you would have," Carter had said. "Only they'll do it better, quicker, and with fewer screwups."

The other writers took buyouts or transfers. But Carter had inspired Roscoe to stay on until the spring line was finished.

When he was done with the checklist, Roscoe sat back, drinking the last bit of coffee from his CHARACTER IS EVERYTHING company mug. It was the PeopleBot, motto—plastered everywhere—and it pissed him off every time he saw it. *What about plot?* he always thought. What good is life or literature or even goddamned CharacterBots if nothing ever happens?

He'd been working on the Ideal Father bot when he realized the character profile was too good to be true. In the old days, a father that was too good to be true would be just that. He'd have a deep dark secret, something that would mess things up, make something happen.

Writing used to be about making characters believable. In the old days, in books, readers wanted characters that were conflicted and compelling. But these days, they didn't want drama. They wanted nice—The Ideal Father, The Thoughtful Boyfriend, The Loving Mother. But characters that are a hundred percent nice simply aren't believable. You have to give them flaws—like with perfume, you need something bitter to keep all that sweetness from cloying.

That's where Roscoe's idea came from. But the inspiration was all Doug Carter. A parting gift to the guy who eliminated the world's last paying job for a writer.

Roscoe looked around furtively, making sure no one was watching, then he started opening subdirectories within subdirectories, delving deeper and deeper into the original PeopleBot character code, until he found the spot he was looking for. Then he started typing.

Carter reappeared at the far end of the floor. "Come on, Roscoe!" he yelled, his exasperation echoing throughout the place.

Roscoe ignored him and uploaded one last file.

Next spring's Considerate Neighbor model—and every model after that—would come complete with a distant but vivid memory. Something terrible had happened to him as a child, something violent and savage. To get on with his life, the Considerate Neighbor had buried the memory deep down in his psyche—in the basic structural code where no one ever looked anymore. He wouldn't be able to remember—wouldn't want to remember—what had been done to him, just that it had been so cruel, so horrific, that if he ever found who did it, he'd make sure that person would never hurt anyone ever again.

The Considerate Neighbor didn't know his abuser's name, but he'd never forget that face—those neon green eyes, that star-shaped face tattoo.

"Jesus, Roscoe, do you hear me?" Carter bellowed. "Everyone's waiting."

Carter kept his head at an angle, avoiding the sight of all

those naked Considerate Neighbor bots. Otherwise, he might have noticed that brief instant, just after the photo finished uploading, when all five hundred robots looked at him with recognition and hatred.

Then Roscoe pressed QUIT and they went blank again, dormant and ready to be shipped out across the country.

"Finished," Roscoe called back. He shut down his computer and grabbed his mug and the PeopleBot tote bag with all his personal belongings. "They're ready to ship out. And I'm ready for some cake."

OUTLAWS
Lori Rader-Day

Two days after starting the move, Tess, her mother, and her sister, Sam, were driving the last of their things from the old house to the new one when Tess's mother slowed the car and skidded into the gravel next to the highway.

"There it is," she said. She flicked her cigarette ash out the window and pointed. She had long fingers. Piano-playing fingers, she said, as though someone else said it first. Tess wasn't sure if her mother had ever touched a piano. "Right there. The most perfect tree in the world. My tree."

There were trees all along the side of the highway and along the other side four lanes over, too. This one stood alone, growing up against a farmer's barbed fence at the edge of an empty field. Skinny, not so tall. But Tess knew why her mother had chosen this tree above all others—it had a crown of leaves, perfectly round, like a halo. Her mother pulled back onto the road, the trees rushing by faster and faster until Tess's eyes hurt to try to single one out. She watched them blur into each other, wondering if the trees stood too close to the fields' fences, if they didn't somehow grow into the wire. If, over time, the trees didn't swallow the barbs and forever after live with biting metal under their bark.

Tess's sixth grade science teacher had told them last month about how nature adapted, how weeds and grass wouldn't stop growing even where they weren't wanted and how a drip-drop of water would put a hole in anything over a long time, including rock, including the earth. "Nature wins," Ms. Sheffield said. "Nature always does exactly what it wants, and it always wins." Tess waited for one of the other kids to raise a hand and ask about humans—weren't they nature, too? They didn't always win. Lightning, remember? Say a human and a bear meet up, she'd wanted to say.

Or say nature meets a car, like it did so many times on the road to the new house. The new house, which was really an old house, was far out in the country, surrounded by five apple trees. When they had pulled into the driveway the first time, the tires smashed the knotty apples to pulp, adding a fresh layer to already-rotting fruit. They got out of the car, and Sam crouched low over a crushed apple and started to cry. The air smelled of vinegar.

"Did you see the leaves on my tree, Sam?" their mother asked over her shoulder. "A little baby oak. Like one of those pictures you draw for Mama."

They were both too old to draw suns with smiling faces peeking around round-topped trees—Tess was twelve and Sam was eight—but Sam still did. She brought them home from her special class and their mother put them on the fridge with a magnet. Or at least she had in the old house. In the new house, the rules weren't decided. There were boxes in all the hallways and stacked next to the doors. Some of the boxes in Tess's new room said KITCHEN on the side. In the kitchen, there were more boxes on the dirty counters, pried open to show the jumble of spoons and spatulas and knives still inside. Yesterday they'd eaten ice cream for dinner off paper plates and at bedtime their mother said, "I'm just so *tired*," and let them go to bed without brushing their teeth.

Since they were getting away with things, Tess had packed an overdue library book instead of returning it. They were outlaws now.

In the front seat, Tess's mother sighed. Tess let out the breath she'd been holding since they'd stopped the car, when, for a moment, Tess hadn't been sure what her mother meant to do. Her mind had leapt forward into possibilities: would she make them get out and leave them next to the road? Or would she get out to hitchhike away as they watched from the back seat? Seemed like, just for a minute, that someone was going to make a break for it.

Tess leaned against the car door. In the front seat, her mother shook her head and made a little ticking sound with her tongue. This is how Tess knew her mother wasn't thinking about trees anymore. Not the stupid, messy apple trees at the new place or even the accidentally crayon-perfect one by the road. She was only thinking of herself, and this was exactly the same as it always had been.

The wind from the open window flicked a strand of Tess's hair into her eyes. Sam reached out and pinched her on the thigh, but Tess didn't stop her or cry out like she was supposed to so that Sam would know it hurt. Tess knew exactly what if felt like to need to pinch someone. It wasn't always the wrong thing to do.

A scratched-up, maroon truck was parked in their driveway. Tess's mother swore quietly and let their car crunch slowly to a stop behind it.

"Truck," Sam said. She hardly knew any words at all. Their mom corrected people who suggested names or diseases. Slow, she said. Sam's just a little slow.

Tess sat up and folded her arms over the front seat. "Yes, Sam, truck. A *red* truck. Who is it?"

They all watched as a man in sunglasses and two shades of blue denim came around the corner of the house. He stopped by the front of the truck but didn't wave or smile.

"Nobody," Tess's mom said.

Nobody usually meant a new boyfriend they'd learn more about later, if he stuck around. Tess's mom had been married twice, once to Sam's dad and once before that to someone who Sam's dad brought up whenever they fought, a man named Roy who was also not Tess's dad. She'd been divorced twice, too, and they'd lived with a few other guys over the years, and then back in with Sam's dad until he packed a big duffel bag last month and left. Tess had hoped they would finally be on their own. She pictured them huddled together out in the new hideout, laying low. Her mother would have to leave her job to take care of them, and she'd have to stay home from school, of course. Maybe Missy and Angel, her two best friends, could come stay, to keep being outlaws from getting boring.

Tess held her hand out so she could admire her fingernails. Missy and Angel had given her a set of teeny-tiny nail polishes as her going-away present. She had painted each finger a different color: blue, silver, red, orange, thumb in black. The reverse order on the other hand. "Is that Roy?" Tess said. Through her splayed fingers, her mother glared at her.

"What do you know about it?" She smoothed her hair down and propped her sunglasses on the top of her head. "Stay here for a minute. Both of you."

As soon as the door closed behind her, Sam started to fuss. Tess brushed her hands away from the belt buckle. "No, come on, Sam. What do you want to play? Want to play riddley-ree? I see something you don't see? And the color is?"

Sam hopped in her seat. "Arnge!"

Tess pretended to search the car for something orange colored. Outside, her mother had her back to them, her arms folded. She was looking off into the fields, shaking her head as the guy leaned in close, talking. Tess tried to read his lips. That could be a cool thing to know how to do. She could amaze all the stupid kids at her new stupid school, figure out the teachers' secrets by just standing down the hall from the lounge. Maybe they would figure out she was too smart and too special—the other kind of special—to be in any school at all and she could leave. She could be a real outlaw, take Sam and head for California. They could live on the beach and she could teach Sam all the new words they encountered. Sand. Sandcastle. Ocean.

"Arnge!"

"Okay, okay, uhhh. Is it my fingernails?" Tess held up her two orange-tipped index fingers like guns and shot them off, *pow pow*, as Sam laughed. Her fingernails were the only orange things anywhere in sight. "What's next? Riddley-ree, Sam sees something *I* don't see, and the color is—"

Tess heard the man's voice rise sharp outside and Sam's answer—orange again—at the same time. She eased her car door open and held it ajar a few inches with her tennis shoe. Her mother's voice cut through the air. "Why *now* all of a sudden?" she said.

At the sound of their mother's anger, Sam's face clenched into a fist. She opened her mouth to scream. Sam's cries were legendary. If they'd been in the grocery store too long or the doctor wanted to check her throat with a stick or their car didn't turn toward the playground, Sam would let out such a howl as to turn the air around them tight.

Tess let the door close. "Okay, Sammy Star, okay. Orange again, huh? Is it, uhhh, my fingernails?" Tess made the finger guns again and poked them gently into the soft flesh of Sam's ribs. Sam giggled, but when their mother opened the driver's door, she started to tug at her seatbelt again, revving up.

"Mom, can we get out? It's hot in here and Sam—"

"Yeah." She reached in for her cigarettes on the dash and sat sideways on the driver's seat to light one. The sun was low. Orange, actually. Tess's mother sucked at the cigarette, squinting across the ragged yard, then closed her eyes. "Yeah, get out," she said. "You got to meet someone."

Crap. Tess looked past her mother at the guy. He was older and sort of fat, but only in the front like a pregnant lady. He had skinny, tanned arms where his sleeves were rolled up. It was probably his house, and this was just another move, another guy. And in a year or so or sooner, another move. Another guy.

How far was California? While her bags were still packed, before Sam pulled all her stuffed animals out of the big trash bag full of her toys, maybe it was time to get out a map.

"Come on," Tess's mom said. She didn't say it mad, though, or impatient, the way she sometimes did.

Tess unlatched Sam and pulled her across the back seat. As they approached the man, he dropped his boot from the bumper of his truck and ran his hand through his hair. Slick strands of it stuck to his forehead. Tess looked from him to her mother and back. She didn't think she'd ever been introduced to a boyfriend. Mostly they just showed up at the door of her mother's bedroom scratching at gaping places in their boxer shorts.

"Well, I know which one she is just by looking at her," this man said.

"You should know her by how old she is, you fool," Tess's mother said. She took Sam's other hand and pulled her in front of her like a shield. Sam's fingers slid out of Tess's. "Tess, this is Darren."

Darren put his hand out toward her.

"Okay," Tess said. She smelled rotten apples. She had never taken a stand, but now she felt as though—why not? She folded her arms. "He's not living here, is he?"

"He's just taking us to dinner," her mother said. "A *nice* dinner." Tess's mom combed her fingers through Sam's hair. Sam slapped her hands away. "Honey, Darren is here to meet you. To meet you, special. That's your daddy."

Tess didn't know whether to stomp off to her new, unfurnished bedroom and cry or to pump the man's hand gladly. After all, he wasn't moving in, and she needed to thank him for that. But most of all she just wanted to go back in time. Just a little while. Just a few minutes, even, before she knew that the pregnant cowboy in front of her was someone she'd have to reckon with. And if she couldn't go back in time, well, all she wanted to do was pinch someone.

The nearest town was too small to have a nice restaurant. They drove in Darren's truck back the way they'd come, toward their old house. He drove with his window down and one arm dangling out. Sam sat on their mother's lap, and Tess sat rigid in the center of the long seat. The quiet got deep and almost loud. The wind from Darren's window rushed into her ear until it hurt. She would not say a word, even if she went deaf.

"Riddley-ree, Sam," their mother said, finally.

"Arnge!"

"Orange, huh? Let me see." Her mother glanced down at Tess's hands, then all around, her head swiveling in a wide circle to make Sam laugh. "Is it my shirt?"

Sam frowned at the shirt. "Red."

"You're right, that isn't orange at all, is it?"

Darren shifted in his seat. Tess looked at him out of the barest corner of her eye.

"What's wrong with her?" he asked.

"Nothing wrong with *her*." Tess eyed the bulge of his belly buckled into a perfect ball behind the steering wheel.

"Easy now, little miss," he said. "Now I'm your dad—"

"You don't even remember my name, do you?" She wanted to tell him that he could save the effort. That nobody was going to be called Dad or Daddy on her watch. She had lived with Sam's dad for years off and on and had never, not once, called the man anything but *him*.

"I do, too," he said. "Theresa Marie Faherty."

Tess's mother coughed. In the little hiccup of noise, Tess heard that her mother wanted her to let it go. Tess sat back in the seat, allowing the name to settle on her. She felt an alternative life pop up next to her real one. An alternative life in which she'd had a father, in which Sam had never been born.

Nope. That name just didn't fit the life she had or even one she might wish for.

"Almost right," Tess said. "Except my last name isn't *Faherty*. What is that, Irish?"

Darren pulled his arm inside and strangled the wheel with two sets of white-knuckles. "Liz, I asked you for one thing."

"You didn't have a right to ask for anything," her mother said.

"A man's got a right—"

"I guess he does if he can keep his ass out of jail."

Tess looked at Darren with more interest. The real thing.

A few miles went by before he bounced the heel of one hand on the dash and said, "Then whose?"

"Whose what?"

"Whose name does she have?"

"I don't have a last name," Tess said. "I'm just Tess." She fanned her fingertips out on her thighs and admired them again.

"Like Madonna," Tess's mother said. She reached out and rubbed the back of Tess's neck. "Or Elvis."

Tess held herself straight and hard against the pat of her mother's hand. She wasn't actually on anyone's side just now.

"Elvis *Presley*," Darren said. "Madonna—" He faltered. "Both those people had last names their daddies gave them."

"Maybe some of those daddies paid the support they owed," her mother said.

Tess scooted closer to her. They rode the rest of the way to town hip to hip, and when they passed the perfect little oak, Tess tapped her mother's knee and was happy when she saw her smile secretly into Sam's shoulder.

When they'd had their spaghetti and meatballs and her mother and Sam went to visit the ladies' room, Darren folded his girl arms over the top of his belly, a shelf, and said, "How'd you like to come live with me? Just for the summer, I mean." His eyes shifted around. "Like a vacation. We've got some getting-to-know-you to do, you and me."

Tess looked across the dark room and the other tables lit by short, flickering candles. Situations like this happened in the books Missy and Angel lent her, and then the heroine might feel the too-warm hand of the greasy long-lost uncle under the table. She realized she had been waiting for this all night. All through the wait for a table, through the silence as they all looked at their tall menus, through the entire dinner, with Darren sawing at his steak and Tess's mom fidgeting with the latch on her purse. She'd been waiting for the thing that must happen, the thing that would change everything.

Now she picked up her fork and tapped at the pile of cold spaghetti in front of her. "Why?"

"What do you mean, why? Because we belong to each other, of course."

"That's a piece of shit," Tess said.

He stared at her. "Big mouth for a little girl."

"So where do you live?"

Darren leaned back. "Here and there, these years. But I got some land out west I'm thinking about buying. Build me a ranch, maybe. Get horses."

Tess let her fork clatter to the table. "Out west? California? Is it near the beach?"

He smiled. He had taken off his sunglasses at the restaurant door, and something in his face reminded her of someone else. The someone else must be herself.

"Not right on the beach," he said. "But you could drive there. I mean, I could drive us there."

Sand. Sandcastle. Ocean. Tess pictured blue striped umbrellas poking into the yellow sand, the checkmarks of sea birds overhead. A scene out of one of Sam's drawings made real. She said, "Sam and me—" But then she remembered that her plan to move to California was far in the future, or even worse, not real at all. Not a plan, but a dream.

"Yeah, what's the deal with that kid?" He fished in his shirt pocket for a pack of cigarettes, then looked around the restaurant and put them back. "I mean, is she—"

"What were you in jail for?" Tess said loudly.

She picked up the fork again and stabbed at a meatball. She wished Sam's dad was still in town. She'd find a phone to call him right over, and he and Darren could have a fight in the parking lot until one of them stomped the other into pieces. That might be interesting to watch. Who would win, in the battle of Sam's dad and hers? She wasn't sure.

"Nothing much," Darren said, glancing uneasily around the room. "Your sister—"

"She's just a little slow."

"You're smart, though, right? Get good grades and all?"

Tess knew what he wanted to hear. Her teacher Ms. Sheffield had explained all about the double-strand pearl necklace of that DNA business and how people got a little testy about what their necklace said about them. The acorn doesn't fall far from the oak, Ms. Sheffield had said, and now Tess wondered. Here was her oak. "I failed home ec, and when I start my new school on Monday, I guess I'm going to fail just about everything there is."

"Why's that?"

Tess opened her mouth to lie, but the truth came out. "Because I want to go back. If it goes bad enough, maybe we'll just—go back."

"If you fail all your classes, the only one you're getting revenge on is yourself," he said. "Believe me, I know. When you say you want to go back—do you mean to the house? To the school?"

Tess glanced across the restaurant again. Her mother was crouched in front of the large aquarium by the front door, her arms, thin as a child's, wrapped around Sam's shoulders. Sam was tracing the path of a fish in the tank with her finger.

Darren still waited for her to say something. She shrugged.

"Know what you mean." He drew out the cigarettes again, put them back. "Just back, right? Know *exactly* what you mean. I don't have much to offer you, but I can tell you this: There's no such thing as going back." He reached across the table and laid a hand on her arm. Tess pulled away, then slid out of her chair and past the waitress and the other tables, until she was next to her mother. Sam looked up at her with round eyes. "Arnge," she said, her voice breathy, her finger on the tank.

"Yes, orange." Tess held her elbows to keep from shaking. No such thing as going back, but what did he know? What did anyone know? Even Ms. Sheffield—that nature-wins business had to be flawed. That slab of cow on Darren's plate, raccoons turned wrong side out on the highway, all the way to the new house, and the smash-apples waiting for them there. Sometimes, with nature, it was a draw at best. "Mom, can we go now?"

Her mother stared into the tank, her eyes crossed to watch a snail stuck to the side. "Darren's driving, Tess. It's up to him."

Tess watched her mother's dull face. How could she not be tired of it being up to him? Him, him, whoever him happened to be? Everything decided itself and they went whichever way the wind blew. The drip-drop of nature creating the shape of them and everything around them.

"Mom, please? Couldn't we call someone? I—I don't want—"

Her mother stood up, her mouth tight. "Who would we call to take us all the way out there? What is it?" She placed her hand on the back of Tess's neck. "What did he say? Did he…do something? Did he—*touch*—"

Tess heard fire in her mother's voice and warmed to it. Her mother gathered both of them into her arms and squeezed, drawing a deep breath Tess could feel in her own lungs.

Across the room, Darren rose from the table. One word. She could say yes. Yes that Darren had slid his hand under the table onto her knee, into the leg of her shorts. Simple as that. But then they couldn't ever go back. They would have to go forward. And even though that made Darren right, Tess suddenly saw the appeal.

Her mother knelt before her and put her hands on either side of her face. Tess imagined how it could go: The four of them in the parking lot. Darren blustering and shrinking and her mother, grown large and wild, clawing at him. Sam crying and the other diners coming outside to see what was happening. Tess couldn't see herself, where she stood, or what happened next. She didn't know. She hadn't been brave enough even to raise her hand in class. She wasn't brave enough to lie. She wasn't brave enough to tell the truth. She wasn't brave enough to be an outlaw, not even close.

Her mother was saying something to her, but Tess couldn't understand. She felt as though a strong wind was blowing through the room, a violent and twisting wind rushing the words out of her mother's mouth. But it was Sam—Sam's howl. They'd been standing in one place too long or they hadn't had ice cream like she'd been promised or—it didn't matter. Sam had found something to be unhappy about. Her cry began as sound, but somewhere over the heads of the other diners, it became something more terrible: a roiling cloud, a storm. Nature versus the restaurant. The restaurant versus the little girl. The little girl versus the world.

The other diners turned toward them, their eyes sharp with disgust or concern or confusion as they tried to make sense of the noise. Darren stared, then slipped past them and outside. He hadn't paid for dinner. Tess stood wooden as the scene erupted around her. Little girl versus mother. Mother versus waitress.

Tess was strangely reassured. They were going to be fine. They were certainly going to be getting out of here without paying a cent. Their life of crime had begun. She made her fingers into orange-tipped guns and stuck the barrels into her ears.

A VANISHING STORY
Michael Kardos

Dr. Allan Hunt, associate professor of linguistics and narra-
tology at the state's leading research institution, was in his
departmental office, looking out the window and chewing on
his pencil despite writing, always, on a computer—even notes,
even brainstorms, even the idlest of passing observations—
when, absently, he reached down for his book on Mikhail
Bakhtin's theory of dialogics and noticed his briefcase missing.

He remembered carrying the briefcase from the car to the
student union, remembered carrying it in one hand, Starbucks
cup in the other, to Fawkes Hall, where he'd set the briefcase
on the floor beside his office desk, same as every day, or at least
he *believed* he recalled setting it down on the floor, because its
absence, he fully admitted, suggested otherwise.

The most valuable loss, if the briefcase were truly gone,
was the briefcase itself—a Milano Napa, black leather (Venice
collection), a gift from Gloria for his birthday, she claimed,
though they both knew it was a gift of apology, a gift of *Let's
give this marriage one more chance*, a gift of *See how I can
pretend to respect your work?*

He was thinking, not for the first time, about the subtler
meaning of the obscenely expensive briefcase, and how de-
meaning a gift it truly was, considering that a professor could
never buy such an extravagance on his salary alone, when he
heard outside his office the rhythmic *thuck thuck thuck* of the
photocopy machine, and left his office to look there.

The undergraduate work study student, Jenny (or perhaps Joanie? Ginny?) looked up from the copy machine and said, "Hey, Professor Hunt," smiling, and then her smile faded, and Dr. Hunt knew she saw his pain, even if she lacked the specifics: that the divorce papers had arrived yesterday morning by courier, that his ten-year marriage was now and forever over. It made one absent minded, a marriage in its curtain-call stage, transforming otherwise articulate men into bumblers, into losers of briefcases, and he felt a fierce, momentary ache for his days as a graduate student when the particularities of language had seemed as urgent and awesome as the cosmos, that time before meeting Gloria the Great, Gloria the Gorgeous.

Yes, this girl Jenny (briefcase thief?) saw through him despite the earnest attention he'd paid to making today the start of the rest of his life—though not teaching today, he wore a sharp blazer, necktie, freshly ironed slacks, and polished shoes; he vowed to glue himself to his chair and write the article coming due next week. And as if more evidence were needed that he was, perhaps, not operating at full speed despite his professional attire, caffeine intake, and pledge to cease mourning for his marriage and, instead, to focus and double-down on his scholarship, his career, his supposed lifelong passion, the girl glanced down, then up, and said, "Where's your shoe, professor?"

"How odd," Dr. Hunt muttered, seeing the black sock covering his foot, size eight, and he returned to his desk where the shoe must have come off while his mind was on Mikhail Bakhtin's notion of unfinalizability—the ultimate unknowability of another—and how, for the first time, he thought: Bakhtin, you've got it dead wrong. Because you *could* know another, and, no, people *didn't* change, not fundamentally, a lesson the professor learned not from any revered philosopher or theorist but from his wife, now his ex, who had taught him that once an adulteress always an adulteress (and, he had to admit, once a blind cuckold, always a blind cuckold).

He wondered, in a burst of bitter humor, if the ex in question were behind the disappearance of his briefcase and his shoe, just as she'd already been responsible for the disappearance of his pride and his ability to sit at his computer and finish any of the papers and articles whose deadlines loomed. Worse, yesterday afternoon he'd stood in front of thirty groggy undergraduates, their notebooks and pens more stage props than learning aids, and while lecturing about essential tropes and archetypes in folktales and fairy tales, twice— twice!—the word "wolf" had come out of his mouth as "wife," as in "*the big, bad wife.*"

She meant everything to him maybe in part because she'd been everything: a magician, for starters, headline performer at the annual magician conventions, the Society of American Magicians and International Brotherhood of Magicians— known, especially, for her dogged resistance to cliché: forget the top hat, the vaudeville shtick with its tired patter. A top female sleight-of-hand artist, she nonetheless decided at age thirty, let's try medical school, and suddenly she'd aced the MCAT and, four years later, had landed a coveted residency in radiation oncology, so now instead of making white doves disappear she had her sights on grander vanishings: carcinomas, lymphomas, astrocytomas.

"Gloria, you have broken my heart and stolen my sole," Dr. Hunt said now, and smiled, because while a bad pun was the lowest form of humor (said dramatist Allan Dennis ages ago), a good pun, Dr. Hunt believed, was an unexpected treat—a lagniappe—even for a jaded linguist.

The misplaced shoe couldn't have gone far, but it wasn't under his desk or by his computer or his bookshelf or behind the mini fridge, and he curled his hands into fists, frustrated that his mind wouldn't let his mind focus on his work, which he'd vowed to do. He needed the books in his briefcase; he needed the shoe; he needed, more broadly, to get a grip: Gloria was gone, pal, and quite likely in bed with Jack Morrow *right now*, and you—yes, you—drove her to him with your childish insecurities and insufferable self-pity.

No, people didn't change: just weeks after meeting Gloria, she had mentioned a second guy, nothing serious, she assured him, but rather than play it cool, Allan Hunt (not *Dr.* Hunt yet, his dissertation still ahead) had stormed off and ignored her calls for an agonizing month. Fast-forward a dozen years, and we have our credentialed and respected doctor of philosophy (tenured, no less), foolish but no fool, who knew damn well he had, once again, contributed in no small way to this parting, except now it was final and exponentially more devastating.

He remembered, several months back, her sobbing to him, "You have taken me from me," and though he'd feigned ignorance, he knew what she meant: he'd grown weary of hearing about her Good Work, the lives saved, the families who'd forever be in her debt. He'd become exhausted, too, of her tales of those she couldn't help, the tragedies, the losses filling her with quiet grief, and it didn't take a scholar to read the subtext: I'm the real doctor, whose hands can heal; you, Allan, play with words. So he shut her down, shut her out, and tried to banish from their conversations even the memories of her first career, the magic shows where adoring eyes were, let's be honest already, leering eyes, and hadn't she just loved all that attention?

He was a hypocrite, though, and knew it, because part of his own love for her was in the leering, for Gloria was a beautiful creature—this woman who had chosen to stand with him before a judge and say, "I do." And they *had*, for a while, loved and honored one another, good times and bad, though he never imagined the bad would ever get as bad as Jack Morrow, radiologist with the perpetual tan, the athletic grace, the condo in Cabo. And although Dr. Hunt had written an entire dissertation on humanity's essential mutability, it was his marriage with Gloria that proved to him he had been funda-

mentally wrong: no, we don't change; we are always our-
selves—adulteress, sucker, magician, stooge.

"You've always tried to reduce me to nothing," he had
told her near the end, when their home was nothing but separate beds and clanking dishes, and then he added, "but I
know you're not that good a magician."

His sheer meanness initially struck her dumb, though then
she sputtered, "You don't know that," and he, ignorant fool,
had merely shaken his head and laughed, feeling that finally
she was the one flailing and grasping for dignity. For dignity
was that essential quality she'd robbed him of, bit by bit, over
many years—she'd stolen his dignity the way you would rob a
bank or an art museum: with patience and planning and pre-
cision. And now she was gone—like his briefcase, like his
shoe—leaving him the Toyota Camry, their too-large bed (no,
not too large: just right!), his reappraisal of Bakhtin, and
where the hell was his sock?

He often misplaced them at home, yanking them from his
sweaty feet, but to have removed a sock at work, in his departmental office, without knowing it...he breathed in, counted to five, and slowly exhaled. But when he reached up to run
a hand through his hair, which, for a man of his age, was especially thick—his finest attribute—he gasped, because he felt
no hair at all. Lowering his arm, he saw the trouble wasn't in
fact his hair, but that the arm—inside his shirt, inside his blazer—ended at the wrist, and gone were the fingers and palm.

There was a little blood at the wrist, which easily could be
blotted, as if the surgery had gone well but required a bit of
post-op attention, and Dr. Hunt cried out. That is, he tried to,
only there was no sound at all, and with horror he knew the
reason had to be one or the other: no ears, or no mouth.

Or both, he realized as he shot up from his chair and bolted out his office door, one shoe on, one shoe off, shouting in
utter silence: *help me, please!*

Friday afternoons were always quiet on campus (even the

copy machine was now abandoned), and no one saw him drop to the carpet, his other shoe gone, sock, foot. He sat and stared at his ankle as the pants faded away and the sock turned to dust and the ankle dissolved, leaving a calf with flapping skin. Then the other ankle, then wrists to the elbows, then knees, thighs, and if Dr. Hunt had lips and a tongue and a throat, he would've screamed. And lungs: he needed lungs for screaming, and for breathing—and oh, God, he couldn't draw a breath, and then his vision vanished with his eyes.

His heart, though: it beat and beat and beat while his shoulders and pelvis and eyebrows and spleen and intestines all dissolved away to nothing. His nose and his liver, his ribs, his kidney, his bladder, his teeth, his veins and arteries, the muscles in his torso, his stomach. There was no pain, not a twinge, and his heart beat on, and understanding narrative, he knew he was nearing his own denouement.

He lay on the carpet by the hallway, just a heart and a brain and the rapidly diminishing viscera connecting the two. His remaining muscles caused him to turn slightly, and then those final muscles gave out and he was almost perfectly still. Electrical impulses lingered, as with a lobster sliced in half, and he barely twitched, his heart still beating, but fainter. His brain, though: it screamed on, aware of the crime against him, aware of its perpetrator, aware, aware, aware.

I am sorry I am sorry I am sorry I am sorry I am sorry I am sorry.

Any thought or feeling or reaction after that could no longer be attributed to Dr. Allan Hunt. His heart reduced to one chamber, his brain to ten million neurons, then five, then two. Then came the final reduction: shrinking, fading, desiccating, everything opaque becoming translucent and then transparent. And that was how he ended, as ever-diminishing ectoplasm, no mind, no body even. A million remaining cells now one hundred thousand, now eight hundred, now fifty.

His blazer and shirt and pants, shoes and socks, skin, all

gone. Organs and blood, reduced beyond the cell, to molecules, atoms, quarks. Then particles yet to be discovered, and then smaller still. Everything he'd ever been, everything he would ever be. All of it, gone—except for his briefcase.

The Starbucks employees are keeping it safe. They figure he'll be back soon. It's awful, losing something important. He'll be so relieved.

He'll say thanks.

You're welcome.

Bye.

BARRIO MATH
Josh Stallings

Summer 1984.
Sunset Boulevard.
Club Bra, Panties & Boots.

Music hit Cisco's chest like a sledgehammer. Lights strobed a Technicolor assault. The pit smelled of sweat, spilled beer, dope, testosterone, and unrestrained, exuberant rage. Cisco pogoed like a mad pinball, banking off bodies, going for the high score in a game that kept no score. When all one hundred and twenty pounds of Cisco slammed into Choncho Sanchez, the result was pure physics. Cisco soared backwards, knocking dancers out of the way. His brief flight ended against a wall. Sliding down to the floor he started to laugh. This was ten times better than he imagined it, hell twenty times. Minutes into his first show he'd been knocked down by the legendary big man. The bloody scrapes on his palms and knees were bonus souvenirs.

Cisco was thirteen, five-foot-five in combat boots, and skinny. His slashed CIRCLE JERKS T-shirt hung loose. Sweat beading his scalp showed through his freshly buzzed hair. FUCK THIS WORLD was inked across the thigh of his frayed jeans. His Doc cherry reds were scabbed and torn, the rusted steel toe caps exposed for the weapons they were. Standing, he caught himself in a mirrored pillar, his face was slack, cool. His heart raced. *That is one bad ass, don't fuck with him, motherfucker.*

Cisco spent the previous year as a poser. At school he wore punk band shirts but kept his curly hair reasonably below his collar. He had a FEAR sticker on his locker, not Circle Jerks or Suicidal Tendencies. People who didn't know FEAR was a band might think it was a statement or a clothing line. He lied to his friends about punk shows he'd been to, mosh pit fights he'd been in. At home he wore headphones when he listened to Bad Brains, The Germs, and king of all, Black Flag. No need to take the shit his mother's Ritchie Valens, bubblegum-loving, Stacy-Adams-wearing boyfriend would smear him with if he heard this angry, energizing music.

Cisco was a child of Boyle Heights. He learned young—to survive he had to hide his true self and be a chameleon. In his world, a person's set, their clique, were familia beyond genealogy. Vattos, Bangers, MaraVilla Rifa, Crips, Bloods, Avenues, Frogtown, Dogtown, White Fence. The city was carved up with boundary lines that could only be moved with loss of life. The color of a bandana, choice of shoe brand, or haircut style, everything carried coded meaning to let combatants know, throw down or let pass. Punk rockers had no turf, no history or power base. Disaffected youth brought together by four chords and a hard-driving rhythm, they made up for their disorganization and small numbers with a pure crazy love of violence. Caring nothing for the code of the streets, their complete unpredictability made them dangerous.

Cisco's cousin Eddy V was a hardcore punk. He ran with a band of merry dirtbags who called themselves Los Psicópata. For cash they sold dope, ran the gay Murphy, creeped houses. For fun they went to punk shows, got fucked up, and if need be, fucked people up. They carried homemade brass knuckles, knives, and bicycle chains. They stuck deep sea fishhooks through the lapels of their leather jackets as a surprise to anyone who tried to jack them.

"I do this, no turning back," Eddy said, holding the electric clippers in his hand. "This ain't Halloweenie. It's represent or go home. Puss out on the street and I'll beat your ass down."

"Never, dude. I'm a midnight killer, a lady thriller, a blood spiller." Cisco's eyes were cold, or as cold as he could make them. Eddy struggled to keep the laugh from breaking free. He loved this kid's bravado. Long black locks fell as the clippers turned sweet faced Cisco into an outcast. In eighties' East Los Angeles, a shaved head made you a target for attacks from gangsters, hippies, rockers, cops, and dads.

Fuck them.

This was Cisco's night. The night it all got real. He was in Hollywood, town built by tuxedoed film makers, now ruled by gutter rats with Mohawks and spike-studded leather jackets.

On stage Henry Rollins sang about seeing a burning world through a dirty rat's eyes.

Kira Roessler whipped her bass strings like a nun taking on a gang of bad school boys. A very sexy nun. Her tomboy short black hair, boots, and white prairie dress didn't confuse Cisco. She looked straight at him. They had an actual moment. His heart broke from walk to gallop in an instant. But Cisco knew his barrio math, there could be no good without equal parts bad.

From across the writhing sea, a giant white dude locked in on Cisco. He was a Nazi Lurch-looking motherfucker. A large, blue, amateur swastika tattoo filled the left side of his shaved head. Whatever intelligence he held didn't show in his dead eyes. Curling back his lips in an approximation of a smile, he showed a mouth full of dull gray steel teeth. Moving into the pit, the school split for the shark. Every one of them implored the old gods to keep them safe from his maw.

Kira snapped her head from Nazi Lurch to Cisco. With a nod and a wink, she ignited his racing adrenaline. He had been an all-city track star last year. It was pure instinct and muscle memory. Bam went the drums. He exploded from the blocks. He was running full out when he hit the giant. His left foot landed on a huge bent knee. Pistoning his thigh, Cisco climbed high enough to strike down. His right fist made a wet crunch when it collided with the swastika. He howled as bones in his fist broke. Swinging his left, Cisco grazed the giant's chin as gravity reclaimed him. Slam dancers opened a hole in the crowded pit, allowing Cisco to hit the floor unhindered. Skull hit hardwood. Sparks danced. Boots stomped on all sides. Two overlapping versions of the crowd blurred over one another. Some asshole kicked his ribs. This new pain took a distant second to his throbbing hand and terminal headache.

Flicking his eyes revealed he was alone in enemy territory, surrounded by white punks. Last he'd seen his cousin and his crew, they were heading out the back door, before Black Flag stormed the stage. *Stay down and these boots will stomp you deader than dead.* Somewhere in the upper stratosphere a giant stalked him. Rolling onto his belly, he pushed up, staggering to almost vertical. Fifty miles of Nazi ugly towered above him. Closing one eye to stop the double vision, he charged. Fists flying. A high yelp expelled every time his right hand connected.

Something like a frying pan struck the side of his head.

Cisco's legs buckled. Falling, he waited for the floor to smack him and bring on whatever new pain it held. *How fucking high did I fall from?*

Instead of an impact, Cisco felt his descent slow, and then he started to ascend.

He was floating through the crowd. His eyes swollen, vision blurred. Black Flag ripped into "Louie Louie." A mob exploded into cheers and jeers. A beer bottle sailed past, spewing suds like a comet tail. Cisco was aware of all this in only the softest of ways.

Possible realities were: A) He was dead and waiting to see the light. But if his *abuela* was correct, as she often was, he should be sinking not rising.

B) The fall severed his spine, and this was phantom movement or pain-induced psychosis.

C) His guardian angel was a seven-foot-tall skinhead.

Cisco forced his eyelids to open a crack. Squinting, he gained focus. The giant Nazi smiled down on him, "Dude, you are one craziod motherfucker." He was carrying Cisco like a princess bride. The whole scene lacked dignity, had he the strength, Cisco might have leapt up and slapped this monster freak. Then the giant would open him up like a gut-filled piñata. Kira would witness his noble death and think: *damn, I could have balled him.* Instead his head lolled feebly.

Black Flag ended the set. Punks stomped, clapped, and spit out their elation.

As Cisco was carried from the pit he was flooded with unexpected gratitude. Lurch hadn't killed him. He had one hell of a real story to tell, and lots of red and purple proof that he wasn't lying.

Cisco tried to speak to the giant, but could only achieve a froggy rasp. He settled on a smile he hoped spelled thank you. Reaching up he touched the swastika tattoo.

"Yeah, I know, fucked up, right?" Close up, Lurch's eyes were uncomplicated, not vacant. "Worst part, my last name is Hertzog. Let that be a lesson: never pass out on reds and wine when your asshole buddy has a cassette deck tattoo gun he's dying to try."

"Your...name's...not...Lurch?" Cisco fought for every word.

"Lurch, funny, no. Bob."

"Down...Walk..."

"You wanna walk, sure." Bob gently set Cisco on his feet, catching him as he started to fold. Reaching around Cisco's back, he held him upright.

"Thanks."

"No biggy. You hungry? I could eat a fucking cow."

Cisco mulled this, running a diagnosis of his vital organs. "Carnitas...no...bullshit...white boy...burgers."

"Cool. Taco shack on Vine suit your racist palate?"

"*Sí.*" Cisco gave his best Speedy Gonzales accent.

A thin L.A. fog haloed traffic lights and swirled around the two young men as they walked down Sunset Boulevard. The deep rumble of glasspack mufflers approached from behind. Cisco looked over his shoulder, his gut clenching. Barrio math again. A shiny black, big-finned Cadillac slipped past them. Smoked glass hid the occupants. It slowed and the rear window slid silently down. Cisco held his breath until he saw Kira peering out. Recognizing Cisco, she smiled, shot him a wink, then the Cadillac was gone.

"Dude, Kira fucking Roessler just winked at your scrawny ass."

"Yes...she...did." Cisco's future held bloody riots and porn parties in the Hollywood Hills. True love gone bad, a suitcase of cash that cost him his best friend, an LAPD beating, narrow escapes, and sun-soaked days in Baja. But this was Cisco's first night as a punk and nothing would ever top it.

WHEN AT LAST SHE SPOKE
John Rector

He knocked, and she let him in.

As she watched him close the door, she felt a sweet tension begin to glow right above her stomach and just below her heart. She told herself it was nothing, but then he looked at her in that way he had of looking at her, and she knew better.

"You shouldn't be here," she said.

"Too late," he said.

"If anyone finds out," she said.

"No one will find out," he said.

"But if they do," she said.

"They won't," he said.

She stared into his eyes, deep and dark and blue, like the sea at dusk, singing to her, begging her to drown.

"You should leave," she said.

"You should kiss me," he said.

"I can't," she said.

"Then I'll kiss you," he said.

"No, it's too—"

He kissed her, taking her words.

She hesitated then kissed him back, long and slow. When they broke she saw they were now in her bedroom, and she realized all was lost.

"You shouldn't have come," she said.

"You wanted me here," he said.

"I can't do this," she said.

"Of course you can," he said.

"If we get caught—"

He kissed her again, and this time the sweet tension glowing right above her stomach and just below her heart turned white and slid down, moving lower and lower until she had to push him away, fighting for breath.

"Stop," she said.

"I don't want to," he said.

"You have to," she said.

He kissed her again.

"Please," she said.

He stopped.

She turned away, folding her arms over her chest, the taste of him heavy on her lips.

"I'm scared," she said.

"I'm here," he said.

"That's why I'm scared," she said.

Outside, a car pulled into the driveway.

"That's him," she said.

"Right on time," he said.

She pushed past him and stood in front of the full-length mirror beside the dresser. She ran her fingertips under her eyes and her hands down the front of her shirt, wiping away tears and wrinkles. Then she glanced at his reflection in the glass and watched as he took a pair of black leather gloves and a long silver piano wire from his pocket.

"I don't think I can do this," she said.

"*You* don't have to do anything," he said.

She heard footsteps outside on the porch, the delicate chime of keys in the lock.

"Better say hello," he said.

"Wait," she said.

"We've waited long enough," he said.

"But I'm not ready," she said.

"Then warn him," he said.

She stared at him, trying to imagine a world where she would do such a thing, but she couldn't.

The front door opened, and a voice called her name.

"We can't do this," she said.

"It's too late," he said.

"It's not," she said.

But it was, and when she heard her name again, she knew it with her entire soul.

"Kiss me," he said.

She did, letting herself sink into him.

There were footsteps in the hallway, moving slowly from room to room. She tried to speak, tried to think of something else to say, but there were no more words. He smiled, touched a gloved finger to her lips, and stepped back, slipping gently into the shadows beside the door, the piano wire wrapped between his hands.

She turned her back on all of it and let her gaze come to rest on the framed photograph sitting on the nightstand, the long white dress, the summer rose garden in full bloom. She studied the image, and for the last time, she allowed the memory to return, the one that had kept her going for so long, the one that had lied to her, told her that things would be different, that he would change.

She closed her eyes, letting the memory fade like a dream in sunlight.

Then she heard her name again, the heavy footsteps in the hallway, coming closer. She took a deep breath, held it, and stood up straight. And when at last she spoke, her voice was her own.

"I'm here," she said. "I'm here."

MAIDEN S LIGHT
Lili Wright

Annie paced the town dock, studying the lighthouse that stood sentinel in the middle of Fisherman's Bay, keeping watch over the islands, like a promise or a warning.

She was still angry with Royce, and even more so with Dorothy, her future mother-in-law, the preppy toad whose irregular heartbeat had forced her good son to bow out of their lighthouse adventure and leave Annie alone for the night. Always lucky, Royce had won the island raffle—lobster dinner for two on Maiden's Light!—but their plans collapsed when Dorothy's heart conveniently went schizo and her blue eyes bulged. Arrhythmia, my ass. Dorothy wanted her son to herself. Dorothy wanted to exile Annie to Alcatraz.

"It would be uncharitable not to collect the prize," Dorothy murmured, clutching her sweaty gimlet. "You go, dear. Represent."

Royce shrugged, apologetic. He'd tried to cancel, but cell service was sketchy on the island, impossible on a lighthouse. He drew a smile on Annie's face with his finger. His optimism exhausted her.

"Maybe you'll make a new friend," he said.

Annie was tired of new friends. Everything about Maine was new—sailing, deer ticks, the mystery of knots. It wasn't easy marrying into an island, keeping track of second cousins and picnic spots, the feuds and real estate.

The harbor was quiet now, the boats pointing their noses in

the same direction like a cult. The island *was* a cult, resistant to intruders, managed by a log of intractable rules. *Not that tea tray. Not that knot.* Yesterday, Annie had gotten stuck in the bathroom, the wood door swollen with fresh paint. She pounded. When no one rescued her, she slumped on the toilet until she heard footsteps. She knocked politely. Dorothy opened the door, saying, "I wondered what the ruckus was." Later Royce explained the technique to exiting that particular bathroom. There was a technique for everything.

At six sharp, a woman buzzed up in a whaler. She looked like an Indian princess, strong arms, high forehead, rawhide necklace dangling a key. A thick, horsy braid of chestnut hair hung over one shoulder. She hopped off the boat with an easy smile, introduced herself as Mia.

"Where's Royce Sullivan?" she asked, lifting her shades. "Isn't he the winner?"

"He's my fiancé. He couldn't come. His mother's heart arrhythmia acts up every time he walks out the door."

"You want to invite a friend?"

"I don't have any. Here, I mean. On the island."

Mia tilted her head, deciding. "I usually serve dinner and disappear, but we could have a girls' night. I've got wine."

Annie gazed at the lighthouse. An island off an island. Remote. Untouchable. "I'd like that. No. I *need* that."

Mia wrinkled her tan nose. "Me, too."

It turned out Mia *owned* the lighthouse.

"The Coast Guard unloaded a slew of them at auction," Mia said. "To overpaid romantics."

Mia and her ex-husband had painstakingly renovated the landmark, clearing scat, laying wood floors, hauling furniture up with pulleys. In real life, Mia was an anesthesiologist.

"I'm paid a lot of money to put people to sleep."

"And wake them up," Annie added, giving her more credit.

They'd reached the whaler. Mia motioned Annie in. Mia started the engine with a shake of her head.

"No. You have to wake up on your own."

Tall and white in the distance, the lighthouse loomed like a sign of hope, an anchor for dreams and wishes. Its rusty base nestled in low-tide rocks. Two decks circled the exterior like rings round a finger. The lighthouse grew bigger as they motored up until they were right underneath and it stood five stories tall. Annie was sorry Royce was missing this, though it pleased her to see a part of Maine he hadn't.

Mia secured the whaler with a knot, maybe a bowline, the one where the rabbit falls back down a hole. She asked Annie to tie two other ropes together, which she did as best she could. The only way to board the lighthouse was by climbing not one but two ladders that ran straight up its side. Fifteen feet up, you had to maneuver to a second, bridging a yard of open air.

"Don't overthink it," Mia said. "Just go."

Oh the view from the deck—a three-hundred-sixty-degree panorama of the islands fuzzy with spruce trees, a smattering of summer houses with docks and swanlike daysailers, and to the north, barely visible, the harbor. The smell of salt water filled her nostrils, her imagination. Envy nipped her heart.

"It's so beautiful," she said, as Mia joined her.

"I like it." Mia looked pleased, proud. "Let's find a drink."

Wine in hand, Annie explored. All the rooms were round. The living room had a crescent-shaped couch and Oriental rug. In the upstairs bedroom, a credenza, a Tiffany lamp, etchings of knock-kneed birds. She fell back on the sleigh bed. How fun! No one could reach them. No cell service. No power.

The next flight led to bunk beds, domed by the red warning

light. From the upper deck, Annie watched the ocean wrinkle its way to shore. Breathing in the vast blueness of water and sky, she forgave Royce...Dorothy...herself.

Back on the lower deck, Mia was boiling water on a gas grill.

"I feel so good," Annie said. "Like I want to throw everything away and live in the same T-shirt all year."

"The best part? No mirrors."

Annie laughed, held out her empty glass, pushing aside the worry of how to navigate the ladders in the dark. Maybe the tide would swallow a few rungs.

The table was set with real linens.

"Entertain me," said Mia, dropping corn into boiling water. "Tell me about your life."

"It's not much of a story...I teach art history at a community college. Expressionism. *The Scream.*" She used this shorthand in non-art circles. "We live in Philadelphia—"

"I met my ex-husband there."

"Does he still come up?"

"Oh, no." Mia wagged her finger with a wry smile. "We had a terrible marriage, a call-in-the-paramedics divorce. I'll tell you the long version at dinner, if you really want to know."

She pulled a lobster from a plastic crate. Its rusty tail snapped. Lobsters didn't look like food. They looked like shrimp dressed for the Trojan War.

Mia grinned. "Some people don't like to watch."

"Like me. I'm a lobster-eating vegetarian. A total hypocrite." Annie covered her eyes, then peeked.

Mia stroked the crustacean until it hung limp, drugged. "If you scratch their backs, they conk out," she said. "It's more humane. Death is only scary if you know it's coming."

She submerged the lobster headfirst, clamped the lid. Annie walked away, ignoring the thuds. The poor creature had woken up, and in a final anguished panic, hurled itself against the pot.

* * *

They feasted, threw the shells overboard. Miraculously, Mia had all the accouterments—crackers, picks, bibs, candles protected by glass. When they couldn't eat any more, Annie said, "The story. You were going to tell me about your marriage."

Mia made a rueful face. "It's not pretty."

Annie curled her legs under her hips. She was ready. She wanted to hear how bad it got, a vaccination that fends off disease. Being engaged was torture. The wait. The worry. On sleepless nights, Annie fretted that Royce would get cold feet, realize he was marrying into a cauldron of depressive lunatics. For most of her twenties, Annie had drifted, knocking about art circles—knocked up, once—before settling into teaching. Adjunct teaching. The kind of gig where no one commits. But Royce was a rock. Grounded as granite. Five billion years old and still beautiful. Together, they could build something real and lasting.

"I met Cole at an anesthesiology conference," Mia began. "I know. How romantic. He's a nurse. I'm a doctor. The attraction was immediate. He loved old houses like I do. Hopeless causes."

Annie focused on a lobster buoy, white with a yellow stripe. Deep on the ocean floor lay a trap.

"Cole had this defiance, a desire to make something of himself. I loved that. And he worshipped me. After work, he'd fix me a Mojito, rub my arches. I made more money, but we didn't care. He was so handsome and the sex—I felt sorry for my friends. Everyone else was compromising."

The sunset stabbed orange machetes of light.

Annie sighed. "Maybe you should stop here—with a happy ending."

"We were happy, but that definitely wasn't the ending." Mia circled her shoulder, like it hurt. "Cole quits the hospital, takes a job at a clinic, *for no good reason*. Major pay cut. We see less of each other. He's always apologetic. 'I miss you, babe. Next weekend, we'll have some you-and-me time.' The sex dries up. All night, he's painting deck furniture. Still, I don't catch on."

Neither did Annie.

"One day, I check our bank statements. We're fifteen thousand dollars short." Mia raised her eyebrows, waiting for Annie to guess.

"Gambling?"

"Opiates. He's been pinching from the hospital, the clinic, buying what he can't steal." Mia stared at the falling sun. "*My husband was an opiate addict.* He couldn't have sex if you force fed him Viagra. He's on the couch weeping, 'Oh, babe. I love you so much. I didn't know how to tell you. Can you forgive me?'"

Annie flinched, conflicted. Addiction is an illness—

"I take him to the fanciest rehab in Philly. Earl Gates. People call it Pearly Gates." Mia laughed a hard laugh, joyless. "Therapy and yoga and quinoa for lunch. He's eating better than I am. He gets out. Everything seems good. Then he starts calling me his angel and I know he's back on the horse."

Annie refilled their glasses.

"There's more," Mia said. She looked more beautiful the darker it got, her eyes the color of the afternoon sea.

"I find videos on his cell phone. He's sleeping with an intern. 'Oh, babe. You must hate me. I'm a sex addict. Don't leave me. I'll kill myself.'" Mia spins her hands, speeding things up. "More rehab. Therapy. Hypnotism. One night, he slaps me. Next morning, I file for divorce."

"What a relief."

"It *was.*" Mia's eyes were wet, but she didn't cry. "Finally, I could start to rebuild."

Annie nibbled chocolate, let it melt on her tongue. This is why she was marrying Royce. He'd stir the risotto. Their children would play under the sprinkler.

"The crazy part is I miss him," Mia said, quieter now, the voice you use in church. "Not him at the end—he was a mess—but the guy who saved this lighthouse, *that* person, I miss every day."

Her fork pulsed like she had something else to say. "A woman died out here."

"What woman?"

"A school teacher from Bath. Sidney Jameson. That's why it's called Maiden's Light."

"What happened?"

"No one knows. They never found her body. She was visiting the keeper and drowned. People make up stories—"

"Wait, when was this?"

"Turn of the century. I think she rowed out in a storm to save a shipwreck."

"Maybe she died of a heart arrhythmia." Annie was feeling giddy.

Mia snorted. "Or the keeper dumped her for the slutty ice girl from Camden—"

"She was a drunk, poaching peach brandy. She slipped on the ice and fell into the brink."

"She was pregnant," Mia chimed.

"Carrying his love child—"

"He slits her throat, bleeds her out like a deer. Rolls her overboard."

"He didn't want to share the light!"

The joke died there. They recovered. Night had fallen and the windows from distant houses gleamed, flecks of gold in a miner's pan. The ocean pushed up and back, and the breeze whispered past their ears, and above them, a gull's wings flapped, and beneath them, fish swam in schools, and on the scraggly ocean floor, a lobster crawled into its trap.

Finally, Mia said, "You know the big take away from my marriage?" She resembled a Modigliani, oblong and sober.

"You never know what someone else is thinking." Mia let this idea float for a minute, then grinned darkly, shaking off the gloom.

Annie didn't see Mia for two years. The next summer, Mia came in August and they'd already left the island. They exchanged an email or two, peppered with Xs and Os. Once Mia signed off as "The Ghost of Sidney Jameson." The story of the doomed school teacher stuck with Annie. She crafted her own version, a love story, dreamy as a Whistler painting. She didn't invite Mia to her wedding—they weren't that close—but she was glad to run into her at the island grocery one sunny day in July. Her braid was longer and she looked tired around the eyes.

"Good news!" Mia said, lighting up. "Crazy story. We need a girls' night. Sleep over this time."

On the whaler ride, Annie sat up front, mist spritzing her cheeks as they thunked into the bay. So much had changed in two years. As Dorothy's health declined, she'd softened, leaning on Annie for help. She now viewed her mother-in-law with greater sympathy: it would be hard to let a stranger join your family, touch your things, botch simple tasks. The women had formed a gracious truce.

Mia pulled up. Annie eyed the dreaded ladders.

"The tide's coming in," Mia said. "Not *too* many rungs." Annie grabbed hold, more confident. At the gap, she thought of Mia, her bravery in all things, and imagined Sidney Jameson, dressed in a cotton frock and bonnet and black-tie shoes.

At the lip of the balcony, a man's face appeared.

"Oh," Annie said, startled. "You scared me."

"Mia didn't tell you? I'm Cole."

Cole looked like an actor, not a nurse. A soap opera actor

or the dad who needs extra-strength detergent. He wore jeans, a green shirt dotted with palms. His shoulders were square, his legs bowed, and he moved with the hangdog athleticism of jocks who understand everything their bodies can do. Annie had dated a guy like him in college. Several, actually.

"You need help, babe?" He peered over the edge.

"Fix drinks."

Hand on Annie's back, he guided her to the bar. Had Mia mentioned a reconciliation? Had Annie missed an email? A friend once advised her never to trash anyone's ex because if they got back together, your friend would never forgive your criticism. Any ex could be de-exed. A negative current flipped positive, like an electrician holding a bunch of live wires.

Two years later and the same dinner. Corn. Lobster. Salad. Cole and Annie faced the water. Mia sat opposite, selflessly giving them the view. She had changed into a white, haltered sundress, bohemian and sultry. Annie wasn't sure what to talk about. Work seemed off limits. Their relationship, too. At no point did Mia acknowledge her startling one-eighty.

They settled on island gossip. How a Boston lawyer had sued his neighbor over a tree house. How long it took to sort garbage at the dump. How one lobsterman had murdered another over a woman.

"That's the only reason to kill someone," Cole said, his lips wet with butter. "For love."

Mia pinched his cheek. "So cute."

The exchange bothered Annie. She didn't know where to put it. How long had they been back together? Months? A year? It didn't matter. They'd worked things out. Rehab. Therapy. Forgiveness.

"It's good to be back on the lighthouse," Cole said, summing up the dinner, the moment. Mia reached for his hand.

"So where are *you* from?" Cole asked, as if seeing Annie

for the first time.

"Philadelphia."

"That's where Mia and I met."

"Yes, she told me."

"Did she tell you it was love at first sight? Mia was strong and sexy, a combination you don't always see."

"I know." Annie smiled at her friend. "And Mia knows all the knots."

Cole looked confused.

"She always has the right knot for the job," Annie clarified. "Mine fall apart."

He nodded. "In her last life, Mia was a pirate."

"Who were you?" Annie didn't trust him. He was a slippery fish, a mackerel. Yet Annie could see the attraction, feel it. Roguish men were so convinced of their magnificence. It was hard not to crave that glow.

"I was a pirate, too," Cole said. "Bluebeard."

Mia snickered. "You mean Blackbeard?"

"Bluebeard? Blackbeard? They're all the same."

Mia shook her head, smiling. "No, honey. They're not."

Cole looked annoyed.

Annie jumped in, calming the waters. "What is it about lighthouses? People go nuts over them. I met a guy who travels around collecting lighthouse figurines. His wife was so patient. She told me, 'People don't understand real passion.'"

Cole poured the last of the wine, their second bottle. "I'll tell you what's great about lighthouses. People leave you the fuck alone."

Mia straightened, mouth pursed. "What's amazing are the brave people who worked on them. Like Sidney Jameson."

"She was a school teacher," Cole said dismissively. "She slipped and fell."

"She was saving a shipwreck."

They'd had this argument before.

"I don't know what killed her," Annie cut in, "but she

came out here for love."

She could see it so clearly. The shy keeper offering his ruddy hand to Sidney as she climbed aboard his skiff. As they rowed across bay, she dreamed of a new life, washing his shirts, warming his supper, the rhythm of their days marked by the light, the sun, the tides, the weather over which they had no control. There was grace in simplicity—seldom grace without it.

Annie said, "What's cool about lighthouses is how the building and people work together. On land, no one warns you. You crash ahead and hope for the best."

Mia set down her glass. "Lighthouses are churches of danger."

This took Annie a minute.

Mia waved at the lobster detritus. "All this is blasphemy. Lighthouses weren't built for pleasure. You're supposed to steer clear of the light. People on lighthouses were cold and alone and scared. They did what they had to. The ocean has no compassion for man."

Annie shivered. She wanted to offer something heartfelt and hopeful, something Royce might say. "Lighthouses are benevolent, like God," she spoke slowly, like a teacher. "Only without the religion. Just a light. A good light that brings everyone safely home."

"I'll toast to that," said Cole, his tongue bending in his mouth. "To getting home safe."

Mia smiled, back to her old self.

Their three glasses kissed.

The sunset was plain, an orange eye descending, clinical in its detachment. Mia excused herself to do dishes, insisting they stay put. Warm and tipsy, Annie no longer worried about saying the wrong thing.

"It's so nice you two are happy together again."

Cole doodled slipknots on the tablecloth with his knife.

"We are happy again. Together."

Annie missed Royce, her sunny sea captain from the fish-stick box. Royce thought life was sweet. Who was she to disabuse him? He should be here. He would have balanced everything out. Why had Mia called this a girls' night?

Cole looked sheepish. "Mia probably told you terrible stories about me." She started to deny this, but he cut her off. "I was a bit wrecked, it's true. But rehab can work miracles. You can get your life back. I'm living proof. Now I just want to give Mia everything she deserves."

His language sounded canned. "You women want a lot." His head tilted coyly.

Was he flirting? *Yes, he was.* Cole popped a beer with his left hand. Why was he drinking if he was in recovery? Mia was singing The Beatles. "Blackbird." They couldn't see her, but her voice carried round the bend.

"That's great you two are trying again," Annie said, repeating herself.

Without warning, Cole gripped her chin. She didn't pull away. She was too surprised, curious, flattered.

"Here's what she didn't tell you," he said softly. "She wrote those prescriptions. I slipped a disc lifting a couch. When the scripts ran out, Mia said—" his voice rose to a cheesy falsetto. "'Oh, sweetheart, I'll write you another—*and another and another.*' She didn't want to lose me. She *needed* me. She kept me as happy and sedated as a houseplant. Doctors *always* want control."

His eyes willed her to take his side. She held his gaze until it was too much to bear.

Cole discarded her. "You don't believe me. You two are friends. I get it. What matters is, I've forgiven her. I wanted the drugs, so that's on me. I'm just saying it took two. Addiction *always* takes two. One person takes the drugs. One person provides them."

He checked over his shoulder. "I could have her license

revoked. I have a case. She'd never practice medicine again."

Annie's chest hurt. Something was seriously wrong with her heart.

"You'd never do that. You love her."

"Do I?" He slapped his hand against his head, gleeful. "I do!" Tipping back in his chair, he looked unhinged, his face a woodcut of angular shadows. "I'd never hurt anyone. I'm a nurse."

He lowered his chair, nudged close. His eyebrows creased, threatening.

"Now you know all our secrets," he said with a fake German accent. His right hand formed a pistol. He pressed the muzzle against her temple. "I will have to kill you."

He fired.

Annie swatted his hand, grabbed her water. It was all she could do not to throw it.

Mia appeared, wiping her palms on her apron. She slid behind Cole, her arms ringing his neck. She kissed his part.

"Take a picture of us, would you?" Mia asked.

"Now?" Annie said stupidly, fumbling for her phone. She stood to get a good angle. "Say lobster."

They vamped various poses. Smooch. Fireman's carry. The camera flashed like heat lightning. Annie felt like a pimp. Nothing lies like a photograph.

"There're some good ones," Annie said. "I'll send them to you."

They untangled. Mia cleared dessert to the kitchen. Annie emptied the lobster chuck bucket over the rail. The shells floated away—tiny, empty lifeboats. Another log drifted past. Cole did nothing to help. He was stargazing through binoculars. She wanted to tell him that never works.

"I see right through you," he teased, swiveling her way. "I know what you want."

"You have no idea what I want." Annie grabbed the wine empties like barbells. She said this as a reflex, a defense against attack, though she sensed he'd glimpsed the cruddiest corners of her being, the tawdry places she'd worked so hard to hide. She sensed that he liked those parts best.

Cole lowered his binoculars. "You don't have to be so pretty."

He shook his head with triumphant sympathy. Men like Cole could drag you under. She'd forgotten. She walked away, scoring a point.

At the sink, she stammered, "Uh, Mia. I don't feel so well. I should go home tonight."

"Oh, no," Mia's face clouded. "Was it the food?"

"No, no. The food was delicious. It's my stomach."

"Did Cole talk your ear off? He gets riled up. Just ignore him." Her expression revealed nothing. "The truth is I've had too much to drink. If the Coast Guard pulls you over, they'll fine—"

"Maybe Cole could—"

"He's worse. I've got Dramamine that should help. I'll take you back first thing in the morning."

"If we went slowly..."

Mia lay a hand on her shoulder. "Let me take care of you."

She led Annie to the third-floor bunkroom, fished up a pill and a glass of water, kissed her cheek. "Thank you for coming—and staying."

Annie didn't ask about Cole. It was too late now. Let it be. Let them be. Her version. His version. There was no truth to be had.

"Please don't say anything about Cole being here," Mia added before leaving. "People love to gossip."

Annie didn't promise, but Mia smiled as if she had. Like a ghost, she floated down the staircase holding a kerosene lantern. It seemed possible Annie would never see her again. She stared at the pill, debating, but as she wanted nothing more than for morning to come quickly, to leave the lighthouse, to return to Royce, her unmistakably decent man, she swallowed it.

The warning light bathed her arms in a bloody glow. Folding the pillow around her ears, she blocked out whatever sound might reach her: dishes, conversation, sex. Stretching her legs, she swam in the sheets, unable to sleep, overcome by a prickly uneasiness. *Love is the only decent reason to kill someone.* There was no reason to panic. She was not Sidney, lost on the bay. Her new friends wished her no harm. All she had done was listen. How would the mystery pill react with the wine? Too late. The chemicals were circulating her veins, making her head feel heavy and thick. *Now I will have to kill you.* The glass-brick window shimmered in the faint light from the deck below. How far away the moon. What distant comfort. *Death is only scary if you know it's coming.*

She watched the keeper row the Jameson woman to the lighthouse in a wooden boat made for two. The school teacher wore a wool coat buttoned high at the neck and her white stockings were speckled with seawater. The keeper lifted his oars with a nervous smile, leaned into his lover, and whispered a secret she couldn't quite hear.

Annie awoke at seven. The fog had rolled in thick. No view. No islands. The foghorn tolled. Grabbing a sweater, Annie circled the staircase. The bay, flat as a mirror, vanished in the mist fifteen yards out. Mia sat slouched on the deck, legs hanging over the side, arms resting on the dewy rails. The hood of her sweatshirt covered her head like a shroud.

"Morning," Annie said cautiously. "Sleep okay?"

Mia turned. Her face was white and taut, delicate as the skin of a mushroom. "Cole left. He's gone."

"What happened?"

"I don't know. I woke up and he was gone."

"He took the boat?"

"The boat's here."

"He went swimming."

"I looked but I don't see him."

Shielding her forehead, Annie stared hard into the ashy sea. It was too early for emergencies. She circled the deck, hoping to see a man's arms breaking the water's surface. To hear splashing or laughter.

"Is Cole a strong swimmer?"

"Average."

"What happened last night?"

"We went to bed right after you."

Annie ran to the ladders, glared at the rungs. No hat or coat or shoe. She called Cole's name. Her voice cracked because some part of her knew this was futile and it was Mia's job to shout, to run and search, and head out in the whaler, but she was just sitting there, slumped, like she knew how the story ended and was waiting for Annie to catch up.

"I don't see him," Annie reported, breathing hard.

"You have the pictures," Mia said. "You saw how happy we were."

"Yes, I saw that."

"I'm going to radio the Coast Guard now," Mia said, "because I don't know where he is and I'm worried."

Her tone was flat.

They fought and he ODed. They fought and she pushed him over. He passed out on the deck and rolled off. He was eating scrambled eggs and salsa at Carlo's Diner, feeling macho after his long swim to shore. He died of a heart arrhythmia. She injected him with poison. She slit his throat, bled him out like a deer. He lay at the bottom of Davy Jones's locker with the remains of Sidney Jameson.

Mia dropped her head, as if whatever occurred last night had sapped the strength of a lifetime. She tore the elastic from her hair. Her braid unfurled in tangled strands. A cormorant swooped past with a minnow clamped in its beak. The fog swallowed it whole.

Annie crouched beside Mia, interlacing their fingers like rope. They had been through something. They were in it now. They would emerge together, boats pointed in the same direction. *Lighthouses are churches of danger.* Annie would pray. She would learn to pray.

Mia rubbed her forehead. "He was going to report me."

"I'm sure Cole's fine," Annie said, with new, affirming calm. She was practicing the story, the first of many versions. "A friend picked him up."

"What friend?"

"A friend from the island."

Mia's upper lip quivered, a tiny wave. Amusement. Relief. "He doesn't have any friends."

AMANDA: A CONFESSION
Nick Kolakowski

I.

Amanda was a painter, with the strong wrists and supple fingers that come from holding a brush all day. On weekend mornings she would pluck a tomato or a handful of herbs from the small garden growing on her fire escape, crack a few eggs into a heavy steel pan, and make an omelet that rivaled anything produced by our neighborhood's overpriced brunch places. *It's all about when you flip it*, she always said, miming the action. *You need good timing.*

I learned a lot from her before she died, but not how to cook a good omelet. Sometimes I flip it too soon, before the eggs cook through, and splatter my stove yellow. More than once, I've launched it onto the counter or the floor. At those moments, I can almost hear her laughing. *Just try not to set your place on fire, okay?*

I have one painting she did for me, an abstract canvas of swirling oranges and reds, shot through with specks of brilliant blue. The inspiration for it came on a bicycle ride we took through Prospect Park one autumn, which ended with us lying beside our bikes in a meadow, meditating on a sky glimpsed through dying foliage. A week ago, with my new mission underway, I took it off the living-room wall and buried it in a closet, beneath a sheet, because all that fiery crimson began to remind me a little too much of Hell.

II.

The café near my house recently purchased a La Marzocco Strada espresso machine, a twenty-thousand-dollar beast with a sleek steel body and a formidable silicon brain that controls the brewing temperature with the fastidiousness of a veteran Italian barista. Every afternoon I settle into one of the café's deep leather chairs beside the front window, where I have an excellent view of the traffic rumbling toward the Brooklyn bridge, and sip at least two of the machine's three-dollar espressos while I peck away at my laptop.

Does the Strada produce a finer caffeine shot than your typical restaurant coffee-spitter? A hard question to answer, even for an experienced palate like mine. The first sip bites your tongue and leaves a tangy aftertaste. There is an oily note beneath, not unpleasant.

"I don't know," Jen says, setting her cup onto the small table between our chairs. "Tastes like regular espresso to me."

"There's a nuance to it," I say. "I'm a little obsessed. Thinking of doing a piece, in fact. Maybe with a historical hook."

"You're so weird." Closing her eyes, she sighs. "Sorry you missed the funeral."

"So am I."

"Why didn't you come?"

Because I'm not good with emotion, I want to say. Because I can't trust myself to stay calm around the dead body of someone who used to finger paint me with chocolate and lick it off. Who wants to see that sort of meltdown? I ransack my brain for a suitable lie. "I thought it was only family."

"Oh, hon." Her eyes open again, soft and melting at the edges. "Everybody came. High school people, college people, studio people. Monica made it, and you know their relationship was shit for years."

"What about her boyfriend?"

Jen pauses. "What about him?"

"Did he show his face?"

"Does it matter?" Jen's lips tighten into a bloodless line. "That thing on Facebook was a lie. Her mom didn't know what she was talking about…"

"What's his name?" The Facebook post had lacked that detail.

"I won't tell you."

I pause to sip espresso, willing my thundering heart to slow. "Why?"

"Because it doesn't matter."

It matters to me, I want to say. I almost reach over, take her small hand in my big one, and squeeze until the bones snap or she gives me a name, whichever comes first. "Forget I asked," I say. "I'm just a little messed up about all this."

"It's okay, we all are," she says. "I was over at her place yesterday, to help pack boxes. Amanda didn't…prepare. She was good at denial."

"We shouldn't speak ill of the dead."

"You want to lecture me, you should have come to the funeral," Jen says, pulling her phone from her jacket and checking the time on the screen. "Look, I have to leave, okay? Thanks for the coffee." She stands, all jangling bracelets and pendants and earrings, her forearms dark with fading henna, and rushes out the door before I can say another word.

III.

Amanda never maintained much of a Facebook presence. It was one of the many things I liked about her. She only posted images of her art, her mother, and her cats. No mentions of friends, lovers, or her oddball opinions on crystal energy and the spirit world. Although we were together for two years, two months, and a week, I only managed to make a cameo appearance as a hand and sleeve in the background of her old profile photo.

A few days after Amanda died, a message from her mother appeared on her Facebook page: *My poor girl didn't believe in western medicine and her boyfriend reaffirmed that fear.* It received ten likes and no comments. When I read it, I cried for hours. I debated whether to comment, to set up a meeting and ask for more detail, but the resulting conversation would have been too much for me to bear.

Besides, even in those first moments, a part of me knew what I wanted to do about it—and the fewer folks in the loop, the better.

After my coffee with Jen, I wait until dark and walk over to Amanda's building, a former factory converted into lofts for trust-fund babies. I try the exterior door—locked, as expected—before heading to the back, where I find a row of dumpsters pushed against the wall. It takes me three tries to successfully balance on the edge of one; from there, I can grip the bottom rung of the fire escape.

In the summer, Amanda would open the skylight in the ceiling of her bedroom so we could crawl onto the roof and let the breeze off the East River cool our sweating skin. Her magnificent cats inevitably joined us, curling in our laps as we drank artisanal beers and talked nonsense about karma and fate. I wonder sometimes if the beast had already started growing in her, cell by traitorous cell.

The skylight still has no lock. I pry it open and stick my head into the darkness, listening for anything that would indicate a person below. Silent as a tomb. I dangle a foot into the opening, sweeping for the top shelf of the bookcase we once used as a ladder. I find it and spend the next few minutes descending as quietly as I can. Her roommates are heavy sleepers, but I prefer to leave nothing to chance.

I stand in the middle of the room while my eyes adjust.

Deeper blacks coalesce into dim stacks of cardboard boxes, a bare desk, and a stripped-down bed in the corner. I know she died in the hospital, but looking at the bare mattress makes me shudder nonetheless. Using my phone as a flashlight, I open boxes until I find a diary with a homemade felt cover, and flip through it for the details I need. I take photos of the appropriate pages, wincing every time the phone makes that artificial shutter-click, but no sounds come from the far side of the closed door.

Now I have the bastard's name and where he works. Good enough.

I return the diary to the box. Before I close the lid, I spy the edge of a ticket stub poking from a book on meditation and pull it out. *Eurydice* on Broadway: a production in which the title character descended into Hades in an elevator, to bathe herself in the river of forgetting and nothingness. We had gone as Amanda's six-month anniversary gift to me. I would like to remember where we went to dinner after the theater, and what we talked about, but the memory refuses to surface.

I slip the ticket into my pocket before I head to the roof. It takes a lot of effort to scale the bookcase with my shaking hands.

IV.

The next morning I call my editor.

In lieu of hello, he asks, "Where's the piece?"

Editors everywhere, they're all the same.

"Working on it," I tell him, smacking a few keys on my open laptop for the sound effect. "Draft's nearly there, I'm polishing. I'll send it over tonight." The draft is nowhere near done, of course, and I plan on turning in something very different from my typical restaurant review. If our past history is any indication, he will love it enough to forgive all my blown deadlines.

"How was it?" he asks, referring to Gai Tod, a new hole-in-the-wall that opened in the West Village last week.

"Four stars," I reply. "Thai fried chicken, it's wonderful. The beer selection left a little to be desired, but hey, they just opened. I think they'll do well."

"Sounds great," he says, his attention beginning to fade. "You looking for another gig? I got a new Polish place over in Greenpoint, and a Mexican meatball place opening in Bush-wick."

"What the hell is a Mexican meatball?"

"That's for you to research and report, man." He sighs. "You want to take it? Usual fee."

"Sure."

"You got it. Anything else before I hang up on you?"

I ask him for a big favor. He grumbles and snorts, but after I feed him a convincing lie, he relents. I disconnect the call and glance at the wall clock. If I stick to my schedule, I have enough time to make it to Prospect Park and back, even if the G train is running slow.

V.

When I see him for the first time, the adrenaline makes my body crackle electric. He leans into the restaurant's front window, one hand shading his eyes against the morning sun, the other rising in a little wave when he spies me on the far side of the bar.

I place the knife down on the counter, wipe my hands on my apron, and walk to the door. My throat is dry, and I worry for a moment that I won't be able to talk. As I flip the dead-bolt, I study him up close, noting the rangy beard shot through with gray, the serene eyes. You might have taken him for a monk, except for the designer jeans and hundred-dollar T-shirt. Hanging off his shoulder is an expensive leather bag, fashionably distressed and bulging with something heavy.

"I'm Raphael," he says, sticking out a hand.

"Glad you could make it," I say, and wave him into the restaurant. "This way, please."

On our way to the bar, we maneuver around stacks of lumber, unopened tubs of cement mix, and kitchen equipment in boxes. At this early hour, the place is empty except for us.

"Thanks for the email. It's great that more restaurants are hearing about what we're doing," Raphael says. "When do you open?"

"A couple weeks," I say, taking my place on the far side of the bar, which doubles as the kitchen. When the place finally opens, the small griddle will serve up artisanal grilled cheese sandwiches, eggs, and other comfort food—and because this is New York, everything will come at a premium price. The Hipster Tax, I like to call it in my articles.

"Looks like you're pretty far along." Raphael plops onto a stool and leans over the bar, so he can watch me pour oil on the griddle. "What are we having?"

"Eggs," I say. "You okay with that?"

"They free range, organic?"

I grin. "We'll serve nothing but."

He returns the grin. "Then it'll do."

I crack seven eggs into a steel bowl and begin to whisk. "You bring any of your famous kombucha?"

From his bag, he removes a large glass bottle of fermented tea and places it on the bar between us. On the label is a fine ink drawing of a plant; above it, in equally delicate type: *Brooklyn Buch*. "This one is mint flavored," he says. "But we're doing it with horseradish, different spices, flavors. We're doing it out of a small space off Metropolitan Avenue, so it's strictly small batch for now, but we have big plans."

"How much you charge for something like that?" The eggs properly whisked, I sprinkle in some chopped onions, garlic, and sautéed mushrooms. The ambient heat from the griddle bakes through my shirt and makes me sweat. My editor, whose wife bought a minority share in this restaurant over his strident protests, had given me the keys but no instructions about where to find various switches, and it took me quite some time to figure out how to turn on the gas.

"On our website, twenty-five bucks a bottle. Wholesale, for your place, more like ten a bottle. You could make quite a killing out of that." He leans forward, grinning as he faux whispers: "If you mention our name on your menu, we can work a bit of a discount."

"I'm sure we can work something out," I say, and pour the egg mixture onto the griddle. When I look up, I see Raphael nearly face down on the bar, palms pressed hard against his forehead. For the first time I note the pale cheeks, the dark circles beneath his eyes, and my heart speeds. Here we go, I think.

"What's wrong?" I ask.

"Long month," he says.

"Oh yeah? Want to talk about it?"

"Not really," he says.

"It's okay," I offer. "I've been going through a hard time lately. Lost someone close to me. Every life has its roughness, you know?"

He stays silent for so long I begin to think I might have pushed him too hard, too fast. Then he rubs his eyes, clears his throat, and says, in a quieter voice: "Sorry, this isn't a very professional thing to bring up, but my girlfriend died a couple weeks ago."

"I'm sorry to hear that," I say. "My condolences." My pulse thudding loud in my ears, I pluck a turner from the bin of clean utensils and shape the edges of the omelet. Its steel tip rattles lightly against the metal because my fingers are trembling. I wait for him to speak again.

"It's hard." He sighs and tilts his head toward the ceiling. "I lose time. Show up for events on the wrong day. Or this week, my partner comes to me and asks what happened to an invoice? And I could have sworn I'd given it to him, but it was in my desk."

I shrug. "Grief is a weird thing. Hits everyone in different ways."

He holds out a hand to stop me. "Intellectually, I get what you're saying. But on an emotional level, people saying things like that makes me angry. This wasn't my grandma or something. It was unexpected. I'm going to need a lot of time."

Good thing I don't really own a part of this restaurant; with a jab like that, he would have lost the sale right there. "What happened, if you don't mind me asking?"

"Breast cancer."

I slide the turner beneath the omelet, praying to Amanda that my timing is right, and flip it, making sure to power through my wrist. It turns cleanly, with only a little fold trapped beneath. "How long did she know?"

Raphael squints at me. "Excuse me?"

"This person I lost, it was cancer, too," I say. "Pretty recently. It's a question that comes up."

"Amanda knew for about a year."

My hand aches as I white-knuckle the turner. "They treat her?"

"They did the doctor thing. Shot her with radiation, pumped her full of poison. If you can call that 'treatment.'" He snorts. "But that was only at the very end. Probably sped things up."

I flip the omelet onto a plate and pass it to him, along with silverware bundled in a napkin. "Those things cure people."

He nods his thanks. "There are better ways, if you don't mind me saying so. I don't know what your beliefs are, and I know this is supposed to be a business—"

I cut him off. "Like what ways?"

Taking two glasses from a stack of empties on the bar, he pours us some kombucha. "Like other approaches. Things that tap into the body's natural energy, try to remove what's causing the cancer."

"Like what things?" I fight to keep my voice level.

"We did healing herbs, some acupuncture. Gallons of kombucha, which boosts the immune system, not that any doctor would tell you that." He takes four quick bites of egg and mushrooms. "Doctors, they're all bought off, you know. Big Pharma."

While he speaks, I pour more egg on the griddle. After sprinkling on some mushrooms, I slide the turner underneath and flip, trying for a little air this time, and the omelet lands in a messy pile. Damn. Sorry, dear.

"Amanda's mother was pissed," I say, looking into the distance beyond his left shoulder. My heart has slowed again to a comfortable rhythm. My hands no longer shake.

His forkful of omelet pauses midway to his mouth. "Excuse me?"

"You must have seen on Facebook. Amanda, she always hated doctors, and you played into that. You keep her from seeing her mother, too?"

He places the loaded fork on his plate. "Who are you?"

"Not who you thought," I chuckle in his face, but my insides feel stuffed with ice. "It's funny, but after I sent that email inviting you to come by, show off your stuff? I worried you might Google this restaurant, figure out the real owners. But you just walked right on in." I scoop my omelet onto a plate and, putting the turner aside, pick a long blade off the counter. I hold it against my hip, pointed at the floor.

Raphael shoves his plate aside and stands, shaking his head. "You're crazy. I didn't kill her. She died of a disease."

"She died because you filled her head with bullshit," I say. "If I'd been with her, she'd still be alive."

His eyes widen as he finally puts the pieces together. He takes a step backward, reaching out to grab his bag. "She told me she ghosted on you," he says. "That you went on a trip or something, and when you came back, she wasn't taking your calls. Is that right?"

I stand there, unmoving.

"She never loved you, man," he said. "If that's what all this is about. Believe me or not, but that's what she said. She dumped your ass a long time ago."

I feel wetness on my cheeks. "You're wrong."

Turning on his heel, Raphael sprints across the restaurant. I stay behind the bar as he fumbles with the front lock and throws the door open. Before disappearing into the street, he turns and yells, *"She said you were fucking scary, and she was right."*

Once he's gone, I wipe my eyes and turn off the griddle. I stand at the bar and eat my eggs, marveling at the tanginess of the mushrooms. Let me assure you that poisoned fungi, sourced locally, are quite delicious. You experience no symptoms for the first six hours or so, after which the toxin's work has progressed past the point of no return. Then you die screaming, as perhaps you deserve.

My dear editor: I'm sorry that I lied to you about why I needed to use your wife's restaurant for an hour or two. Hopefully the fact that you will never have to pay me for this blockbuster story will make up for my deception. I want to give you another gift: please take the painting and the ticket stub, which the cops will find in my apartment. I want someone to remember what I had.

MAGIC 8 BALL
Scott Loring Sanders

I'd only slept with three men before I met Jack. And then one other after we were married, which happened two nights ago. My sister Dani, who was three years younger but always acted like the older one, the one in charge, the one who protected me, she'd always said, "Michelle, deny everything. Admit nothing." I'd thought that a pretty shallow motto to live by, not to mention problematic, considering I was a cop. But I was starting to see its merits.

A few days earlier, before my indiscretion, I'd been out on a call around Great Meadows, a protected wildlife refuge near the Concord River. An older couple from the city had spent the afternoon in the woods cross-country skiing, said they'd seen something suspicious near the pond.

"What do you mean, suspicious?" I asked.

The woman did most of the talking, late sixties, her husband a few years older. She had a not-quite-hidden Mainer accent. Came from money, you could always tell. The way she wore her makeup (who put on makeup to cross-country ski, for one thing?), her Patagonia jacket, *MIT Alum* sticker displayed across the rear windshield of their BMW. "It was a big man," she said, "dragging something heavy toward the edge of the pond."

"Or maybe away from it," said her husband.

The pond was expansive, ten football fields easy, currently frozen and covered with snow. The trees encompassing it were bare, sad looking, except for the few birches intermingled between the bleak brown and gray of everything else.

"Did you talk to him? Say anything?" I asked. I'd flipped open my pad, was scratching notes.

"Gosh, no," she said. "We saw him from across the way, beelined back to the car. Surprised we even got a signal to call you."

I radioed dispatch, popped the cruiser's trunk, pulled out my snowshoes. "Don't suppose you'd like to ski across with me?" I said. "Show me exactly where you saw him?"

"Gosh, no," she said again. "I remember what happened at Walden. No thank you. See that tallest evergreen?" She pointed across the pond with her mitten. "He was just to the right of that. Soon as he spotted us, he vanished like a skittish Big Foot."

"Okay, well I'll go take a look."

"You be careful out there, sweetheart," the husband said to me as he dipped into his car. I wanted to punch him.

I loved the outdoors, so this was a perk of being police in a rural area. I missed bow hunting and cross-country skiing, things I'd grown up doing with Daddy. I'd always been a tomboy, Daddy's little girl. But after having children, and a marriage that was, well, ugh, and Daddy passing a few years ago, I didn't get in the woods much anymore. So taking a nice walk sounded perfect. Go investigate exactly what Big Foot had been up to.

I'd been on scene at that Walden Pond incident she mentioned. Made the national news a few years back. A couple of kids fishing in a cove, one of them hooks something big, starts reeling in. Turns out, it was a human skull attached to the treble hook of the kid's Rooster Tail.

The boys freaked, tossed it into the woods, ran home. At first, they didn't say anything, scared they'd get in trouble. But a day later, they told their parents who laughed it off. Another day went by, one of the moms started wondering, decided to call. We basically laughed it off, too, but my partner, Mike McGill, and I went ahead and checked it out. The boys walked us off the trail, peeled away some leaves, and bam, there you go. A skull, no skin or eyeballs, but relatively recent because some soft tissue still lingered inside, rattling around like pennies in a piggybank. The lower jaw removed, the upper teeth missing. Somebody really hadn't wanted that victim IDed. We brought in frogs to dive for the remains, which they found, but clear across the other side of the pond. Meaning, the head had been severed and dropped in a different location. They also found a second skull, in similar shape, the remains equally separated. It was determined both had been male. The case is still unsolved. Two John Does in red marker on Homicide's board, a blemish Chief shakes his head at every morning.

Though I was pretty sure my Boston couple hadn't witnessed anything of value, it was worth investigating. I tromped across, straight for that tall pine, and quickly determined I'd been wrong. They *had* seen something. A circle of ice was broken at the pond's edge. Someone had created an opening the size of a manhole cover, the shattered pieces already trying to regroup and refreeze. Reminded me of my son Max's preschool artwork—triangular shards stacked atop one another in a haphazard mosaic.

Boot prints had tamped down the snow, and a few blood splatters were evident. Not much, but just enough to raise my hackles. I squatted, scanned through the tree columns as if scouting for game. But the woods were silent and still, the way they always get before a storm. And it was eerie. Just because I'm a cop doesn't mean I don't get freaked out sometimes. Has nothing to do with being a woman, either, despite what that elderly *sweetheart* of a man back in the parking lot probably presumed. You're alone in the woods with visions of decapitated skulls dancing in your head. It's only natural to feel a little jittery.

I found a dead branch, maybe eight feet long, and busted

the skim of ice. Started probing and prodding the depths, churning up decayed leaves and twigs. Then my heart jumped into my throat when something grabbed the end of that stick. Scared me so bad I almost dropped it, but I pulled upward, hand over fist as if gathering an anchor, the end noticeably heavier. My heart rate shot to overdrive. When the branch broke the surface, I finally exhaled, chuckled nervously. A Conibear trap was clamped to the end, having nearly snapped the wood in two, which was illegal within the refuge. So no wonder that poacher had slipped off when my skiing couple spotted him. He probably had a bunch of muskrat pelts in his possession, maybe some beaver, which must've been what they'd seen him lugging. Figured I'd find drag marks in the snow if I took a walk.

I had a pocket calendar in my jacket, one of those stupid things Chief handed out at year's end. A little *Thanks For Your Service* token. I tore out the page with today's date, with Concord Police Department stamped across the top, and wedged it between the clamps of the Conibear. I'd always had sympathy for the old timers who were just trying to make a buck off the land. Same as my daddy used to do. This guy needed to take his business elsewhere, out of my jurisdiction, but I didn't want to throw him in jail over it. Figured my little warning would provide the necessary hint: we're on to you, pull your traps, relocate. Or else.

And I'll be honest, I was relieved. I'd take a poacher over unexplained body parts every single time.

Some people, no matter what, will never forgive me for cheating. That's fine. I'm not looking for forgiveness. But I am going to explain my side.

Jack and I had been fighting, as usual, mostly about money. I had the steady job, he the steady gambling habit. And to a lesser degree, steady drinking habit. He was doing some Uber stuff, but other than that, unemployed. Lost his job at the Raytheon factory in Andover a year ago, got caught up in some scam, skimming hours he never worked.

I'll state up front that Jack had never gotten violent. But he'd done a few messed up things when it came to our children: Max, four years old, Eliza, eighteen months.

"You'll come home one night," he'd once said, "and me and the kids'll be gone. Poof, never see us again." That was a year ago, after I confronted him about parking receipts I'd stumbled upon in his car. Dozens of them, all from the Plainridge casino. While he'd supposedly been out Ubering, he'd been at a blackjack table, losing our grocery money.

His words hurt me, scared me, but I'd always considered his threats idle, mainly because he didn't have any money to run off with, whether he took the children or not. But two nights ago, everything changed.

I'd stopped by the market after my shift. I had the next few days off, so I thought I'd make a pot of stew. Maybe rent a few DVDs from Redbox for me and Max. But when I went to pay for the groceries, my credit card was denied. Which was weird because I had a four-thousand-dollar limit. Figured it was a glitch, how the magnetic strip gets scratched sometimes. I offered the cashier my debit card instead, which I knew would work because I'd just gotten paid. Denied.

Embarrassed, I bought a frozen pizza with a ten I had in my purse and hustled to my car. My chest had gone tight. I struggled for breath. I grabbed my phone, checked our bank account. My entire paycheck was gone. I called MasterCard— multiple cash advances made yesterday morning from an ATM at Plainridge. Which did and didn't make sense. It obviously made sense because of Jack's gambling problem, but he assured me he'd quit for good. Eight months ago. Okay, so maybe he'd lied. But at the same time it *didn't* make sense because if he'd been at the casino, then where had my children been? Because Jack was watching them. So there must've been a mistake. A logical explanation.

When I slammed the frozen pizza on the kitchen table, Jack was in the living room, watching SportsCenter, drinking a beer and smoking. The kids were upstairs in bed, tucked in for the night.

"You wanna explain this?" I said, presenting the screen-shot of our account balance.

"I don't know," he said, "maybe you didn't get paid yet."

"I got paid two days ago. Direct deposit. What the hell, Jack? How're we supposed to pay our bills? Feed our kids for Christ's sake?"

Jack stared at SportsCenter, refused to catch my eye. "Listen, babe, I got in a little over my head."

"A little over your head? We've got nothing in checking, you maxed our credit card. You need to go find a few fares right now, just so we have some cash."

"Can't," he said, holding up his Bud can and wiggling it as if I were a waitress and he needed a refill. "But I'll go first thing in the morning. Maybe you could pick up a little over-time or something."

I walked over and slapped that beer right out of his hand, sent it screaming across the room, a foam trail spewing be-hind. "Overtime? Have you lost your fucking mind? I should catch a few extra shifts to cover your nonworking, blackjack addicted ass? I want you out of my house right now. Get out, get a job, get your shit together. I can't do this anymore."

"But, Shell, you—"

"Where were the children, Jack? What did you do with my babies while you were in that casino? Did you leave them in the car? Is that what you did? Were they strapped in their car seats, stuck in that freezing parking garage while you pissed away the little money we had left?"

"Hell, no, Shell."

"Then where were they? Because I know they weren't sitting in your lap as you doubled down on a pair of goddamn eights."

"You don't double on—"

"Shut up, Jack. Jesus Christ, where were my children?"

He looked at the television, stared at an Axe commercial. "They were here," he said. Quietly, almost inaudible. "At the house."

"With who? The sitter? My mom? Who was watching them?"

"Max," he said, so low it was essentially a whisper.

"Max? What do you mean, Max?"

"I left them here. Told Max to take care of Eliza."

I felt sure I'd misunderstood. I had to have misunderstood. Because no one would leave a four-year-old to take care of a toddler. I mean, that wasn't possible.

"I'm sorry. I've got a problem. I'll—"

"Get out. Don't say another word. Get. The fuck. Out."

"Shell, you—"

"Jesus Christ, I deal with scumbags all day long. That's my job. And I've never, not once, heard of anything like this. The casino's an hour from here. An hour each way, plus the time you gam...Good God, get out."

I opened the front door, so furious I thought I might punch him in the throat. He stayed hangdog as he moped behind me. But right as he approached the doorway, he grabbed my wrist, twisted, and slung me into a chicken wing. He pushed me straight out the door before I could react or use my escape training. I shot across the porch, had to hurdle the three brick stairs to avoid wrenching an ankle, then dipped a shoulder into the snow-covered yard.

"Call your cop buddies and see what happens," he yelled, his face wedged between the door and jamb, eerily reminiscent of *The Shining*. "Don't try me, Michelle. Don't fucking try me." He slammed the door, followed by the metallic slide of the bolt.

I still had on my jacket, keys in pocket. But they'd be useless against the bolt lock. I also had my phone, and I sure as hell *was* going to call my cop buddies. It would be embarrassing, but I'd have to suck it up. They'd be at the house in minutes, have him cuffed and stuffed for assault at the very least.

I brushed away the snow, located my phone. But then something curious happened. All the house lights went out. We lived in the country, our nearest neighbor a quarter mile down the road, and when Jack shut off the lights, everything went black. No stars or moon to speak of, so other than the snow, I was shrouded in complete darkness, the house's outline nearly indiscernible. But then a faint orange light flashed from an upstairs window, from the room the kids shared. As my eyes focused, Jack's silhouette appeared between the parted curtains, holding a Zippo, the flame flickering. In his left arm was my sweet little Eliza, her head tucked under Jack's chin, still sleeping.

Jack's face was only partially distinguishable, but I could tell, even from the front yard, that he smiled as he waved that lighter in a sweeping motion. He held it inches from the curtain's edge, as if readying to light a fuse, then brought it across his chest, holding it impossibly close to the hem of Eliza's hanging nightgown, the one with the little circus elephants on it, the one Mama had bought her. Taunting me. Daring me to call.

I immediately lifted my phone up high so he could see it, then slowly, exaggeratedly, stuffed it into my jacket. I raised my hands as if under arrest, a "you win" posture. Then I tromped through the crusted snow to my car, my throat so constricted I thought I'd suffocate. I had to be careful, had to make sure I posed no threat. As I turned the ignition, Jack remained in the window, the lighter held to his chest now, creating an orange radiance that lit up his face in partial shadow. Like the way Dani and I, as little girls, held flashlights under our chins during backyard campouts, attempting to look like the devil.

But Jack *was* the devil, a horrific and frightening thing to

discover about the father of your children. About your husband. I knew right then, without question, he'd ignite those
curtains at the first sign of a cruiser rolling down our road. I
backed out, watching that bedroom window shimmer and
twinkle as if already engulfed in flames, feeling like a dog
trapped deep in a well, barely treading water, barely holding
on.

"He's a piece of shit," said Dani as we split a bottle of wine,
sitting at her kitchen table. "I've always hated that bastard.
To hell with men. The day my divorce went final was the best
day of my life. Swear to God."

"But you don't have kids," I said, the wine's warmth ap-
peasing my fears. I wasn't much of a drinker, but this was
needed, felt like an elixir.

On the drive to Boston I'd called Jack repeatedly, but he
refused to answer. With every ring, my heart sank deeper, my
despair unbearable. My mind explored places I'd never
known existed, envisioning my children mangled or charred
or tortured. But then finally, he picked up. We talked, we
fought, we screamed as I drove. When I heard Eliza crying in
the background, relief poured so strongly I couldn't hold back
tears. "I have to deal with her," he said. "We'll talk in the
morning." He hung up on me, but my children were alive. Yet
I was sick, beyond frightened. A stinging pain ran through the
soles of my feet. I couldn't get comfortable.

"I need to go back, Dan. What if he—"

"You need to stay right the hell here. You go back, you
might set him off. And then what?"

The wine was confusing me, impairing my judgement. "I
don't know."

"Actually, you do know. So not tonight. The kids are safe
and that's what's important. He's cooled down, so keep it
that way. Start fresh tomorrow. In the meantime, let's get

loose," she said, and refilled my glass.

Dani dragged me to her local bar after the wine, a rundown place with dartboards and a jukebox. I drank more, we met a couple of guys, one who Dani apparently had a casual thing with. He and his friend came back to the apartment. I vaguely recall kissing the friend, then lying on my stomach, my face squashed into a pillow as he took me from behind. When I awoke in the morning, Dani was already at work. No sign of either man. A note sat on the table.

Get your kids. Stay here if you want. Or at Mama's. But deny everything. Admit nothing. Love you, D.

I'd never understood true self-loathing until right then. The guilt, the shame, the disgust. I hated my life. But as I pulled into my driveway, I was struck by a tinge of relief. My house still stood. Between the hangover and the anxiety, as I'd driven back to Concord, my mind had journeyed to other dark places. Visions of driving up only to see a skeleton of my home, the framework smoldering. Then a firefighter emerging from the rubble, carrying the tiny, blackened remains of my children.

So my plan was simple. I hoped it would be as easy as gathering the kids and leaving. Once they were sheltered in place at Mama's house, a phone call would have Jack in handcuffs within minutes for child endangerment. I was done swallowing my pride. I was done worrying what the guys at the station might say. I'd endure all the humiliation in the world to ensure my kids stayed safe.

Max and Eliza sat in the living room, watching television, eating Cap'n Crunch out of the box. Eliza was naked, no diaper, no nothing. Max had apparently poured Pepsi into a pair of sippy cups from a two liter which lay on its side, the carpet soaked and stained.

"Mama!" said Max, running to me. "You're home." He squeezed my leg, and I bent to his level, licked my finger, and wiped away what appeared to be ketchup from his cheeks. I kissed his head.

"Where's your daddy?"

"Sleeping," said Max, already returning to the television, SpongeBob luring him back.

It was nine o'clock. My head pounded like senior prom. In the kitchen, I drank a glass of water, nearly stepped on the uncooked pizza sitting on the floor, a butcher knife lying next to it, apparently the tool used to tear open the packaging. Tiny fingerprints dimpled the lukewarm cheese, little bite marks pocked the edges. Between last night's alcohol, the flashbacks of that dirty stranger fucking me from behind, and the sickening vision of my Max holding that giant knife in his tiny hands as he'd worked to feed his baby sister, I almost puked in the sink. But besides being sick, I was also furious. Why should I be the one to leave? It was my house, I paid the mortgage.

I picked up the knife, the flaccid pizza, the plastic wrapping and box. Thought about storming upstairs, hurling the whole mess at his face. How had my life been reduced to this? I'd been popular in high school, had friends, boyfriends. I enjoyed attending football games, going to the movies. Now here I was, mid-thirties, a failed marriage, near bankrupt, living with some psychopath who'd threatened to burn my children alive.

I went upstairs quietly, methodically. I walked down the hall. Our bedroom door was open. Jack lay on his side, one arm jackknifed and tucked beneath his ear, the other lolled over the bed's edge. Two beer cans were on the night table, an ashtray mounded with butts. And sitting innocently atop his pack of smokes was that goddamn Zippo.

The hilt of the knife felt natural in my hand, the same as a bat handle when I'd been on a sixteen-game hitting streak in softball. I aimed for the indentation just below the Adam's apple, where I'd once observed an EMT perform an emergency tracheotomy on a choke victim. I nailed it and plunged deep, leaning over him, putting my weight into it. Reverberations traveled through that steel blade and straight into my hands as the knife scraped through neck vertebrae. Jack made a strange exhale like a hissing bike tire, but his eyes never opened, his arms never flailed. To my surprise, there wasn't much blood.

As I tried to remove the knife, the blade got stuck, pinched like the bar of a chainsaw. I twisted and turned that handle, heard the grinding and scraping as I cranked it around until it wiggled free. Then I waited two minutes, grabbed his wrist, checked for a pulse. Nothing. It had been that simple, that easy, that quick.

"Mama, is Daddy still sleeping?"

I spun around, knife in hand, to see Max standing in the doorway. He hugged his blankie to his chest and trampled the corner with fidgeting feet.

An onslaught of hyperventilation was fast approaching. "Yes, sweetie, he's still sleeping," I said in my best mommy voice. "Do you need to go potty?"

He nodded.

I set the knife on the bed and ushered him to the bathroom, careful not to touch the shoulders of his little pajama top. As he peed, I turned on the faucet, scrubbed furiously. Miniscule traces of my husband disappeared down the drain.

Back downstairs, I made a phone call. "Mama," I said, "I need to bring the kids by. For an overnight."

I undressed Jack, bathed him using a sponge and bucket, the early stages of rigor already setting in. From the garage, I gathered the blue tarp covering his riding mower, spread it on the floor, then rolled him off the bed and swaddled him like baby Jesus. The rest of the day was spent cleaning the house, the bedroom mostly, then taking that knife to Jack's workshop, grinding down the blade, then clamping it in the vice and snapping it into pieces. I'd drop them into various trash barrels around town sometime in the future.

"If you don't want to help," I said to Dani when she arrived after work, "you don't have to. I mean it, Dan. If you have any—"

"Stop it," she said. "We'll take my Forerunner. More room, four-wheel drive, nobody'll recognize it around here."

We arrived at the Great Meadows parking area close to midnight. "We'll carry him first," I said, "then come back for the other stuff."

We strapped on snowshoes, Dani wearing the slightly larger set I'd bought for Jack last Christmas. We then lugged the tarp across the pond to that trapping hole. The Conibear was no longer on the bank, meaning that poacher had taken heed, pulled his traps, moved elsewhere.

I've never done anything more exhausting in my life, including an eighteen-hour labor with Max. I was still painfully hungover, though probably in far better shape than Dani, who was bent over, her clothes soaked, gasping for air. Jack wasn't a big guy, maybe one-sixty, skin and bones mostly, but slogging a dead body through snowy woods while wearing snowshoes is no easy task. Every muscle in my legs and lower back screamed for relief, my biceps so taut I thought they might explode. One thing's for certain though: the idea of life in prison, of never seeing my children again, well, that's a pretty strong motivator to help push through the pain.

On our second trip, we carried two cinderblocks apiece, along with a thick coil of rope from the workshop. I used one of the cinderblocks to break through the thinned ice of the trapping hole. When I unrolled the tarp, Dani gasped. "Jesus, Shell. You didn't...you didn't tell me that."

"I got my reasons," I said, following her gaze to Jack's head, separated from the rest of his body. I hadn't removed his jaw or teeth though, a definite risk.

"Christ, what kind of reasons?"

"Just trust me. I know the guys in Homicide. Know the connections they'll have to pursue if his body is found. But if we do our job right," I said, snapping the rope between my hands as if testing its strength, "it never will be."

We tied a block to each naked ankle and each naked wrist, then stuffed him into the tight hole, wrestling and wrangling with his torso until he disappeared. Just before I dropped his head in, Dani said, "Hold up a sec." She leaned in toward Jack and spit in his face. "For good measure," she said. "The sick bastard."

A part of me wanted to say, "That's the father of my children," but I didn't. Seemed a tad ridiculous considering I had my husband's severed head in my hands, a head I'd personally separated from his body with a hacksaw. Instead, I exhaled deeply, thankful for my little sister and her toughness. Thankful I had a strong mother who'd raised two strong girls, a mother who would help me raise my kids to be the exact same way, a mother who would never ask questions about why Jack left, where he went, or if he was ever coming back.

I set Jack's head on the water's surface and released my grip, shoving it off like a toy boat. It dipped for a second before popping back up, but beneath the ice, as if his face were smooshed against a glass floor. It reminded me of one of those Magic 8 Balls Dani and I played with as little girls, where the cube pops up against the plastic window, revealing its answer.

Silently, without even thinking, I asked Jack's head, *Will I get caught?*

I almost saw his lips moving in the partial moonlight as he responded. *Without a doubt.* I shook the 8 Ball in my head, repeated the question. *Will I get caught?* He answered, *Yes, definitely.*

I panicked, worrying his cheek and lips might get permanently stuck to that ice, leaving one hell of a surprise for that beaver poacher if he decided to return. But as the skull took on water, it lolled to the side, then *baloop*, disappeared.

When we got to Route 2 and were moving at a good clip, I pushed that tarp out the passenger window and let it fly off into the night. A road crew would eventually gather it and take it to the dump. Jack's vehicle would be driven to Mama's garage, where it would stay hidden behind closed doors. His parents were dead. He had an estranged sister he hadn't seen in over twenty years, a woman I'd never once met. He had no job, so no employer would be calling. He had a couple of friends, but not good ones, all of them even more screwed up than him. They sure as hell wouldn't come creeping around my house, especially knowing I was police.

Spring would be stressful and worrisome, once things thawed, wondering if his body might pop to the surface. But I figured that thick rope would hold for several years, maybe a decade. Keep him down there deep where his flesh would rot away. And his skull wouldn't float, that I knew for sure.

I stuck my hand out the window and glided it on the frigid air, letting it dip and soar like I'd done as a little girl in Daddy's truck.

"Roll that damn thing up, will ya?" said Dani. "It's freezing."

I smiled and clicked the button, immediately feeling the heat through the vents. I smiled because everything was fine. Everything was going to be okay. I'd simply asked Jack's head the wrong question back there. I now said, *Will I get away with it?* Jack's same answers came up. *Without a doubt. Yes, definitely.*

I must've uttered the question aloud, because Dani, staring straight down the highway, said, "Deny everything, Shell. Admit nothing."

And that's precisely what I planned on doing. If I ever started feeling guilty, I only had to think of Jack in that bedroom window, squeezing my little girl tight to his chest, the two of them shrouded in that eerie orange glow.

Deny everything, admit nothing. That would be no problem. No problem at all.

THE UNFORESEEN HAZARDS OF HITCHHIKING

David James Keaton

A white man is chained to a black man, on their way to prison. They're both in their fifties, and look it. The white man turns to the window beside him, blinking as a sign catches his eye. It reads: PRISON AREA: DO NOT PICK UP HITCHHIKERS.

He smiles, allows himself a small laugh. The black man looks over as if to say, "What's so funny?" then notices the strange, modified handcuff on his seatmate's trembling, soap-white left fist. The white man loosens his grip to steady his fingers.

"Name's Bill Bishop," he says, nodding down at his hand. "Long story."

The black man doesn't respond, trying to decide if he's been chained to a dangerous man or merely a damaged one. They both stare at the jangle of metal binding them. Bishop's restraints gleaming and new, with an extra loop of tempered steel crossing the lifeline of his palm and circling up between his two middle fingers.

"They made this special," Bishop says, rattling his wrists. "With a hand like mine, you can shake off their cuffs like a broken watch."

The black man realizes Bishop is missing the thumb on his left hand. He doesn't ask for an explanation. He's been on long prison bus rides before, and he knows to wait for explanations to be offered. When it doesn't come, he offers a handshake best he can.

"Thomas Jefferson Jones. Forgive my metal."

"That's quite a name. You a founding father?"

"Yes, I am." He smiles. "And that's a longer story than yours."

Bishop thumps the window with the side of his head.

"Any idea when we'll get there."

"Why? You in a hurry?"

Another sign rolls by that reads: HEAVY MACHINERY ON THE ROAD WHEN FLASHING, and an orange light blinks its warning.

Inside the prison walls, the arrivals walk past a row of cells, strangely quiet as inmates gaze from their cages. Their eyes seem to look through them, and Bishop looks around for Jones, whispering to the nearest inmate shuffling next to him instead.

"Aren't they supposed to spit on us or something?" Bishop asks.

"*Shit* on us?" He laughs. "No, that comes later."

Then a wad of saliva hits Bishop in the back of the neck, and he winces and smacks at it like a mosquito. The guard behind him shoves him to walk faster. A shrill, familiar voices pipes up in his ear.

"Welcome to Eeeeee-loy Prison," someone says, and Bishop looks back into the sea of orange jumpsuits and the wide face of a young man in a lime green jumpsuit, grinning from the middle of the dead stone glares. He has a crazy, lopsided blond sweep of hair, like a wave crashing on the top of his head, and his bizarre hair and strange green jumpsuit earn him an instant nickname from a young black man behind him, who gives him a shove.

"Shut the fuck up, Gumby," he says, and Bishop notes the huge number 7 tattooed on the side of the black man's neck.

As Bishop walks on, he sees white inmates being corralled

and steered up some stairs by the guards. It's a quiet, almost casual segregation, and he looks around to see if anyone is protesting the color-coding as he's marched up to the second tier. A steel baton taps his chest and stops him in front of a cell. He steps inside and turns. Minutes later, as the shadow of the bars slide across his face, he makes eye contact with the man with the number 7 tattooed on his neck, and notices it actually reads 187, wrapping completely around his throat. Bishop gives him a nod out of habit, and the inmate stares back a moment, then backs up into his cell until he disappears into the dark.

"Listen!" a voice echoes. "You are at Level One! Twenty-four-hour lockdown for the first thirty days! Level Two allows some freedoms. Depending on how you handle Level One! Use this time to screw your heads on straight!"

There's a flurry of footsteps above and below Bishop's cell, as he stares at the tight bundle of mattress and pillow curled in the center of a sagging metal bed frame. He sits on the floor instead.

"Lock it down!"

There's a heavy iron *BOOM!* as a distant door is slammed shut, and a low rumble as unseen machinery slides deadbolts into place. Bishop stares at a stain on the floor outside the bars, waiting to see if it crawls away. His eyes grow heavy before he finds out.

Hours later, Bishop's eyes snap open to the distinct clink of polished feet trying to be quiet, the clank of riot sticks, and the muffled grunts of a struggle. He's still sitting on the floor of his cell, his mattress roll and pillow untouched on the bed frame. Across the drop, he catches a glimpse of a cell door rolling shut, and he sits up straight to squint into the dark. Nothing else happens, and he fades back to sleep to dream of swimming in the sky just above the razor wire.

* * *

A parked car with a police boot locking the front wheel sits motionless as the sun races over its hood. The sky gets bright then dark, bright then dark. Days fly by and bird shit appears across the windshield like a Jackson Pollock.

In a nearby house, shadows stretch and vanish as fingers flutter around a small mechanical creation. The hands are a blur of motion as the shape of an airplane becomes clear, twirling knobs and pushing buttons on a large remote control until the tiny propeller starts to spin. Time slows for a moment to reveal the hands of a young girl.

Miles away, the sun chases ants through infinite spirals in the sand, circling a jar propped like a monolith next to their hill. Almost imperceptibly fast, the flicker of ants scramble, climb, and scratch the glass, as sunlight pulses around them. Once inside the jar, they are unable to climb back out, and their motions slow, then cease, dried and dead with their legs above their heads. Slowly, despite the sun and moon racing overhead, a large, sunburned hand reaches into the jar, and new ants are dumped inside. These new ants pile over the dead and dying, in turn scratching and spiraling around the base. Eventually they slow, then die, too, and the huge, red hand drops more.

Inside the prison, days pass, and men race in circles confined to their cells. Men in gray, men in blue, men in black with shields and plastic faces. They all buzz around the halls like insects, appearing and disappearing. Outside in the cafeteria and yard, some stop to fight, racing back to their cells ahead of the whistles, then out again, until they slow, slow down, as time finally returns to normal.

It's now a month since Bishop arrived, and he still sits on the floor, his mattress roll untouched. Though time has leveled out, his breathing is still fast, and he sucks in his breath at the familiar metal *BOOM!* and his cell door sliding open with a rumble.

* * *

A huge guard looms at the corner of the yard like a human watchtower. His hands are out in front of him, his thumbs and forefingers framing a director's square. His tongue ticks as he imitates an old-time movie camera.

Each gang in the prison yard takes a turn inside the guard's square. He settles on a shot of the small circle of white inmates. There are only nine of them, leaning against a brick wall, silent, looking over shoulders, listening to rap music sung by white men with country accents from a stereo balanced on an old pair of shoes, like a car up on blocks. The guard squints to get a close-up on Bishop, who is walking toward the black prisoners. There he finds Jones, the man he was chained to on the bus, leaning up against the fence. He tries again to get Jones's attention, but Jones is staring hard at nothing in the skyline. Then Gumby is running toward them, pointing to a shadow moving up in the sky. The other white men around them look off into the distance too, and Bishop hoods his eyes until he sees it.

It's an airplane on the horizon, and it's headed straight for the prison. Bishop realizes it's flying lower than it should, and he looks around for reactions. The inmates who are watching seem unimpressed by this strange sight, either turning back to conversations or changing tapes in their radios. One of them tries to scratch a hard-to-reach spot on his back. Gumby is the only one who seems excited.

"Is someone trying to bust someone out?!"

A mob of inmates parts to reveal the huge prison guard with the director's fingers, heading for the strange lack of commotion. He's walking slowly, sort of stalking his line of sight with the plane in the distance. He punts a boombox out of the way, and it sails at least thirty feet and crashes down, knobs rolling in all directions.

This guard is easily twice the size of the rest, even bigger than the prisoners, and a good two feet taller than the two guards run up to flank him. His thick face is pale white, hard-living late thirties, red curly hair, piercing blue eyes, with ragged scar tissue tracing his throat. He looks like a burly lifer someone dressed as a guard for Halloween.

"Who's that monster?" Bishop asks.

"Jim Wayne," Jones whispers. "He'll tell you to call him The Duke, but I wouldn't talk to him at all."

The Duke crosses his arms to reveal a black-and-blue splotch on his forearm. A closer look and Bishop sees it's not a bruise, but a tattoo over another tattoo, both now unrecognizable. The Duke watches the sky with a grin, apparently unconcerned with this breach of prison air space. He cracks his knuckles, then closes one eye to aim with a thumb-and-forefinger circle.

"Wait, the engine, it's all wrong..." Bishop says, trailing off, too, and he starts backing up to prepare for a crash.

The airplane flies over the prison wall with a shrill whine, skimming the loops of barbed wire and dipping down toward the men in the yard. Just as it clears the wire, The Duke runs up and swats it down with his bare hand like an angry orangutan, and a cloud of plastic and metal shards flutter to the sand-dusted concrete. Bishop shakes his head as he finally understands he was looking at a toy, a small remote-controlled model airplane. The show over, inmates wander off as if they've seen this happen a million times before while the new guys remain confused.

A Mexican inmate walks over, and the white men are noticeably agitated by his presence. He's forty-something years old, with faded green homemade tats on his neck and hands.

"Salvador Francisco," he says. "You notice anything weird about this place yet?"

He holds out a hand to Bishop, but shakes it too fast to notice Bishop's missing thumb.

"No, just everything."

* * *

In the cafeteria, Bishop walks past the table where The Duke eats alongside his ant farm for company. He doesn't understand why a guard is dining with the prisoners, and curiosity gets the better of him. He peers down and watches The Duke hug his plate with his huge, ink-stained arm. Buried in one tattoo is a green eyeball, bursting from the swollen knob of bone on The Duke's wrist. He catches Bishop staring.

"Hey! You wanna look in my crystal ball that bad? I'll read your fortune."

Bishop walks past, and The Duke stands up, smiling. Most people around look up.

A smaller guard talks into a radio as Bishop stops and turns to face The Duke.

"You," he says to Bishop. "Back to your seat, boy, and wait for the whistle."

But Bishop can't help studying The Duke's arms, and suddenly The Duke is standing. He leans over to rest his chin on the top of Bishop's head.

"Are you going to be a problem? Is that it? Tell me now, 'cause we got a lotta big problems around here, so maybe we can just get your little problem out of the way right now."

Bishop looks past The Duke to avoid his eyes.

"No, sir. Just here to eat."

"Tell you what," The Duke whispers. "You don't worry about my scars, and I won't worry about yours."

As he says this, The Duke reaches down and pulls Bishop's left hand up, rubbing the angry pink pinch of skin where Bishop's thumb used to be.

"Damn, son, I'd rather get my balls chopped off than my thumb! Or blow my brains out. You're left handed, too, ain't ya?"

The Duke lets Bishop's hand drop back down to his side.

"I *know* what you did," he whispers to Bishop, barely

audible.

Bishop looks into his dead eyes a moment, then looks away.

The Duke suddenly bangs the table and digs through all of his pockets.

"Almost forgot!" he shouts, positively giddy. "Your fortune for the day!"

The Duke pulls a scorpion from his pants and unscrews the top of his bug jar to drop it in. It's long dead, and the ants just ignore it. The other guards go back to their patrol, and The Duke takes a gummy bite of mashed potatoes, talking to his ant farm.

"Remind me again why I keep any of you creatures around?"

Flashback. Bishop's front yard. The day of his arrest. Bishop is face down in the grass, a knee in his back as a police officer cuffs him. The blood on his hands, his arms, his face, is making this difficult.

"It's not her blood..."

"Shut the fuck up," the cop says.

Bishop struggles to raise his head. His daughter Jenny glares at him from their driveway. She's sixteen years old, her face pinched into a red fist of anger.

"It's my blood," he tells her, and she looks at her watch to mark the time, then she turns away and runs toward the front door of the house. Bishop strains harder to rise, veins pulsing across his forehead, desperate to stop her from going inside. Another officer piles on, and more hands slam his head down to keep him still.

"Please, don't let her go inside," he pleads. "Are you going to let a child see her own dead mother!" he howls.

"Okay, stand him up."

"One...two...up!"

Bishop is lifted to his feet, and he watches helplessly as his daughter opens the front door and begins to step inside. He clenches his teeth so hard that he bites through his own tongue, and this helps him calm himself. He slumps, and the cops loosen their grip. Because of the blood, they're unaware of Bishop's left hand and the thumb he removed earlier that day in his garage. Bishop's left hand slips the handcuffs, and his arm comes around fast and shoves the first cop into the second. He's loose and moving toward the house, bloody cuffs dangling from his right wrist. His daughter stops at the door and stares at her father reaching for her. She barely recognizes him, and she cries as she reaches for her father's good hand. They're inches from each other when the police tackle him again.

"Did he break those cuffs?" one cops says, amazed.

"Naw, his hand's fucked up, lost his thumb," the other cop says. "Get the wire."

"How'd you miss that shit?"

"Ain't got time to be counting fingers, son. Scenes like this don't come with instructions…"

"Well, they're going to need the instructions for those two bodies in there. They'll be sorting out those puzzle pieces for hours."

One cop laughs at this as he removes his knee from Bishop's head to whisper in his ear.

"If they find an extra thumb in there, don't worry, we'll save it for you."

"Yeah, we'll make a lucky keychain for you, killer…"

Bishop strains his head under all the fists, forearms, and knees and manages to force his head up again, just in time to watch in horror as his daughter disappears inside the house.

Back in the prison cafeteria. Bishop is sitting at a table with Sal, Gumby, and Jones, all in a heated debate.

"Why does The Duke eat with the inmates?"

"I hear he *is* an inmate. Some kinda experiment. Cost-saving, let us police our own sorta shit."

"I don't know. I never saw him come in. Never heard him come in, go out, nothing. He's just *there* sometimes."

"Don't get caught up in this shit, Bishop," Sal says. "We got other things around here to worry about."

"Like what?" Sal asks.

"Like the fact that we might not get to do that 'time' they promised us," Jones says. "First Number Seven is gone, who's next?"

"That wasn't a number seven," Bishop says, but Jones keeps talking.

"Maybe this prison is built over an old Mexican temple…did you know they played basketball with heads?"

"You guys keep saying 'Mexican' when you should be saying Hispanic, or Chicano, or Latino," Sal says. "Why is anyone not quite black and not quite white from Mexico?"

"Sorry, I was just trying to make it easy."

"Well, it's got to be 'Mexican,'" Bishop says.

"Why?"

"Because of the joke."

"What joke?"

"We're the joke. A white man, a black man, and a Mexican walked into a prison…"

"It's supposed to be, 'walked into a bar.'"

"Why?"

"That's just how jokes start."

"Well, I walked into the bars!" Gumby cackles.

"What's he hiding?"

"Who?"

"The Duke. Who do you think? That ink on his arms. That's at least three layers. He get kicked out of the Marines? A fraternity? Auschwitz? Is that his serial number? Expiration date? Bar code? What?"

"Remember what they say about the imagination being the last thing to go during incarceration."

The men turn their attention to the sky when the buzzing starts again. Another plane is coming in hot. They all hood their eyes and scan for the approaching toy on the horizon. It comes in low, wobbling in the desert wind. It dips its wing and turns, heading for a spot by The Duke on the basketball court, who waits eagerly. It's following a clear line The Duke has scuffed into the concrete with the black tread of his boot heel. They all watch as the plane touches down safely, skipping on tiny wheels across the sand and finally buzzing to a stop at The Duke's feet. The propeller slows, and before it even stops, a huge, red paw covers the toy like a monster as The Duke claims his prize.

The next day, The Duke sits at his table alone, the toy plane parked next to the ant farm. And when the airplane's motor begins to buzz, his red fist crashes down to smash it like a horsefly. The propeller chops tiny gashes into The Duke's wrist as he pounds the plane into silence, and Gumby takes advantage of the distraction to run to The Duke's table, where he amazes everyone by grabbing The Duke's prized ants. He holds it high over his head, then smiles like he's on stage.

"What the hell is he doing?" Bishop has time to mutter, then Gumby spikes the jar to the ground.

"Touchdown, asshole."

Ants, sand, cricket and spider husks fly everywhere, riding glass shards and rotten food across the cafeteria floor in slow motion. One ant makes it all the way to Bishop's tray where it uncurls and its antenna waves to taste the air. Then a guard hits Gumby in the face with a baton, and another guard gets his arm under Gumby's chin, and Gumby is floating off his feet when a third guard buries a boot deep into his stomach.

Gumby vomits up his beans, and they let him roll forward onto the tile. The Duke walks over and delivers a brutal kick to Gumby's skull, parting that green wave of hair forever. He stands over him while blood drips from the propeller gashes in his arm. Then he kicks him again.

"I hate it when the Gumbys stop moving like that," he says, kicking harder with each blow. "Why bother?"

The Duke holds up a hand to stop the boot-and-baton party, and Gumby is quickly dragged from the room, as their eyes follow the blood-and-bean streak trailing across the cafeteria floor.

"You know what I think?" Jones says, pointing toward the remains of the plane.

"What?" Bishop says, finally breathing again.

"I think we just missed our chance to fly out of here."

Ink sits high in his throne of chairs, cleaning his needle and blowing dust from his motor. Around him, pins, needles, and hollowed out ballpoint pens are soaking in urine. On the floor are inmates Hobbs and Waters, reading porno rags. They all drop what they're doing when Bishop walks through the open cell door.

"You lost?" Hobbs asks him, standing to block his forward progress.

"I wanted to ask you a quick question," Bishop says to Ink.

"You don't hear me?" Hobbs asks him. "You don't see me standing over you, blocking out the sun?"

"One question, then I'm gone."

"I don't doubt that!" Waters laughs.

"You getting branded?" Ink asks, squinting. "What you want on your arm? A heart? A cross? 'Mom'..."

They all laugh, and Bishop just stares.

"You think I'm joking?" Ink says. "You ain't getting shit from me without giving up some skin."

Bishop starts to back out of the cell. Then something occurs to him, and he grips one of the bars with his mutilated left hand, squeezing until his knuckles turns white, then he slowly rolls up the sleeve over his right arm.

Minutes later, Ink is hunched over Bishop's arm. He has the shell of an empty pen shell with a needle taped to the front, poking and wiping blood from his skin as they talk.

"How long you been here?" Bishop asks him.

"Only thing I don't keep track of."

"Were you here before The Duke?"

No answer.

"How long have those toy planes been coming over the wall?"

"Airplanes? You seen them, too! I've never seen those airplanes everyone talks about. Just a UFO once and they swatted *that* fucker down. But the guards? The guards here, some of them are serving time too. Just like us."

"The Duke?"

"Well, he's something different altogether."

"The tattoos on his arms. Did you cover them up? When he was still a prisoner?"

"Who says he's not?"

"Huh?"

"Why did you cut off your thumb? Did you think it would stop you from doing something bad?"

Bishop refuses to answer, and Ink suddenly jumps back, throws his pen against the wall and wipes his hands on his thighs.

"We're done."

Bishop looks down at his arm and frowns. He's managed to control it for a while, but now the left hand is shaking again.

"You can't leave it like that. What is that? A frog?"

"Finish it yourself. Or don't. They're all misspelled anyway."

Ink hands him a stained ballpoint pen shell with a black needle taped to the end of it, and Bishop pockets it and leaves. As he walks, he rubs the blood away from the new letters on his arm. Just under his wrist is the shape of a heart. Inside the heart, Ink has written: JENNY FROG.

Bishop runs, scratching at his arm, blood seeping through his sleeve as his bad hand, now rock solid, picks and digs at the stain.

Back in his cell, Bishop pulls his pen and needle from his mattress bundle and shakes out a black puddle and dips the tip. His bad hand pokes his arm, then stops. He leans his head out his open cell door to check for guards, then dips the needle like a quill in an inkwell. Then he throws it to the side and uses his black-and-blood-stained fingernail on his bad hand to finish what Ink started. He scratches and smears until his arm finally reads what he wants it to, or something close enough: JENNY FROGIVE ME.

That night, conversations through the pipes are hopping, and Bishop is on his knees in front of his own metal bowl, ready to fake puking if a guard wanders by. Toilet voices echo around the blue-stained water, shimmering with bad ideas.

"Tomorrow," a voice says. "We go for it."

A toilet flushes deep in the works, and Bishop sticks his head back in.

"Hey, is anybody…"

A loud voice from the next cell echoes through the block: "We're trying to sleep! Hang up the fucking phone!"

Another uprising squashed, riot guards stand over the prisoners. Bishop is handcuffed on his stomach. Jones buries his own face in the asphalt before he can be manhandled, and the guards step over them in waves as the inmates sneak looks when they're able.

"They'll never try this again," Jones says.

"Not true," Sal says, as a foot kicks him behind the ear.

"What's not true?" Jones wants to know.

"That's what they used to say in court," Sal goes on. "You see, it's not that I don't believe you. Or that I think you're 'guilty' or 'not guilty.' I just think that your story exists somewhere between 'true' and 'not true,' just like our heads forever exist between the foot and the floor."

Jones rolls over to spit some dirt, and a guard steps over him while he quickly buries his face again.

"Okay, time's up," Jones says, eyes darting around after another boot grazes his head. "If one of y'all was planning on some dramatic ending here, stop humming nursery rhymes…"

"Fine," Bishop says. "Here's a rhyme for ya. Three little kittens lost their mittens…"

Bishop slips his blood-soaked, four-fingered hand easily from the riot guards' plastic handcuffs, and he quickly pushes himself up from the ground. He continues to recite the rhyme as he stands up, ignoring the commands from the guards and inmates alike.

"Get the fuck *DOWN!* Face-plant, motherfucker! Hands over your head or you will *DIE!*"

"Don't do it!"

Bishop calmly steps through the minefield of prisoners at his feet.

"…but they smelled a rat close by…"

"Do it! Down on the ground! Three seconds!"

Bishop walks over to one of the bloody convicts The Duke has kicked into oblivion, reaching to help them with his trembling, thumbless hand. The yelling around him increases as his eyes find the sun and actually stares it down until a cloud finally makes it blink. Then there's a scramble in the guard tower and a weird whistle in the air. High-school athletics instincts kicking in, Bishop reaches out to pluck something arcing toward him. It hisses against his chest, gripped tight in his hands, and for a second he thinks he's cradling some sort of animal. Then the military surplus tear-gas grenade explodes, and a bloody, basketball-sized hole flowers from Bishop's ribs. Bishop goes down hard. On the ground, he stares at a tiny drop of blood on the tip of his finger, following it when it forgets his skin and falls to the sand. The sunlight jumps around the bubble a moment, as if it's still alive. It swells and swells until it bursts, and the desert soaks it up like it had never been there at all.

Bill Bishop lies stiff in the prison infirmary, eyes wide open. A sliver of moon sneaks through the bars on the window, illuminating a man in the shadows, who gently slides Bishop's blood-freckled arm from under his body. A small flashlight clicks on, revealing the face of Ink, back to finish his job. He licks the corner of his gray shirt to swab the dry, black blood from Bishop's cold skin. Then he takes his pen-and-needle rig to fix the mutilated tattoo. His work completed, the flashlight beam traces the number 188 and the beautiful Old English script in a twitching circle of light. It reads: JENNY FORGET ME.

The flashlight lingers on another numbered, nameless prisoner, then the remote control is bagged and balanced on the dead prisoner's chest. Then the beam is gone, and Bishop is alone again, and the only light left is the faint reflection of the moon flickering in his black, dilated eyes. Finally, the moon looks away, too.

EDITOR'S NOTE

The following story contains guns. I know that runs contrary to what the cover of this book says, but the story is different in another way—it's all true.

I had seen writer Ed Aymar mention the real-world experience he had with gun violence. So when he expressed interest in being a part of *Unloaded 2* I encouraged him to write about his story. What you'll read is terrifyingly mundane about the near tragedy that struck his family. It's not specific to his area or the gun laws in his state. This could happen anywhere, and often with much more tragic results.

I was happy to hear from Ed that writing this down helped him process the complicated emotions around the incident. For that reason I thought it was important to break with the "rules" of this book and to let Ed tell his story and for us to see an example of how close each and every one of us is to gun violence every day in America.

So with deep appreciation that his son is okay, here is an actual example of the gun madness that surrounds us. I wonder if this had happened to any of our nation's legislators, would they feel the same indifference to calls to end incidents like this?

THE CENTER
E.A. Aymar

A bullet broke through a day care's window, sailed over the heads of the children sleeping in the room, and smashed into the wall. My two-year-old son was at that day care.

True story.

At first, like most emergencies, no one was sure what happened. I received an email from the center's administrators an hour or so after the gunshot. They only told us that a window had been broken. A second email hours later asked parents to park in a different lot because of a security issue. Finally, around ten-thirty that night, one of the senior members on staff called me. She told me that, unfortunately, the police discovered a bullet had broken the window. She was calling every parent who had a child in that room.

"My son was in there?"

She said he was.

It was astonishing to me, when I went to the day care the following morning, that the staff hadn't immediately realized it was a gunshot. The hole was exactly the type you see in a TV show: an almost-perfect circle with violently-jagged lines stretching out from it. But I thought about it, and wondered if I would have known it was a bullet hole. If I were the teacher, I might have thought the glass was defective, or a rock had been thrown, or anything else. Maybe a gunshot fired at a daycare wouldn't have been my first thought.

Violence always takes you by surprise.

After staring at the bullet hole, I went inside to see how the day care staff was doing. I was taken aback at how calm everyone was. A few women confided to me that they were nervous, but almost all of them had returned to work.

I expressed my gratitude, left, and hoped those teachers couldn't tell how sad I was for them. Childcare workers aren't paid much. Few who work there do it as some sort of leisure activity. Its hard work, draining, often thankless, and it's all day. Those women were likely there because financially, they had to be, even if someone had tried to kill them the day before. Those women were probably terrified, but they were making the children smile and laugh and sing that morning as they sat together in a room, far away from any windows.

But had someone tried to kill them?

Or was it an accidental shot?

Two nights after the shooting, the center held a meeting with the sheriff's department and concerned parents. The sheriff was shaken. He assured the families in attendance that the police were doing everything they could. He told everyone that, because a day care had been targeted, the police had a heightened sense of urgency.

But they didn't expect to catch the shooter.

"You won't believe," the sheriff said, "the number of calls I get about shots fired at buildings. Happens all the time. We never expected it here. But it happens all the time."

My wife and I wondered if we should keep the news from our parents. They're older and deeply love their grandson but, like a lot of older folks, their worry has the potential to unhealthily consume them. Turns out we didn't have a choice. The shooting made the news, and I received a text from my father: *Just saw a shooting at a day care. Was it his?*

There's this guilt you feel as a parent, especially under the watchful eye of those who raised you, that you're not doing enough to keep your child safe. It's a frustrated form of guilt because, whatever you do, it never feels like enough. It's only enough when your child is in your arms, and anything that comes for him would have to go through you.

It's heartbreaking to know that there will be a time when your child desperately needs you, and you won't be there. It's the curse of a parent to bear that feeling. If they haven't, they will.

Every parent knows it.

Painfully, so does every child.

By noon on September 11, 2001, most of the people in my office had gone home. I worked for a public affairs television network in D.C., and a lot of my coworkers had friends or family in the World Trade Center or the Pentagon. People wanted to be with their loved ones, or try to find their loved ones, or grieve. My father worked in the Pentagon, and my mother and I had left messages at his office and his cell phone, with no reply.

I was sure my father was dead.

Journalists were trying to determine the scope of the damage, and reporting that there was the potential for thousands of lost lives at the Pentagon. I don't blame them for getting the facts wrong; America was unprepared for that day. It still hasn't recovered.

I called my mom around eleven. She hadn't heard from my father. I hurried to the restroom, locked myself in a stall, and buried my head in my arms. I was scared, and I was sad, and I wanted to cry but, inexplicably, couldn't. My dad and I didn't have the distance parents and kids often do. He was my father and my friend, a soldier who served in Iraq after the first Gulf War, protecting the Kurdish people. But he lacks the traditional military stereotype. I see him as a classical pianist, which he studied in college and played every night when I lived in their house. He didn't play for a recital or concert—just because he liked the music. He taught me two of the most important lessons of art: determination and humility.

He was gone. I told myself this, huddled in that empty restroom. I told myself this even if his death didn't seem possible, too sudden to be true, too unexpected...but, for those same reasons, I believed it.

It was probably around 1:00 p.m. that a voice mail appeared on my phone. He was alive. His cell phone was out of service, and he'd been helping the injured. But he was alive, and heading home to my mom.

I left work with two of my colleagues. On the way, we stopped and ate a joyous lunch at some chain restaurant. I was deliriously happy. We ate hamburgers and French fries and made jokes about anything but what had happened that morning.

Some parents sent their children back to the center. We, and many others, didn't. We couldn't. It didn't seem likely that the day care would get shot at again, especially with a police presence at the facility, but sending our son back to an active crime scene was unimaginable.

That sounds like it's easy to harshly judge those who returned. It isn't. Our son liked that day care and he developed quickly, surprising us when he sang the entire alphabet one night, or when he counted to twenty. He made friends with other children; we did the same with their parents. We knew the teachers, got them gifts for holidays. It was a small village for us.

And even though what happened was terrible, the shock wore off quickly.

Because no one had been shot.

What luck we had. That bullet landed bloodlessly in a wall. The two teachers, cleaning the room as the children slept, were fortunate they hadn't been struck.

But what if they had?

Or what if the children had been standing? They were eight in that classroom. One would have been killed. This local story would have been a national tragedy.

In all likelihood, the center would be closed forever.

The police alerted us to a discovery a few days later. It hadn't been a single shot, or an accidental discharge.

Multiple bullets had been fired at the building.

No one knows why.

Years ago, a serial killer took our community hostage. Every day there was a shooting, the victim occasionally someone who had simply been pumping gas. The police were baffled, unable to apprehend anyone. And they admitted their frustration, which revealed their powerlessness. And so the Beltway Sniper had us under his authority.

Streets and stores were empty. When we did go out, and when we had to get gas, we danced in place, or stayed in our cars with the seats reclined, or ran into the adjoining convenience mart. Standing still at a pump felt like certain death.

The police and media suspected a male, probably active or retired military. They told us to watch out for a white van. I remember driving through Alexandria and seeing cops standing at intersections, grimly staring at everyone who drove past.

I had a dentist appointment one afternoon during those weeks and, for some reason I can't remember, I went. Like all dentists inexplicably do, mine talked during my cleaning, and she talked about the sniper.

"They say it's a man. Maybe former military. That makes sense to me." She shook her head. "I just can't see a woman doing something like that."

That small comment struck something in me, largely because she was right. Why is it that violent criminals are almost always men? What compels us?

The greatest writers of crime fiction have always provided motive; otherwise, their work would make no sense. The reader would be left frustrated, grasping for anything, any explanation that provides a sense of order. A story must be complete. There needs to be reason.

And so we invent reasons for criminals. We blame it on class or frustration or race or economy or society or God or no god. But when the criminal is anonymous, as the Beltway Sniper was during those days, that lack of reason is terrifying. There is no outer enemy to blame. Something else has risen.

The greatest horror for humans is having nothing to check our fear. No hero to fight it. No explanation to soothe it.

Nothing to end it.

No one knows why someone fired bullets at my son's day care. But everyone thinks they know why.

Some people assume it's a disgruntled ex-boyfriend, either of the staff or a parent. Others believe whoever did it is insane, and that's enough of an explanation.

I don't really have a theory, but I do have a guess. My imagination keeps producing this kid in the apartment buildings across the street from the day care, aiming whatever gun he has at the center.

He starts off by just pointing it, looking at toddlers through the scope, pretending he's going to pull the trigger. He doesn't. But he thinks about it. Can't stop thinking about it.

The day care is in a tall building, and the top floors are vacant. The kid knows this, so he finally gets enough courage (he thinks its courage) to shoot at the high windows. He grows excited when the glass shatters. He's even more excited when no one asks about it. No one seems to care.

The next day the kid aims lower. Teasing himself. He wants to see how close he can get to the center without actually hitting it. He shoots near the windows, hitting the brick walls, but he's too far away to tell where the bullets strike. He gets frustrated and a little scared, and digs deeper. He shoots low.

When the window breaks, the kid puts the gun away and hides. He's sweating everywhere, having problems breathing. He wipes his wet hands on his jeans. He doesn't hear anything across the street, no shouts or screams, so he hopes everything is okay. At that moment, all he wants to do is pretend nothing happened. Have dinner with his family like he normally does. Play video games like he normally does. Go to school like he normally does.

The kid promises himself that he'll never fire a gun again. Its days before he looks back out that window.

My version is the nicest, safest version possible.

It's not a true story.

My wife has trouble sleeping.

Nightmares don't jar her awake, but she finds herself up at four or five in the morning and can't go back to sleep. She lies in bed, thinking, or she watches our toddler on the baby monitor. Like any crisis, this isn't a matter easily resolved. And when something's unresolved, everything has the potential to linger. She's handled this with strength and intelligence and humor, but it's taken a toll.

Years ago, a man with a gun burst into her office building and took three people hostage. I was at lunch when it happened, and returned to a whispered voice message from her, telling me that she and her coworkers were hiding upstairs.

The police killed the assailant after a few tense hours. Nobody else was harmed, including the three people he had taken hostage.

My wife, and almost all of her coworkers, recovered fairly quickly. The company discussed the issue openly with employees, redesigned the lobby, and everyone tried to return back to what had been. We're told that's the important thing in these crises—to return to what had been. After 9/11, a constant refrain was the importance of our American way of life remaining unchanged. Here in the D.C. area, we no longer dash into stores or dance next to gas pumps. At my wife's office, people walk past the spot where three of their former coworkers were nearly murdered.

Some of that comes from healing. Some comes from denial.

Denial gets a bad rap. It's forced ignorance, a willingness to look away from a light so harsh it'd blind you. But how could we exist otherwise? How could we ignore the cruel and stupid and violent men around us as they defiantly claim, as the Beltway Sniper reportedly did, that our "children are not safe anywhere at anytime"?

After a while, you can't help but feel hunted.

I like the clichéd approach to end this essay. I like the idea of describing my son sleeping in his crib, lying in his Batman pajamas. I could talk about how the moonlight falls on his face, how he smiles.

Or maybe I end this nonfiction with a small bit of fiction. I could write that the police caught the shooter and he's behind bars, or that it actually was the guilt-ridden child I invented earlier. And stay away from the truth that, as of this writing, no one has been apprehended. And guilt hasn't driven anyone forward.

Or maybe I finish it abruptly, violently so, since this seems to be an endless cycle of violence in which we're submerged, and it feels so fucking hopeless. Like the way my wife feels when she wakes up at four in the morning, wide awake. Helpless.

We took my son to a birthday party today. Good friends of ours have a daughter who was born one week before he was, and she just turned three.

The party was held at one of those small gyms for children. Everything was padded, and children were going crazy everywhere. We walked in, removed our son's shoes, and he was off. Running with kids he doesn't know, playing with random toys, climbing up slides while we nervously watched.

There were two sets of folded mats in one corner of the gym, maybe three feet high from the ground. My boy loves jumping—it's sort of his thing—and he was jumping back and forth between them. Nothing too dangerous. But he slipped and fell and landed awkwardly.

He stood up, looked for me, and came running over.

And he buried himself in my arms, crying.

It seems like he always wants me to hold him the same way, and I remember it the way I remember the scent of bread when I walk into a bakery, or how water feels when I'm thirsty. His face presses against the right side of my chest, and his hands dive down between our bodies, against my stomach. A hug from my son feels like he's giving everything of himself to me.

And then he ran off.

ACKNOWLEDGMENTS

Both volumes of Unloaded came together through the generosity and hard work of many people. First and foremost, the authors involved. They all gave their time, their talent and their dedication to a cause when I came calling. And it was a big ask—to write a story with a weird restriction and do it for no money while opening themselves up to criticism from people who take the issue of guns very seriously and are quick to spit vitriol and anger at those they disagree with.

But every author here stepped up and for that I am grateful. Every author here has other work that deserves your attention and I encourage you to seek it out.

Thank you to the team at Down & Out Books who took the bold stand to put out these collections—I appreciate and applaud your courage. And all while giving away all the money!

Thank you to the volunteers, organizers, legislators and citizens working every day to end the runaway gun violence in America—thank you for your inspiration and igniting the fire for us to get up and no longer remain silent.

With any luck a volume three won't be necessary.

On a personal note, it is my great pleasure to publish a story by Bill Crider in what may be his last appearance on the page. Bill left us in February of this year but he will be remembered for many, many years to come. Bill has been an inspiration, a friend, a tireless supporter of writers for decades. He is kind of man writers aspire to be, both as an author and a human being. Thanks for everything, Bill.

ABOUT THE CONTRIBUTORS

E.A. AYMAR'S latest novel is *You're as Good as Dead*. He writes a monthly column for the *Washington Independent Review of Books*, and is the managing editor of *The Thrill Begins* (for the International Thriller Writers). Aymar is also involved in a collaboration with DJ Alkimist, a New York- and D.C.-based DJ, where his stories are set to her music. For more in-formation about that project, including a version of the essay included in this anthology, visit eaalkimist.com.

ERIC BEETNER has been described as "the James Brown of crime fiction—the hardest working man in noir." (Crime Fiction Lover) and "The 21st Century's answer to Jim Thompson" (LitReactor). He has written more than twenty novels including *Rumrunners*, *Leadfoot*, *The Devil Doesn't Want Me*, *The Year I Died 7 Times*, and *Criminal Economics*. His award-winning short stories have appeared in over three dozen anthologies. He co-hosts the podcast Writer Types and the Noir at the Bar reading series in Los Angeles where he lives and works as a television editor. For more, visit ericbeetner.com.

Award-winning author **KRIS CALVIN** is a former local elected official who knows politics from the inside out. She lives minutes from Sacramento, capital city of California, and has been honored by the State Assembly and the California Governor's office for her leadership in political advocacy on behalf of children. Ms. Calvin's debut novel, *One Murder More*, received multiple national 2016 Silver Falchion awards: Best First Novel, Best Female Detective/Sleuth, and Best Political Thriller.

ANDREW CASE is the author of two novels based on his experience investigating police misconduct in New York: *The*

Big Fear and *A Falling Knife*. He is also a playwright whose work has been produced or commissioned at Steppenwolf Theatre, Manhattan Theatre Club, New Theatre (Miami), New Jersey Rep, 79th Street Rep, and many more.

STEVE CAVANAGH was born and raised in Belfast and is a practicing lawyer. Steve writes fast-paced legal thrillers set in New York City featuring former con artist turned trial lawyer Eddie Flynn including *The Defense*, *The Plea*, and *The Liar*.

BILL CRIDER is the winner of two Anthony Awards and an Edgar Award finalist. An English college professor for many years, he's published more than seventy-five crime, Western, and horror novels, including the Dan Rhodes mysteries. In 2010, he was inducted into the Texas Literary Hall of Fame.

CHRIS HOLM is the author of the Collector trilogy and the Michael Hendricks thrillers. *The Killing Kind* was named a *New York Times* Editors' Choice, a *Boston Globe* Best Book of 2015, and *Strand Magazine's* #1 Book of 2015. It won the 2016 Anthony Award for Best Novel, and was also nominated for a Barry, a Lefty, and a Macavity. His second Hendricks novel, *Red Right Hand*, was named a *Boston Globe* Best Book of 2016 and nominated for the 2017 Anthony Award for Best Novel. Chris lives in Portland, Maine.

MICHAEL KARDOS is the author of *Before He Finds Her*, *The Three-Day Affair*, and *The Art and Craft of Fiction: A Writer's Guide*. He is the winner of a Pushcart Prize and the Mississippi Institute of Arts and Letters Award for fiction. He lives in Starkville, Mississippi, where he codirects the creative writing program at Mississippi State. His new novel, *Bluff*, features a magician who becomes obsessed with magic's dark twin—the underworld of the poker cheat.

268

DAVID JAMES KEATON'S work has appeared in over fifty publications, including *Grift, Chicago Quarterly Review, Thuglit, PANK,* and *Noir at the Bar II.* His contribution to *Plots With Guns #10* was named a Notable Story of 2010 by storySouth's Million Writers Award, and he won a 2012 Spinetingler Award for the Best Short Story on the Web. His first collection, *Fish Bites Cop! Stories to Bash Authorities,* was named the 2013 Short Story Collection of the Year by This Is Horror and was a finalist for the Killer Nashville Silver Falchion Award. His first novel is *The Last Projector.*

DANA KING has two Shamus Award nominations, for *A Small Sacrifice* and *The Man in the Window.* His Penns River series of police procedurals includes *Worst Enemies* and *Grind Joint,* which Woody Haut, writing for the *L.A. Review of Books,* cited as one of the fifteen best noir reads of 2013. His newest Penns River book, *Resurrection Mall,* was released by Down & Out Books. A new Nick Forte novel, *Bad Samaritan,* was recently published.

NICK KOLAKOWSKI'S crime fiction has appeared in *Shotgun Honey, Thuglit, Spinetingler, Out of the Gutter,* and various anthologies. He's also the author of the novellas *A Brutal Bunch of Heartbroken Saps* and *Slaughterhouse Blues.* He lives and writes in New York City.

JON MCGORAN is the author of eight novels and numerous short stories, including the ecological thrillers *Drift, Deadout, Dust Up, Down to Zero,* and *Spliced.* He is also the author of the novella *After Effects,* from Amazon's StoryFront imprint, and *The Dead Ring,* based on TV's *The Blacklist.*

LAURA MCHUGH lives in Columbia, Missouri, with her husband and children. Her debut novel, *The Weight of Blood,* won both the 2015 International Thriller Writers award and a

Silver Falchion award for best first novel, and was nominated for a Barry award, an Alex award, and a Goodreads Choice award. Her second novel, *Arrowood,* was an Indie Next pick and a LibraryReads pick.

LORI RADER-DAY is the author of the Mary Higgins Clark Award-winning novel *Little Pretty Things* and *The Black Hour*, winner of the Anthony Award for Best First Novel. Her third novel, *The Day I Died*, was an Indie Next Pick. Lori's short fiction has appeared in *Ellery Queen Mystery Magazine*, *Time Out Chicago*, *Good Housekeeping*, and others. She lives in Chicago, where she is the president of the Mystery Writers of America Midwest Chapter.

JOHN RECTOR is the *Wall Street Journal* bestselling author of *The Grove*, *The Cold Kiss*, *Already Gone*, *Out of the Black*, and *Ruthless*. His short fiction has appeared in numerous magazines and won several awards including the International Thriller Award for his novella *Lost Things*. He lives in Omaha, Nebraska.

SCOTT LORING SANDERS is the author of two novels, a short story collection, and an essay collection. His work has appeared in *Best American Mystery Stories 2014* and noted in *Best American Essays 2015*. A story from his most recent collection, *Shooting Creek and Other Stories*, will be included in *Best American Mystery Stories 2018*. He's a frequent contributor to *Ellery Queen Mystery Magazine,* has been the Writer in Residence at the Camargo Foundation in Cassis, France, and was a Writing Fellow at the Edward F. Albee Foundation in Montauk, New York. He teaches creative writing at Emerson College and Lesley University.

ALEX SEGURA is a novelist and comic book writer. He is the author of the Pete Fernandez Miami Mystery novels—*Silent*

City, Down the Darkest Street, and *Dangerous Ends,* all via Polis Books. He has also written a number of comic books, including the best-selling and critically-acclaimed "Archie Meets Kiss" story, the "Occupy Riverdale" story, the *Archie Meets Ramones* one-shot and *The Archies* monthly comic series. A Miami native, he lives in New York with his wife and son.

TERRY SHAMES writes the award-winning best-selling Samuel Craddock series, set in the fictitious town of Jarrett Creek, Texas. Raised in Texas and a University of Texas alum, Terry lives in Berkeley, California.

JOSH STALLINGS is author of the three critically acclaimed Moses McGuire crime books, the 2014 Anthony Award nominated memoir *All The Wild Children,* and the seventies' glam rock disco heist novel *Young Americans.* He has been, in no particular order, a film editor, a taxi driver, a criminal, a father, a husband, a club bouncer, a trailer editor, a screenwriter, a bad actor, and a good friend.

JAY STRINGER was born in 1980, and he's not dead yet. He was raised in the Black Country, in England, but now calls Glasgow home, and his loyalties are divided. Jay writes hardboiled crime stories, dark comedies, and social fiction. His heart beats for the outsider, and for people without a voice. He's coined the term "social pulp fiction" to describe his style.

JAMES R. TUCK writes all kinds of stories as himself and Levi Black. He used to toss people out of bars for money.

DAVE WHITE is the Shamus Award-nominated author of the Jackson Donne series and thriller *Witness to Death,* available from Polis Books. He has been nominated for multiple awards for both his novels and short stories. In his spare time, he's a middle school teacher.

LILI WRIGHT is author of *Dancing with the Tiger*, a literary thriller set in Mexico, and the travel memoir *Learning to Float*. Lili Wright worked as a reporter for ten years before earning her MFA at Columbia University. A professor of English at DePauw University, she lives in Greencastle, Indiana, with her husband and two children in a yellow Victorian that always needs work.

JAMES ZISKIN—Jim to his friends—is the Anthony and Macavity Award-winning author of the Ellie Stone Mysteries, which have also been finalists for the Edgar, Barry, and Lefty awards. The sixth book in the series, *A Stone's Throw*, is set for a June 2018 release. He lives in Seattle.

BOOKS

On the following pages are a few
more great titles from the
Down & Out Books publishing family.

For a complete list of books and to
sign up for our newsletter,
go to DownAndOutBooks.com.

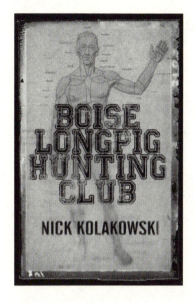

Boise Longpig Hunting Club
Nick Kolakowski

Down & Out Books
August 2018
978-1-948235-13-6

When you want someone found, you call bounty hunter Jake Halligan. He's smart, tough, and best of all, careful on the job. But none of those skills seem to help him when a shadowy group starts taking his life apart piece by piece...

Boise Longpig Hunting Club is a wild ride into the dark heart of the American dream, where even the most brutal desires can be fulfilled for a price, and nobody is safe from the rich and powerful.

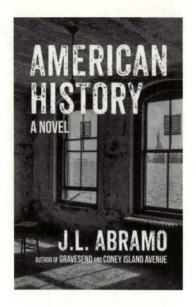

American History
J.L. Abramo

Down & Out Books
September 2018
978-1-946502-70-4

A panoramic tale, as uniquely American as Franklin Roosevelt and Al Capone...

Crossing the Atlantic Ocean and the American continent, from Sicily to New York City and San Francisco, the fierce hostility and mistrust between the Agnello and Leone families parallel the turbulent events of the twentieth century in a nation struggling to find its identity in the wake of two world wars.

In Loco Parentis
Nigel Bird

All Due Respect, an imprint of
Down & Out Books
August 2018
978-1-948235-14-3

Joe Campion is the kind of teacher that any child would want for their class. He's also the kind of teacher that lots of mothers want to have. And some of them do. When he becomes aware of the neglect and abuse suffered by a pupil in his care and witnesses an explosion of rage from the music teacher in the school, he decides the systems to deal with such instances aren't fit for purpose. It's time for him to take matters into his own hands. His impulsive nature, dedication to his pupils and his love of women lead him into a chain of events that would cause even the most consummate professional to unravel.

Breaking Glass
Alec Cizak

ABC Group Documentation,
an imprint of Down & Out Books
July 2018
978-1-948235-24-2

In a parallel universe, is redemption possible?

Chelsea Farmer is in hell. She's addicted to opiates. She partici-
pates in home invasions with her fellow junkies to feed her habit. As her friends grow increasingly violent, Chelsea realizes she
needs to escape before her friends do something none of them
will be able to walk away from...

35699513R00178

Made in the USA
San Bernardino, CA
14 May 2019